THE FOUNDING FATHERS OF FRAUD

THE FOUNDING FATHERS OF FRAUD

INDEPENDENT INDIA'S FIRST SCANDALS THAT ROCKED THE NATION

BHASWAR MUKHERJEE

An imprint of
Srishti Publishers & Distributors

Srishti Publishers & Distributors
A unit of AJR Publishing LLP
212A, Peacock Lane
Shahpur Jat, New Delhi – 110 049

editorial@srishtipublishers.com

First published by Bold,
an imprint of Srishti Publishers & Distributors in 2024

10 9 8 7 6 5 4 3 2 1

This is a work of non-fiction based on the author's research about the subject. While due care has been taken by the author and publisher to verify contents at press time, any inadvertent miss that is brought to their notice shall be duly verified and updated subsequently. Actual names of people and places have been used with a view to provide firsthand information. The views expressed in the book are the author's own and are not intended to hurt the sentiments of any individual, group, community, sect or religion.

Printed and bound in India

CONTENTS

ACKNOWLEDGMENTS

In a world of AI dependence, sourcing authentic historical information is challenging. I must say that I found generative AI fraught with errors. I am deeply grateful for the wealth of knowledge available in our wonderful libraries and museums. All the books, journals, reports, papers and legal cases which form the bedrock of this book have been mentioned in the references. Without these, reconstructing these twin true crime events and the various political, economic, and legal forces at play would have been impossible. A debt of gratitude to Nasir Tyabji sir, an astute economic historian whose seminal work on the sociopolitical fabric at the time of India's independence helped me understand the context of this book. A special thanks to Neelima Dalmia Adhar ma'am, who helped me procure a copy of her book, based on a single phone call from me, a stranger.

I am also deeply grateful to the following without whose invaluable support and direction this effort wouldn't have seen the light of day.

To Suhail Mathur of The Book Bakers, my literary agent and guide, who, after our last successful outing with Telgi, threw the challenge of exploring another true crime. I am glad that I picked up the gauntlet! The climb was steeper this time though…

To Srishti Publishers and Distributors, who gave this ambitious project a platform and provided the wind beneath my wings. Arup Bose, thank you for patience and counsel, Stuti Sharma Gupta and Alisha Verma Chopra, thank you for your valuable inputs and guidance. Thanks to the Srishti team for the diligent editing, cover ideas, presentation and channel distribution.

To my son-in-law Arjun, daughter Anuta and wife Saswati for their constant support and understanding, allowing the wood of my desk to grow into my soul while they managed the family front. This was especially challenging, since my daughter's wedding took place in November 2023, while this work of nonfiction was in the throes of its creation. Earlier, my daughter made a trip of over forty-five miles to Berkeley, twice, just to access a journal I needed, the sole copy of which was available in the university library!

Finally, dear readers, my gratitude to you, as you hold this book in your hand. I sincerely hope that you will enjoy this telling of the 'Founding Fathers of Frauds' as much as I have enjoyed putting it together. Please do provide your feedback liberally, laudatory or otherwise, via email, for that is the only way I can ever hope to become better at my craft.

INTRODUCTION

An internet search for scams and scandals since India's independence seventy-seven years ago reveals about two hundred and fifty-seven events. From modest single digits between the 1940s to '80s, the numbers jump to twenty-three in the '90s, and 218 in the 21st century. Since we wrested our sovereignty from the British in 1947, scams have grown exponentially, encouraged perhaps by opportunism, an effete justice system for white-collar crimes, and a fair share of political indulgence. Barring a few indiscretions like the Jeep scandal case or the Cycle scam in 1948 and 1949 respectively, the first corporate scam to be recorded was the Haridas Mundhra (Mundhra) event, which erupted in 1957.

Surprisingly, Ramkrishna Dalmia's (Dalmia) name doesn't figure anywhere in this long and unenviable list. Dalmia was the patriarch of the Dalmia-Jain group, which saw a meteoric rise in fortunes since the 1930s and was a major contributor to the industrialization efforts of independent India. The group was able to build a conglomerate with interests in varied industries, and at one time, the Dalmia-Jain empire ranked third after the Tatas and the Birlas. Dalmia was accused of fiscal misdemeanours, of pauperizing wealthy joint stock companies by financial manipulation and integral fund transfers through a labyrinth of interlocking companies into his private entities, and of embezzling funds from his insurance company. Notwithstanding, Dalmia's contribution to India's industrialization efforts post-independence remains undisputed, unlike Mundhra's devilry of fundamentally being a corporate raider, with self-aggrandizement being his only driver.

Mundhra hailed from a family of traders and went from trading commodities to trading companies with consummate guile and ease. Mundhra's is the story of wheeling-dealing in publicly listed shares and the leveraging of commercial banks to borrow large sums for his acquisition against the pledge of shares (including forged ones) of companies acquired. He kept repeating the process until he had built a tottering Ponzi scheme, which devolved into a crisis with the falling fortunes of his companies. His crowning of evil glory was his ability to influence the government and make Life Insurance Corporation (LIC) invest in his companies at irrational premiums. The aftermath and the revelations caused the first significant financial and political scandal in free India.

Dalmia and Mundhra were as different as chalk and cheese. Where Dalmia had established himself as an industrialist with diverse business interests, Mundhra was a 'nobody from nowhere'[1]. Strangely, though, the twin episodes of Dalmia and Mundhra in exploiting the managing agency system, and India's fragile banks and capital markets were linked.

This book explores the trajectory of their wrongdoings and the strange connections that their separate lives had. These include the nationalization of the insurance business in India (prompted principally by the adverse findings in Bharat Insurance, a Dalmia company) and the formation of the LIC, an institution under

---

[1] A term used to define Mundhra's dubious background and questionable ethics. Mundhra had earned various epithets from many quarters for his murky dealings. In his parliamentary speech in the Lok Sabha on 16 December 1957, Member of Parliament Feroze Gandhi, who questioned the LIC investment in Mundhra shares called him "the mystery man of India's business underworld."

government ownership, exploited by Mundhra only a year later! We will discuss the role played by parliamentarian Feroze Gandhi, (Pandit Jawaharlal Nehru's son-in-law) in heaving the Dalmia and Mundhra crimes into political and public consciousness, converting the scams to scandals. Inquiry commissions instituted by Prime Minister Nehru for Dalmia and Mundhra, respectively, were both chaired by the same justice Vivian Bose, though in Mundhra's case, primary investigations were helmed by the Chagla Commission. Ironically, despite Mundhra's charges being adjudged far more serious than those of Dalmia, and him being awarded a prison term of twenty-two years, he managed to secure release in three years, closer to Dalmia's awarded and served prison term of two years. Notwithstanding these curious connections, the modus operandi and the driver for these two founding fathers of frauds in India were quite different.

The Indian economic and political landscape in the years before and after 1947 presented myriad opportunities. Indian policy makers sought to harness these opportunities and desired a self-reliant and vibrant industry based on Nehru's socialistic approach of wealth distribution away from the capitalist approach. Many Indian entrepreneurs (albeit grudgingly) supported this as well. Our stories are, however, about the deviants who exploited the opportunities.

The demand to replace and rebuild war devastations and address shortages following the Second World War (WWII) provided the perfect opportunity for cornering personal wealth by business owners. The repatriation of British interest and capital lured Indian businesspersons into acquiring existing firms. This diverted the scarce industrial wealth necessary to build new capacities and create employment as envisaged in the Five-Year Plans. Organic industrial development in India stuttered as a result. The political flux created by the transfer of power by the British to independent India, the nascent legal systems and underdeveloped capital and financial markets added to the opportunism.

While many chose to fatten their privy purses even when they were building Indian industry, few like Dalmia were prosecuted. We will try to examine why the tax evasions of the Tatas and the Birlas were considered as lesser evils and why Dalmia's dark deeds were subject to the Commission of Inquiry. To a degree, the state of polity and the proximity of India's capitalists to the then political leaders were responsible. The indiscretions of Mundhra became more notorious because of their rapacious character and the fact that they embroiled the government as well. Thus, though Mundhra is often labelled as India's first scamster, our story is incomplete without understanding the intricacies of Dalmia's indiscretions. In terms of size, scale, and complexity, Dalmia's was simply much bigger.

This book seeks to explore the machinations of Dalmia and Mundhra, what the similarities and differences were, and how their respective arcs impacted the polity and legislation thereafter in many ways. Allied developments in the corporate and financial world caused by the seismic upheavals of these swindles, insurance nationalization, and the demise of managing agents are also essayed. The role played by commercial banks in creating leverage for the scams has been explored, as have the distinctions between merchant (trading), usury (money lending) and industrial (production) capital, and how these played out in blurring the lines between greed and greatness.

Before we dive in, we need to put our story in the context of those times of India's independence in 1947, understand the construct of the managing agency system, which was demised in 1970 by the Indira Gandhi government, as well as the industrial climate before and after independence. These have been provided in the appendix and familiarization of these would be useful for the reader. Key findings and recommendations of Dalmia's Commission of Inquiry being too voluminous have been provided as an appendix as well. Many of these were later incorporated in the Companies Act and Industrial Policy documents.

To benchmark the value of these frauds with those that we see today, we have used the inflation-indexed purchasing power of the rupee as provided by the data from the Organisation for Economic Co-operation and Development (OECD) and the World Bank.[2] This yields the value of Rs 100 in 1958 to about Rs 9,163.80 today. As a thumb rule therefore, we can conservatively use a multiplier of 92 times, for the values dealt in this chronicle, though it would be higher (about 95 times) were we to scale back to 1947 or so when Dalmia's indiscretions began.

The methodology of the frauds described in this book has been refined and honed since then, in line with extant practices by fraudsters. Loopholes in law and controls have been exploited over the years within corporations. Justice as a deterrent has continued to play "catch up" and newer frauds have assailed the collective human consciousness, with rapid strides in digitalization and the advent of cybercrimes.

A 2020 study[3] revealed that in the 2504 cases examined from 125 countries from across the world, which had caused losses of USD 3.6 billion via frauds, three primary reasons had been identified. Asset misappropriation, which involved an employee stealing or misusing the employing organization's resources,

---

[2] India Inflation Calculator: World Bank Data: 1958-2023: https://www.in2013dollars.com/india/inflation.

[3] 2020 Report to the Nations. Copyright 2020 by the Association of Certified Fraud Examiners, Inc.

occurred in eighty-six per cent of the fraud schemes. Corruption, which includes offenses such as bribery, conflicts of interest, and extortion, came second occurring in forty-three per cent of cases. Financial statement fraud schemes, in which the perpetrator intentionally causes a material misstatement or omission in the organization's financial statements, were the least common at ten per cent. These figures changed only marginally in the 2022 report by the same organization. And these were the principal reasons of why even the Dalmia and Mundhra frauds were perpetrated about seven decades ago! A 2022 study[4] by PricewaterhouseCoopers LLP (PwC) which examined 1296 global organizations – of which 112 were from India – representing thirty-two diverse industries also reiterates that asset misappropriation was a major contributor in their findings.

Of the 2504 cases examined in the 2020 study by ACFE, 77 cases were examined from India and South Africa each, second only to the US, which accounted for a lion's share of 829 of the cases. While there could be regional biases, the number of cases selected from these three countries puts India well ahead in the map for global frauds and scams. This is also reflected in India's poor showing in the 2023 Corruption Perception Index (CPI) report by Transparency International.[5] This report ranks 180 countries and territories across the world by the perceived levels of public sector corruption. Although one could argue that corruption is not synonymous with fraud and scams, it can be an indication of the overall integrity and risk environment within a country. India's ranking dropped to ninety-three from her rank from eighty-five achieved in the 2022 CPI report.

---

4 PwC's Global Economic Crime and Fraud Survey 2022 - Pricewater houseCoopers International Ltd.

5 https://www.transparency.org/en/cpi/2023.

DALMIA'S DARK DEEDS (THE DALMIA-JAIN GROUP)

AN ARDUOUS CLIMB

The chief architect of the Dalmia-Jain group (the DJ group henceforth), Ramkrishna Dalmia, was born on April 07, 1893, as the third child to Harjimal Dalmia and his wife Jadia Devi, in a small village Chirawa in Rajasthan. Manmeri and Basanti were his two elder sisters and Godaveri, his younger. Ramkrishna began school at the tender age of four. He was an exceptionally gifted child, with a head for numbers and adept at the Marwari dialect. To escape poverty, the family resettled in Calcutta (now Kolkata), the then business capital of India.

Ramkrishna was nine when the family settled in a small rented room in Calcutta. Just after a year, despite performing very well and securing a double promotion, Ramkrishna left his new school in Calcutta to join his rich maternal uncle Motilal Jhunjhunwala with a job as a cashier. Motilal was a successful merchant and under him, Ramkrishna learned the ropes of trading commodities well. When Ramakrishna was eleven, Jadia Devi delivered her son Jaidayal, with whom Ramkrishna immediately developed a great bond. Given their considerable age gap, Ramkrishna was more of a father than a brother to Jaidayal. A few months later, Ramkrishna was married to Narbada, eleven months older than him and someone who, by his own admission, he would physically abuse.

By the time he was fifteen, Ramkrishna was earning in commissions more than double his father's salary as a cashier – of sixty rupees a month. Soon, however, tragedy struck, and Ramkrishna lost Narbada to tuberculosis when she was sixteen.

Depressed and contrite for having tortured her when she was alive, he chose to leave for Uttarpara along with his father where they tried to make a living in cloth trading. The business failed, and they had to sell their shop and return to Calcutta where Motilal again employed Ramkrishna for a meagre salary. Soon, he began to handle cash and keep accounts, aided by his innate skill in mathematics and an elephantine memory for numbers. This also allowed him to observe his uncle's bullion business up close (Motilal had earned the nickname of "Silver King") and he learnt to decipher coded telegrams received from bullion agents in London. The riches of speculation enamoured him, and outside of work, he tried his hand in trading in commodities like jute, cotton, and silver. Soon the lucre of the *satta bazaar*[6] beckoned him, and he dived in recklessly.

At eighteen, he married Durga, who later gave birth to their first child Rama. Rama would later marry Shanti Prasad Jain. Four years later, Ramkrishna lost his father. The burden to support his family comprising his grandmother, mother, three sisters, a brother, and a wife, fell upon his young shoulders and he struggled to make ends meet with his fickle returns from speculation and a poor salary. Additionally, he had ratcheted up substantial debts in the *satta bazaar* and earned himself a dubious reputation as a defaulter.

Ostracized, uneducated, deep in debt – at this nadir of his life, Dalmia met Seth Baldeodas Dudhwawala, one of Calcutta's wealthiest merchants, who had risen from very humble beginnings and was a highly venerated member of the community. Baldeodas took Ramkrishna under his wing as a 50:50 partner for profits alone and agreed to bear any losses. He even offered his own creditworthiness to reinstate Dalmia's credibility. Baldeodas had only two conditions – one, that he was never to be deceived and

---

6 Betting and gambling markets and syndicates.

the second that Ramkrishna would stop betting and gambling. Desperate, Ramkrishna embraced Baldeo's largesse, agreeing to the conditions. Regrettably, so steeped he was in the intoxication of gambling that he belied Baldeodas's trust time and again. Every transgression was forgiven by Dudhwawala, but Dalmia failed to reform. Dudhwawala had a profound influence on Ramkrishna, who devotes both his career choices and goodness to his mentor. In his memoir[7] he writes, "My career was greatly influenced by my association with the late Seth Baldeo Dasji Dudhwawala… Whatever goodness I have in me is the result of what I learnt from Seth Baldeo Dasji and inherited from my forefathers." A large defaulter in *satta bazaar*, Dalmia became a pariah in the market and no one, not even his relatives would lend him five rupees. He was scared for his life and limb with the creditors baying for his blood. Reportedly, he was also once physically assaulted by an incensed loan shark.

Despondent, he turned to Pandit Motilal Biala (of Fatehpur, Rajasthan), a reputed astrologer. The pandit poured over Ramkrishna's horoscope and foretold that in six weeks, his misfortunes would end, and he would soon earn over one-lakh rupees. To assuage Ramkrishna's disbelief, the astrologer even wrote his prediction on a paper and signed it.

In his days with Motilal, Ramkrishna had independently developed contacts with bullion agents in London. There were only four agents in London then, authorized to advise overseas investors by cablegram about market trends in precious metals. One of them sent Ramkrishna a cable informing him about an expected increase in silver prices. Ramkrishna convinced Panditji (the astrologer, for

---

7 Dalmia, Seth Ramkrishna. *Some Notes and Reminiscences (A Guide to Bliss)*. Delhi: National Printing Works (The Times of India Press), 1959.

Dudhwawala too had given up on him), to invest in silver worth 7,500 pounds (a little over 1,12,000 rupees at that time) and agreed that his own commission would be only a 100 rupees. Panditji also gave ten rupees for sending the necessary cable for the purchase of silver, as Ramkrishna didn't even have that sum. However, the next day, Panditji reneged on his agreement, as his well-wishers had advised him not to trust Ramkrishna. It appears that the astrologer had little faith in his own prediction! Ramkrishna spent two harrowing days petrified that a drop in silver prices would obliterate him. Though the price dropped on the first day after the transaction, it soon recovered thereafter. In Europe, hoarding and governments using the metal for their war efforts largely caused the disappearance of gold and silver coins from circulation. Prices of silver shot up and Ramkrishna was soon sitting on a profit of four thousand rupees.

This was the enigma of the man. Instead of selling immediately and booking profits, his greed got the better of him and he stole his wife Durga's only piece of jewellery and provided it as security for a loan of two hundred rupees. This he used to cable his second agent to purchase more silver worth 10,000 pounds. His profit grew five times over the next few days. Dalmia kept buying the silver. Soon, his book profit swelled to 75,000 rupees. He cabled one of his agents to sell all the silver he had bought and another one to buy an identical amount. Quirky fortune continued to smile upon him. The first cable for the "sell order" got garbled in transmission and his agent sought a clarification. His "buy order" however went through. The market shot up again and Dalmia finally squared up his position by selling all his silver holdings and making a profit of 1,56,000 rupees, an amount significantly larger than that predicted by the astrologer! Ramkrishna immediately paid 5,000 rupees to the astrologer and the same amount to the bank's *munshi*[8] in gratitude. He also cleared up his debts in the *satta bazaar* and even the dues of his departed father to Motilal.

Emboldened, he began speculating in other commodities, always ensuring to settle his credits promptly and not repeat his past mistakes. Bit by bit, he rebuilt his reputation and success in business. Though he lost and won many times in his speculative activities, he gained a new respectability in the market. His crowning glory was when he formed a syndicate with his uncle Motilal and others and cornered all the silver in the market. The transaction was for one hundred lakh rupees. Despite pledging all the silver to raise the necessary loans for the purchase, the syndicate was still short of ten to fifteen lakh rupees. In a stroke of resounding luck, the government of India was, for the first time, stocking silver for India's coinage and bought up the entire holdings of the syndicate. Had the deal failed, the syndicate would have been wiped out. The deal netted Dalmia several lakhs. For some time, Dalmia, along with Dudhwawala, also controlled the share market in Calcutta.

With the seminal changes taking place globally by the late 1920s, Dalmia realized the need to graduate from being a speculator to an industrialist. Though manufacturing would require a greater investment, profits too would be higher than the wafer-thin margins his commodity trading was yielding. He leveraged his experience as a commission agent in Dinapur (later Danapur), Bihar, and his good connections. He joined hands with a well-known local zamindar named Nirmal Kumar Jain (of Arrah) to set up his first manufacturing venture in 1932 in Bihta near Dinapur – the South Bihar Sugar Mills Ltd. It was the biggest sugar mill at that time

---

8 A bookkeeper. Banks would employ bookkeepers in those days. This munshi had introduced Ramkrishna to the London agents and had also provided a favourable credit report for him.

with an unlimited supply of raw material from the many adjoining sugarcane fields that it owned.

Simultaneously, he transitioned to a strict Gandhian, embracing vegetarianism and practicing religious duties. He spurned all British-made goods and clothes, wore only handwoven and hand-spun khadi and rejected alcohol. All family members were instructed, "to adhere to Gandhian principles of *satya*[9], *ahimsa*[10] and *swadeshi*[11]."[12] He regularly donated cash to Sadaquat Ashram in Bihar run by Gandhi's followers and his association and proximity with Gandhi lasted till the latter's assassination in 1948. Dalmia's support to the Indian National Congress grew, as did his stature as a wealthy and successful industrialist.

Ramkrishna Dalmia was a study in contrasts. In many ways, he could be described as a promiscuous puritan. He is believed to have desired women outside his six marriages. These included Kamla, who spurned his offer for marriage (and who bore a striking resemblance to Narbada, his first wife), and Fatima, Jinnah's sister. He even developed feelings for a distant relative and pestered his first wife, Narbada, to arrange a meeting! His sixth and last wife Dineshnandini (who he believed was a reincarnation of Narbada) had discovered him in questionable circumstances in a New York hotel in 1948 with an American lady Juliana during their 'One World' peace mission championed by Dalmia after WWII.

He was a staunch Hindu who refrained from consuming alcohol and meat and championed the crusade against cow slaughter, a cause for which he gave up the use of shoes and watchstraps made

---

9 Truth.

10 Compassion.

11 Of one's own country.

12 Dalmia Adhar, Neelima. *Father Dearest: the life, and times of R.K. Dalmia*. New Delhi: Westland Ltd, 2017.

from leather and the consumption of cereals. Yet, he was a close friend of the unapologetically unorthodox Mohammad Ali Jinnah. After the split of the DJ group's family assets (described later), this astute businessman, based on some advice from an astrologer Haveli Ram, in an irrational act, sold his lucrative drum-manufacturing factory in Bombay for a pittance and disposed two textile mills in Bombay at throwaway prices. In the words of Dalmia's fourth child from his sixth wife, "The multiplicity of Dalmia's persona swung him perpetually like a pendulum from the spiritual to the carnal, from the saintly to the sinful, and from the sublime to the worldly, taking in its sweep a wide gamut of sharply conflicting emotions."[13]

The year 1932 was also significant, as Ramkrishna's daughter, Rama married Shanti Prasad Jain, from Najibabad (UP), who was her private tutor. Shanti Prasad was intelligent, well educated and a quick learner. Dalmia loved his son-in-law and under his tutelage, Shanti Prasad learned the ropes of business quickly, soon becoming a befitting partner to Dalmia's rapidly expanding business empire and ambitions. In due course, Shanti Prasad oversaw the group's interests in Bengal, Bihar, and Orissa (now Odisha). The wedding also led to the rechristening of the group's name to 'The Dalmia-Jain group of companies'.

Shriyans Prasad, Shanti Prasad's brother, looked after the concerns of the group in the then Central Provinces, the Bombay Presidency, and Southern India. Jaidayal Dalmia, Ramkrishna's brother, formed the fourth person of the tetrad, whose heart was in technology rather than in commerce. He was tasked with managing all technical aspects of the group's factories in Dalmianagar (an enormous industrial township in Rohtas Bihar named after Ramkrishna, that later housed many of Dalmia's companies) and with sourcing the latest technologies and procuring state-of-the-art machinery available

[13] Ibid.

globally. The core think-tank of the group comprised Ramkrishna Dalmia, Shanti Prasad Jain, and Jaidayal Dalmia.

A second sugar mill was soon set up at Dehri-on-Sone in Rohtas, followed by SKG Sugar Ltd in Saran, and another in Champaran, Bihar; the Raza Sugar Co Ltd, and the Buland Sugar Co Ltd in Rampur.

The DJ group then forayed into cement, with a network of plants in key locations around the country in Dalmianagar and in Shantinagar (a township near Karachi, now in Pakistan, named after Shanti Prasad Jain) under the Dalmia Cement Ltd. Dalmia Cement owned a couple of smaller plants as well; one at Dandot (now in Pakistan), another at Dalmiapuram, in the then Presidency of Madras as well as a plant at Dalmia Dadri (now in Haryana). The principal objective for this diversification into cement appeared to be their desire to challenge the monopoly of the then-reigning Associated Cement Company (ACC) Ltd. The various other industries and companies under the DJ umbrella were as under:

INDUSTRY NAME	YEAR	COMMENTS
FINANCE AND INSURANCE		
Bharat Insurance Co Ltd	1936	
National Safe Deposit and Cold Storage Ltd	1937	A chain of strong rooms with massive iron vaults and storage facilities in Calcutta, Lucknow, and Kanpur.
Bharat Fire and General Insurance Ltd	1943	
Bharat Bank Ltd	1943	India's first private bank. Grew to 292 branches by India's independence. According to Neelima Dalmia Adhar, the financial wizardry of Ramkrishna Dalmia enabled to set up the bank within twenty-four hours.

INDUSTRY NAME	YEAR	COMMENTS
TEXTILE		
Andrew Yule Jute Mills	1944	Acquired majority stake in three mills - Albion, Lothian and New Central Jute Mills Ltd.
Madhowji Dharamsi Manufacturing Co Ltd (MDM)- Cotton Mill	1946	
Sir Shapoorji Broacha Mills Ltd (SSB) - Cotton Mill	1946	
MEDIA		
Bennett, Coleman & Co Ltd	1946	Dalmia's love for the media has been detailed later.
Automotives		
Allenberry & Co Ltd		
Dalmia-Jain Airways Ltd		
OTHERS (NOT EXHAUSTIVE)		
Patiala Biscuit Manufacturers Ltd		
Lahore Electric Supply Co		
Rampur Distillery & Chemical Works Ltd		
Rampur Maize Products Ltd		
Shevaroy Bauxite Products Ltd		
Govan Brothers Ltd		A British managing agency acquired by the DJ Group. Had several firms in its portfolio.

While the DJ group's interests spanned the country, east India was their home. Dalmianagar, their 3,800 acre industrial township that housed the mammoth Rohtas Industries Ltd, remained their jewel in the crown. In addition to a sugar factory, a cement plant, a chemical plant, a plywood factory, a paper and hard-pressed board factory etc., Rohtas Industries, an umbrella organization, also housed a 12,000 KW powerhouse that supplied power to both, the group's factories and to the Bihar government.

The chronicling of the group's diverse companies and portfolios becomes necessary, as many of these companies were the subject of investigations by the inquiry set up by Nehru in 1956 under the Commission of Inquiry Act 1952.

The meteoric rise in fortunes soon placed the DJ group as the third largest industrial conglomerate behind the JRD Tata group and the GD Birla group, even as trouble was brewing within. The first was the family split and then came the Commission of Inquiry.

Sharp differences began to surface between the Dalmia family and the Jain family in the late forties, as detailed later. The parting of ways first divided the group between the Jains and the Dalmias, and then between the brothers Ramkrishna and Jaidayal. Interestingly, the Commission of Inquiry found no documented agreement for the split, which appeared entirely unofficial and, to a great degree, amicable.

However, Shanti Prasad Jain, his family and Jaidayal sought to distance themselves from the inquiry pleading that after May 1948, they had nothing to do with Ramkrishna. Justice Vivian Bose, who headed the Commission of Inquiry observed that the Dalmia-Jain group's affairs "were so interlocked and complex because of black money and secret, undisclosed assets and undetermined income tax liabilities that this (dissolution or partition) was not found to be easy." Yet the isolation of Ramakrishna Dalmia by the Jains and his brother also meant that he had to bear the major burden of guilt as ascribed to the group by the revelations of the Commission of Inquiry.

In the division of assets, Ramkrishna didn't interfere except seeking to retain *The Times of India* (Bennett Coleman & Co Ltd; yes, he loved the media!) and Sawai Madhavpur Cement Company, losing both eventually. The blows of the family partition, the findings of the Commission and the charges of embezzlement, which earned him a prison sentence, hurt Ramkrishna Dalmia's fortunes irretrievably. He could never reclaim his halcyon days in business. He was incarcerated in 1962 for a period of two years for tax evasion, perjury, and criminal misappropriation of funds. His business empire then, with assets of over one hundred crore rupees, cracked up on revelations of corruption.

After his death in 1978, his business was divided among his seventeen surviving children born out of four of his six marriages. His daughter Neelima Dalmia Adhar's biographical recount of her father[14] provides the family tree and the names of the eighteen children he had sired. In her 'no holds barred' book, she paints a rather scathing indictment of her father who she appears to have loved and loathed with equal passion.

Ramkrishna Dalmia was a strange admixture of puritanism and profligacy. "Much like his own divided personality, he kept his three surviving wives Saraswati, Asha Devi and Dinesh Nandini, and their respective children in three palatial buildings in Delhi, all within a kilometre or two of each other. The children went to separate schools and avoided social contact until they grew to man their estates and were ready to fight out a last lacerating battle with each other over the ruins of their father's empire. It definitely was in ruins, because apart from most of his companies and property being in liquidation, the grand old man left personal liabilities worth rupees six crores. Moreover, all his eight marble-floored, gothic-

14 Ibid.

pillared, and chandeliered houses, spread over Delhi, Calcutta, Hardwar, and Varanasi, turned into disputed property before long." (*India Today*, October 15, 1980)

In a weak redemption, politicians and industrialists lamented Ramkrishna's demise, notably Jayaprakash Narayan, Jagjivan Ram (the then Union Minister for Defence), KN Modi and Sitaram Jaipuria. Yet, perhaps Dalmia's greatest deliverance was the condolence from the former Prime Minister Indira Gandhi, the daughter of his once bitter opponent, Jawaharlal Nehru, who said, "His services in the industrial and social spheres of the country will always be remembered... he was very large-hearted and philanthropic, and his demise will be equally mourned by his family members and countrymen."

The legacy of the Jain family – principally the media powerhouse Bennett, Coleman & Co Ltd – and that of Jaidayal Dalmia, which passed on to his son Vishnu Hari Dalmia, (Dalmia Brothers, Dalmia Bharat group and the Renaissance group) has proved to be more enduring and continues to flourish.

SETTING THE CONTEXT

Political and economic developments during and after the WWII saw Indian businesses use the opportunity to line their privy purses. Offenders included the DJ group, even the Tatas, and the Birlas.

India's involvement in WWII was as *fait accompli* as she was a part of the empire when Britain declared war on Germany. Agriculture suffered from lower exports of groundnuts, raw jute, and raw cotton. Producers and traders sought to compensate for the loss of export revenue by increasing domestic prices. Although demand for food in India had increased because of war evacuees, prisoners, and a large foreign army, the fear of the rupee depreciation stymied imports of necessary food grains. Expectation of further price rise led to hoarding and stock building by consumers, traders, and farmers. The situation took an ugly turn with the fall of Burma in April 1942 and the resultant scarcity of rice supplies. The government failed to take adequate measures to de-hoard stocks proactively and ensure their equitable distribution, while speculators took advantage. This resulted in the infamous Bengal famine in 1943 and 1.5 million lives were lost before the government acted.

Indian industry, on the other hand, prospered as demand to replace and rebuild war devastations grew. Industries such as cement, cotton textiles, sugar, iron, and steel expanded. Newer capacities were created in diesel engines, pumps, machine tools, and chemicals. The small-scale firms flourished too, as blankets, tents, camouflage nets, boots, socks, etc., were needed for war supplies. Increasing demand led to rising prices of industrial produce and established manufacturers reaped rich dividends. The average profits for textile mill owners, for example, rose eleven times between 1939 and 1945.

Sadly, the government did not engage proactively to harness such windfall to spur industrial self-reliance and growth. While they allowed the profits to be freely spent on munition effort (strengthening war supplies to the countries of the British Empire), they inexplicably resisted the use of such profits in furthering industrial investment. Proposals to manufacture automobile and ships, for example, were turned down even as the government continued to place large orders for these, overseas.

The twin impact of inflationary prices in agriculture and industrial produce hurt the common person, while the privileged class flourished. Yet the government continued to appease business interests and failed to control the price rise. Until 1942, the prices of cloth and coal were controlled only for government orders and fixed at government dictated 'reasonable' prices. Prices of all commodities in the civilian market were allowed to rise unfettered. Higher prices translated to increased profits for those in business.

Though the Excess Profits Tax (EPT)[15] had been in force since 1919 and was raised between 1940-47 to harness the unusual profits of WWII, it failed to fill the government coffers due to under reporting of profits by businesses. The five times rise in prices (in both open and black markets) should have translated to profits for the textile industry of over Rs 300 crore for the year 1943-44 and

---

15 The Excess Profits Tax was enacted as a wartime measure during WWI to generate additional revenue for the British government. The tax was a levy applicable to companies and businesses operating in India that exceeded a specified threshold of "standard profits".

over Rs 200 crore (lower, as certain price control measures had been instituted) for the year 1944-45. However, the actual declared profits for these years were estimated at Rs 93 crore and Rs 117 crore, respectively (calculated from the actual EPT collections of Rs 62.25 crore and Rs 78 crore respectively).[16] This clearly indicated the practice of under reporting profits and the resultant tax evasion in both years.

Thus, in addition to post-war shortages resulting in rampant black marketing by both traders and manufacturers, manipulation of accounts for tax evasion, (as evident in the Birla and the Tata cases discussed in the next chapter), seemed to be prevalent, with attendant accumulation of unreported wealth by the industrialists and traders.

Between 1946-47, while the government was pandering to the business class, losing opportunities to channelize their capital for industrial growth, it was also grappling with multiple issues of the 'Transfer of Power' and the looming onus of self-governance after independence. It was in the third quarter of 1946 that an interim government by the Congress-Muslim League assumed office. These were two parties with divergent support groups in an uncomfortable coalition. While the Congress had received considerable help in its growth from Indian business interests and was controlled by political leaders who had many connections with these businesspeople, the other political party, the All-India Muslim League was supported by dominant zamindars (feudal landowners) and was indifferent to the fortunes of the capitalist groups.

Liaquat Ali Khan, finance member of this interim government and representative of the ethos of the Muslim League, presented his budget on February 28, 1947. In his budget tax proposals, he

---

16 Tyabji, Nasir. *Forging Capitalism in Nehru's India: Neocolonialism and the State, c 1940-1970*. New Delhi: Oxford University Press, 2015.

introduced a special income tax of 25 per cent (Business Profits Tax) on businesspeople (industry, professionals, and occupations) whose profits exceeded one-lakh rupees. He also increased the rates of corporate taxation and introduced a capital gains tax. A commission was also proposed to examine the accounts of those who had accumulated wealth during WWII and to tax them heavily (Income Tax Investigation Commission).

Even before the completion of the budget address to the Central Legislative Assembly, many in the visitors' gallery staged a walkout, including GD Birla, a recognized patron of the Congress and one of the big five captains of Indian industry. Over the next three weeks, the protests included the prolonged closures of the Bombay, Calcutta, Delhi, and the Madras stock exchanges to sustained campaigns in both national and regional press.

While most papers welcomed the pro-poor slant, they had misgivings that both markets and industry could label the government as 'anti-business'. The Birlas-controlled *Hindustan Times* reported 'the consternation among businessmen assembled for the annual session of the Federation of Indian Chambers of Commerce and Industry (FICCI) and by legislators who had examined the budget details.'

The DJ group-controlled *The Times of India,* which supported the proposals, argued that India's financial position was not strong and thus the interim government was right to mop up extraordinary profits from businesses. Their indulgent view was possibly prompted by Liaquat's proximity to Jinnah, the leader of the Muslim League and a close friend of Ramkrishna Dalmia. The *Times* viewpoint was ironic, for, as we shall see later, this paper became Dalmia's mouthpiece to speak against the Congress.

Soon, however, the adverse reaction of the business community became 'public criticism' using the platform of the Associated Press of India agency, where most media turned negative. Yes, the use of the media to fuel popular public opinion by the business houses is as old as our independence!

While Liaquat Ali's scheme of scaling down business profits with increased business and individual direct taxation could be tolerated for development plans, capitalists balked at the adverse impact on their decimated dividend payments and the debilitation of personal wealth. They were also worried for the shape and powers that the proposed Income Tax Investigation Commission would assume and how it might impact them and their business.

Eventually, after prolonged debates, on his last day as viceroy, Lord Wavell persuaded the finance member, and the Business Profits Tax was reduced to 16.67 per cent. The event highlighted the capitulation of the political will in the face of serious business opposition, driven largely through the efforts of the FICCI. Measures such as the investigation commission and the control on the pricing of shares (issued with the Capital Issues Control Act to prevent the siphoning of resources through manipulated share price increases) nevertheless survived opposition from businesses. However, they helped little, as the government's policy of pacifying industrialists continued.

With the expiry of the Defence of India Act in September 1946, most of the wartime-induced controls lapsed. The government introduced expensive (and limited) import and export licences and only those with the right connections and means to corner these licenses ruled the roost and secured enormous profits for themselves. In tandem, tax evasion by industrialists and traders grew. These evasions led to a growing concentration of wealth in the hands of a few, an antithesis to the socialistic determination of the government.

The phenomenon of widespread tax evasion assumed serious dimensions as some of the names under investigation by the income tax authorities were among the most prominent leaders of Indian business. The government was worried that the revenue leakage from tax collections would stymie planned investments in the public sector. And while Indian business had managed to carve out significant industries to be awarded to the private sector or to public-private partnerships in the Industrial Policy Resolution, 1948, they were unwilling to commit the large investments required to be made by them.

By the beginning of the first Five-Year Plan in 1951, greedy capitalist behaviour was endemic. In addition to tax evasion, malpractices were rife in diverting companies' investable funds towards trading in managing agency rights and using these to purchase shares in the open market to acquire control over other well-established firms. Once acquired, the object was then to use the cash resources and liquid reserves diligently built up by these target companies over the years, to buy shares and gain control over other companies or to engage in speculative activities in share or commodity markets. Sadly, the focus shifted away from an industrialist's mindset of expanding and developing new undertakings/lines of business to that of a short-term trader and speculator in company shares.

Policymakers and parliamentarians voiced their fears that the objective of the industrial revolution, if not accompanied by a moral revolution, risked damaging the economy more than poverty and ignorance had. So much power in the hands of a few large industrial firms was undesirable, and the measures adopted to stem the tide were ineffective.

The Income Tax Investigation Commission (ITIC), though well intentioned, did not achieve the success desired in bringing offenders to book speedily. Rather, the most it managed was some clawback for government revenues by inducing the suspects to reach a settlement. However, here too, they were cautious in estimating the degree of concealed income and thus the quantum of revenue and penalty payments due to the government remained sub-optimal. A large part of the problem was the challenge faced in tracing financial transactions between firms that were interconnected through common managing agent(s).

In 1951, for example, the ITIC estimated the concealed income of the DJ group at Rs 458 lakhs for the eight-year period from 1939 to 1947.[17] An order of the income tax officer for the accounting year September 30, 1952 alone shows that the ITIC computed the concerned assets of the DJ group in the shape of concealed shares in limited companies to the order of Rs 420 lakhs.[18] This seems to mirror the meteoric rise in the group's fortunes, as they had increased their controlling interest in shares in both acquired and new enterprises nearly four-fold, from Rs 393 lakhs to Rs 16 crore between 1939 and the early fifties.

In other cases of two prominent businessmen from Kanpur, Uttar Pradesh (UP); Padampat Singhania and Ram Ratan Gupta, political correctness was chosen to ensure that the government dealings with them could not be criticized. Padampat Singhania's matter was settled with the UP government with a token penalty amount of Rs 2.5 lakhs, principally as the Home Ministry had faced a setback in a Bombay court. Allegedly, all witnesses had been bought by Singhania. A similar course of action with Ram Ratan Gupta was proposed, since protracted investigations had failed to build up a case strong enough for the courts.

---

17 Ibid.

18 Report of The Commission of Inquiry (Inquiry on the administration of Dalmia Jain Companies).

Both the finance minister and the chairperson of the ITIC strongly opposed this leniency as the option to settle without prosecuting was morally indefensible and could be legally contested to be compounding a crime.

In some other cases, though, the ITIC was more successful with the settlement and penalty amounts, like the case of Surajmull Choteylal, the vice chairperson of McLeod and Co, a large managing agency.

Notwithstanding the negligible prosecutions and the muted recoveries, the ITIC laid bare the various modus operandi for funds diversion and hiding profits.

BENCHMARKING WITH THE BIGGIES

Tax evaders included members of the two top industrial houses, the Birlas and the Tatas. And yet, they escaped relatively unscathed, compared to what the DJ group had to endure. Laying bare Dalmia's misdemeanours may be unfair without this detour to the instances of misdeeds of the Birlas and the Tatas.

In March 1950, the Bengali weekly *Yuga Bani* published an article on the nexus between the West Bengal sales tax department and the GD Birla group. It alleged that the Kesoram Cotton Mills, a Birla group company, had evaded sales tax payments of a considerable sum. A Bombay-based English periodical named *Current*, republished excerpts from this article. Yet it did not create a ripple within political circles. Only when in the Nasik session of the Indian National Congress, later that year, a book titled *Mystery of Birla House* was distributed, did the Government of India wake up to the seriousness of the matter. This book alleged various business malpractices within the Birla group.

In September the same year, Nehru wrote to Harekrushna Mehtab, the Minister for Industry and Supply, that the business community was openly resenting the preferential allotment of import and export licences to the Birla group of companies. Also, he felt that the West Bengal Chief Minister BC Roy was hesitant in expediting the investigations into the sales tax evasion issue, which had been in public glare without any action having been taken.

Birla reportedly had 'excellent personal relations' with the finance minister of West Bengal, Nalini Ranjan Sarkar.

It was also worrying that the West Bengal government had transferred the official (assistant commissioner, sales tax department) dealing with the Kesoram Cotton Mills tax case. For two years before his transfer, he had attempted, without success, to obtain information for the sales tax assessment and the tax payable. To make matters worse, someone leaked the correspondence between him and his superior to the press, which contained his allegations against the system. His replacement, in contrast, had 'successfully completed' assessments from 1945-50 within a year!

Nehru was upset that instead of probing the alleged connivance that had resulted in the leak in sales tax revenues, the Bengal government seemed more intent on investigating the source of the press leak. He then took up the matter directly with the West Bengal chief minister.

In response, BC Roy forwarded the official notes prepared by the sales tax commissioner and the finance secretary. The finance secretary averred that the question of tax evasion did not arise. During the post-war years of 1944-45, 1945-46 and 1946-47, the sales tax department had undertaken no assessment of tax payable. The sales figures provided by the company had been accepted in good faith and the tax paid by them treated as the correct amount leviable. It appeared that the allegation of sales tax evasion was first made by the Central Board of Revenue, which too was unable to find evidence in the matter. They had also accepted the tax payment by the company as correct, presumably based again on the data provided by the mills.

This explanation did not convince the finance ministry in Delhi. Nehru voiced his worry to BC Roy that public and popular opinion were already prejudiced against business, particularly for their propensity for tax evasion.

What had weighed the scales against the Birlas was that when the assistant commissioner had asked for the manufacturing records of the mills, Kesoram had protested that such a request was unreasonable and harassing. At a later stage, when the request was repeated, this time with the support of the state government, the mill responded that the said records had been destroyed. The sales tax commissioner's report favoured the Birlas and stated that the assistant commissioner was biased against the Birla group and had thus been transferred. There was a clear indication of the sharp division within the sales tax department itself.

The Central Board of Revenue opined in the matter that rich and influential taxpayers complained of harassment and inconvenience whenever an inquiry was initiated. However, every such complaint was investigated impartially, and appropriate action was taken. This helped in sustaining the morale of the officials tasked with extracting the taxes due from influential taxpayers.

The board also noted that those under scrutiny must cooperate in order to complete the investigation quickly. Thus, it was difficult to lay down a time limit for assessment completion. The only option then was to abandon the line of investigation or have the scope of the inquiry limited by senior diktat.

Two weeks later, Nehru wrote again, escalating the matter to the attorney general, providing him a copy of the book *Mystery of Birla House*. The latter recommended a judicial inquiry into the circumstances, which had led to the transfer of the assistant commissioner. At the risk of crossing swords with the state government, Nehru urged the West Bengal government to accept the attorney general's advice, mentioning to BC Roy that a public judicial enquiry might have to follow.

The *Current* had reported that goods (parachutes made in Canada) bought from army surplus stores and subsequently sold in three equal quantities to three registered dealers had been omitted in the tax returns of the Kesoram Mills. Although the Bengal commissioner for commercial taxes had earlier opined that valuable evidence had been suppressed, the Bengal government explained that as the mills were registered as a dealer rather than a manufacturer. And since sales from one registered dealer to another were not taxable, hence no tax revenue was lost!

Further, BC Roy refuted Nehru's suggestion of a judicial inquiry, arguing that there was no case. The commissioner confirmed that the said transfer was recommended by him and approved by the government, purely on grounds of insubordination and hampering the progress of the case. The West Bengal government refused to be coerced into sitting in judgment on its own actions.

The matter, however, had spiralled beyond differences between the prime minister and the chief minister. Nehru reverted to BC Roy's note that public charges of administrative impropriety had been made and the case had gained the status of high notoriety. A centrally sponsored high-level enquiry was necessary, whose focus would be the evasion of taxes by Kesoram Mills, and the way government officials had connived in this. The assistant commissioner's alleged disobedience would also be scrutinized in the course of this inquiry.

The Bengal government moved swiftly, evidently to prevent such an inquiry. Not only did they ensure the completion of the assessments for the years 1944-45, 1945-46 and 1946-47, but also managed to get production data from Kesoram Mills, measured in terms of bales of cloth. The mill continued its refrain that since it was unable to convert bales (a measure of weight) into yards of cloth (a measure of length); their earlier plea that production data was unavailable was not compromised! With the data provided by the mill and the bale-yard conversion ratios obtained from the textile commissioner, the sales tax department was able to identify serious discrepancies in the figures of production given to them and to the textile commissioner. Over the three-year period, unreported production of the value of Rs 70 lakhs was identified, and an additional tax of Rs 2.7 lakhs was levied. BC Roy did not explain how the production figures were suddenly made available when the earlier position of the mill was that the manufacturing data had been destroyed. Four pages of his six-page letter were devoted to reiteration of the circumstances that had led to the assistant commissioner's transfer. More than the quantum of the misdemeanour, this event laid bare the business-government nexus, and that possibly, the Bengal government by acting swiftly, had averted an embarrassing central judicial probe.

Some years later, MO Mathai – personal assistant to Nehru – expressed the concern that the perception of the proximity of senior board members of the Tata group to Nehru had prevented the Central Board of Revenue from taking punitive action against tax evasion by the Tata Group companies. In particular, JRD Tata (group chairman) and PA Narielwala (then advisor in Tata Chemicals, a Tata Group company) were on a first-name basis with Nehru; JRD Tata was invited to a meal every time he was in Delhi and Narielwala had apparently free access to Nehru without an appointment and was a frequent visitor to Nehru's residence.

The Tata Iron and Steel Co Ltd, (TISCO) was said to be the single largest case of evasion in the entire history of Indian income tax administration during that period. During 1940-46, the central board of revenue "had identified Rs 350 lakhs of unreported profit, implying an evasion of Excess Profit Tax (EPT) of Rs 225 lakhs and income tax of Rs 50 lakhs on the EPT. Together with penalties and interest, this amounted to Rs 775 lakhs, of which Rs 450 lakhs were still leviable."[19]

According to the revenue board, they had evidence that the Tatas indulged in tax evasion despite written protests from their auditors. The methods of tax evasion were ingenious: undervaluation of stocks, stores, raw materials, charging capital expenditure to revenues by illegal methods and claiming excessive tax relief for deferred repairs through false statements and misrepresentation of facts.

The income tax authorities argued that tax evasion by manufacturing concerns had existed in most countries during and after the war. However, the most effective panacea in all cases being dealt with by special schemes (whether amnesty or punitive in nature) had one common feature that accounted for their success. This was the decision to make an example of the *biggest* offender, the criminal prosecution of the *most* glaring cases. Tax experts were unanimous that it was impossible for any investigation in any country to detect more than a few cases, and tax evasion would continue unless there was evidence of very severe consequences for transgressors. The deterrent moral effect of even one serious prosecution would be far-reaching. If this were so, then in India, the Tata group's tax dodge should have been showcased. However, this did not happen.

The Government of India promulgated the Indian Companies (Amendment) Ordinance 1951 on July 21, 1951. For the first time, the government assumed extensive powers to intervene directly in the affairs of the company and extended the powers of the court to take suitable action when the affairs of a company were being conducted in a manner prejudicial to its interests. It was intended

---

[19] Tyabji, Nasir. *Forging Capitalism in Nehru's India: Neocolonialism and the State, c. 1940-1970*. New Delhi: Oxford University Press, 2015.

to prevent the passing of control of well-established and reputable joint stock companies into unscrupulous hands. The ordinance was replaced with some changes by the Indian Companies (Amendment) Act, 1951.

After the failure of the ITIC, the government floated the Voluntary Disclosure Scheme in 1951, with draconian prosecution for offenders who did not declare their concealed income. Till the end of 1955, it was estimated that, on an average, Rs 100 crore was evaded every year or an aggregate of Rs 500 crore during the plan period. Regrettably, few were punished.

The government was frustrated with its failure to control the spate of corporate wrongdoings that had marred their dreams of an industrially vibrant India. Corporate swindles of tax evasion, and using unaccounted wealth routed via a labyrinth of private companies/managing agencies to acquire large stakes in wealthy joint stock companies, (with the intent to pauperise them) made the audit trail of the funds difficult. The wrongdoings were aided further either by the apathetic attitude of the very shareholders whose interest and wealth were being decimated, or by their inability to put up a united front of resistance.

In 1956, Nehru instituted an inquiry under the Commission of Inquiry Act 1952 into the affairs of the DJ group. Much has been written about why the prime minister singled out this group when financial misconduct was found in the Tatas and the Birlas as well. A significant part of the next chapter has been devoted to providing the reasons for this. Some argue that it was the extent of the exploitation, which was discovered by the Commission of Inquiry in the malfeasance of the DJ group, which was much more than that of the Birlas and the Tatas. This argument appears flawed, as an inquiry was never instituted into the house of the Tatas or the Birlas to learn of the extent of their wrongdoings. Some argue that the Birlas and the Tatas took advantage of the loopholes in regulations and were within the ambit of law, while the DJ group abused it unlawfully.

"Jawaharlal Nehru, a westernized Fabian socialist whose contempt for businessmen, particularly those of the *desi* variety, was well known. In fact, throughout the Nehru regime (1947-64) Tatas were closer to the prime minister and the government than Birlas who were generally kept at a distance."[20] Nehru seldom saw eye to eye with Ghanshyam Das Birla, and we have already seen that through the government in West Bengal, he had persecuted the Birlas for tax evasion.

In the pre-Independence days, Nehru believed that Birla supported the Hindu lobby within the Congress, which he felt was bad from a secular standpoint. Additionally, unlike the religious Birla, Nehru was agnostic, dismissing any place for religion in public life. Birla, on the other hand, resented Nehru's leanings towards the Soviet Union and resented his socialist stance. After Mahatma Gandhi's shocking assassination on January 30, 1948 by Nathuram Godse on the lawns of Birla House in New Delhi (Gandhi stayed in GD Birla's home in the last four months of his life), Nehru was keen that the house be converted into a national monument, which Birla opposed. Post Independence, Birla's plan to set up a steel plant in Durgapur was thwarted by Nehru at the last moment as he determined that heavy industries such as steel would be in the ambit of the public sector rather than the private. GD Birla never forgave Nehru (for the Tatas already had a steel plant) for this, and the relations between the two were never quite the same again.

When he was short of money after his father's death, Nehru had toyed with the idea of working with the Tata group. He had

---

20 GD Birla, A legend in his lifetime – *India Today* archives, June 30, 1983.

apparently even used a Tata aircraft during his campaign in 1937. Despite his fondness for the Tatas, fractures in the relationship began to emerge soon after Independence. The Tatas did not approve of Nehru's economic policies, especially his socialistic decision to reserve industries for the public sector. Reportedly, when the Tatas voiced their displeasure that the public sector didn't make a profit, Nehru is reported to have retorted, "Never talk to me about the word profit; it is a dirty word!" Another businessman Nehru respected was Lala Shri Ram of DCM. He was well known in business circles for his pro-labour policies, high ethical standards, and staunch support to swadeshi. When Lala passed away, Nehru was one of the first visitors at his residence.

Though Nehru's relationship was initially cordial with Dalmia, it would sour over time until it reached a point of no return. Be it political backlash, or an unfair hand of fate or justice delivered for his dark deeds through the Commission of Inquiry findings, or then his incurable streak to speculate, which led him to embezzle funds from his insurance company, they all severely damaged the fortunes of one of the largest industrial groups of India and brought an ignominious end to Dalmia's business aspirations.

THE TRIGGERS AND THE TIPPING POINT

Ramkrishna Dalmia was an ardent supporter of the Indian National Congress (INC) and enamoured by Gandhi's crusade on patriotism and self-reliance. Upon Gandhi's call for non-cooperation and civil disobedience movement, in a show of solidarity, Dalmia even withdrew his fifteen-year-old brother Jaidayal from school. The school was government (the British then) recognized and therefore anti-national. Reportedly, at a rally addressed by Gandhi, the crowd willingly courted mass arrests, and Jaidayal, who was a minor, was soon released.

Dudhwawala (discussed earlier), who had a profound influence on Ramkrishna's formative years, was often approached by the INC workers, including Madan Mohan Malaviya and Gandhi, for monetary support. In Bihar, the Sadaquat Ashram, supported by Dalmia's donations (Dalmia in his memoirs reveals that he often even borrowed sums to donate for the Congress cause) became the nucleus of anti-government activities against the British. In a crackdown once, many Congress leaders were arrested. At the behest of Hasan Iman, the first Muslim president of the INC and a friend, Dalmia, accompanied by Rama, his fifteen-year-old daughter and holding aloft the Congress flag, marched from Danapur to Patna, shouting slogans against the government. The crowd of a few thousands swelled to over a lakh by the end of the journey.

Dalmia harboured political ambitions and desired to contest elections as a Congress nominee from Danapur for the legislative assembly. However, he had to make way for another candidate (who was Dr Rajendra Prasad's choice and whose campaign was financed by Dalmia!). Dalmia contested as an independent and lost, on account of the adverse propaganda by the Congress. He was deeply embittered by the treatment he received at the hands of INC, as he had openly and wholeheartedly supported the party when industrialists were afraid to overtly support the revolutionaries, although they did secretly make generous donations to the party. Dalmia's resultant standoff with Gandhi and Dr Rajendra Prasad was resolved by the intervention of industrialist Jamnalal Bajaj. This hiccup notwithstanding, Dalmia remained steadfast in his support for the Congress and in his friendship with Gandhi till the latter's assassination in 1948.

Dalmia's ability to get an audience with Gandhi is evident from the time that Gandhi had to entertain his strange request. Dalmia's promiscuity as well as his obsession with his first wife Narbada (who died young) has been well documented. Once, when he had travelled with his second wife, Durga, to Bhagwat Bhakti Ashram at Revadi for the latter's naturopathy treatment, he sighted Kamla, the daughter of a sanyasi. He was immediately besotted with her on account of her resemblance to Narbada and wanted to take her as his wife. When she rejected him saying that "I would rather marry a dog", Dalmia was deeply distressed and travelled to Delhi to meet Gandhi, aware that Kamla worshipped Gandhi like a godfather. Dalmia's request to Gandhi to champion his candidature for Kamla came a cropper. Kamala wept before Gandhi and said, "Ask anything of me, Bapu. I shall not hesitate to give my life for you, but I cannot agree to become Dalmia's wife." Dalmia went into an abyss and was reportedly depressed for a period of five years thereafter, believing

Kamla's rebuff to be proof that Narbada had not forgiven him for the excesses that he had inflicted upon her.

As Dalmia's acquisitions grew, so did his heady sense of power. All the rich and the famous – Jamnalal Bajaj, JK Birla, the maharajas of Bikaner, Jaipur, Darbhanga, Jodhpur, Jamnagar, the Nizam of Hyderabad – had sought his friendship. He was on good terms with most of the leaders and revolutionaries, which included Sardar Vallabhbhai Patel and Jayaprakash Narayan. He knew Dr Rajendra Prasad well, as both were from Bihar. Subhas Chandra Bose even visited Dalmianagar and stayed with him, as did Muhammad Ali Jinnah, with whom he was especially close and whose bungalow at 10, Aurangzeb Road he later bought at the time of the Partition for a regal sum of two lakh rupees. This residence of Jinnah's in Delhi was only five minutes from Dalmia's, and they often spent time together. In her 1949 book, *Halfway to Freedom*, American photographer Margaret Bourke White attributes the Jinnah proximity to the fact that Dalmia was locked in perpetual one-upmanship with Birla. "Somehow, the younger, more personable Birla always managed to be first. Birla had adopted Gandhi; Dalmia began backing Jinnah."[21] Many felt that Dalmia in a sense had backed the wrong person, which contributed to his downfall.

The only person with whom Dalmia failed to see eye to eye was Jawaharlal Nehru, who proved to be more than a match. In fact, both Jinnah and Dalmia resented Nehru in whom "they both perceived the cunning of a self-absorbed 'pseudo-socialist' who had never really discarded his essentially British ways."[22] Jinnah's angst was directed at a personal level at Gandhi as well, for he blamed

---

21 Ramkrishna Dalmia first spoke out against cow slaughter – *Business Standard*, August 25, 2015.

22 Dalmia Adhar, Neelima. *Father Dearest: the life, and times of R.K. Dalmia*. New Delhi: Westland Ltd, 2017.

him for favouring Nehru and thwarting Jinnah's political aspiration to lead the country into independence as her first prime minister.

In his memoir, Dalmia however doesn't speak ill of any Indian leader, including Nehru. He recalls that despite his own precarious finances then, he had sent 5,000 rupees to Jawaharlal when he learnt that Nehru's financial health was not very secure following the death of his father, Motilal Nehru, in 1931. Nehru returned the cheque enclosing his response that despite his difficulties, he would rather work as a labourer than take money from a friend. In the letter, he requested Dalmia to allow him to use the money for the cause of the farmers. The incident enhanced Dalmia's regard for Nehru.

The second and more important touchpoint in the arcs of Dalmia's and Nehru's life occurred in the late 1930s when Nehru wanted to establish a newspaper, *The National Herald* from Lucknow. Dalmia was in those days supporting the Congress newspaper *The Searchlight,* with a monthly remittance of 500 rupees. Nehru, aware of Dalmia's proclivity for the print, despatched a prominent Congress worker to Dalmianagar to offer Dalmia a stake of 25 per cent in the proposed newspaper, an amount that would support the operating expenses of the *Herald*. Further, if Dalmia became a prominent shareholder, others would follow suit, believing that it presented an attractive investment opportunity. Dalmia surprised Nehru by offering to take up 30 per cent of the shares for 10,000 rupees, advising that no amount could be large enough for a patriot like Nehru. *The National Herald* was born in 1938. The paper, however, had its fair share of problems. In 1942, when the Quit India movement started, its publication was suspended for its refusal to submit to censorship. The paper resumed its publication in the latter part of 1946. In a meeting held on September 22, 1946, Feroze Gandhi, Nehru's son-in-law, replaced Nehru on the Board of Directors as Nehru had become busy with his engagements with the interim government. Dalmia later picked up an additional 25 per cent stake when funds became necessary to sustain the paper, and at 55 per cent, was the largest shareholder. He appointed Shanti Prasad Jain as the director of the newspaper.

Feroze joined the Associated Journals Ltd, which published *The National Herald,* on February 16, 1947, and turned around the fortunes of the paper even as he handled the editorial content. When Dalmia refused additional monetary support, Nehru sent him a nasty note accusing him of going back on his promise. Clearly, Nehru was ill-informed, for Dalmia had invested far more than his initial commitment. Dalmia, offended with Nehru's note, retorted, "I would rather forfeit all my shares than listen to this… I have done nothing to earn this ire and do not deserve your ingratitude for I have not gone back on my word. In fact, I have more than honoured it!"[23] Little did Dalmia know then that Feroze Gandhi would later be responsible for bringing him down.

Despite Dalmia's deep friendship with Jinnah for which he was tagged anti-Hindu, he did not fail to deride Jinnah when the latter's call for a separate Pakistan and 'Direct Action' a year before independence led to a wave of violence and bloodbath across the country. "You are selfish and ambitious Jinnah," he said. "You want to become like the Caliph of Turkey in independent Pakistan. The Hindus think you are a demon and retarding the progress of the country…"[24]

Personal aspirations aside, Jinnah's demand for a separate state also stemmed from his belief that the narrow-minded Congress leaders would make no concessions for their Muslim brethren. Dalmia was hopeful and made one last-ditch attempt to stall the

---

[23] Ibid.

[24] Ibid.

partition of India. He tried to get the leaders onto the negotiating table and entreated Dr Rajendra Prasad and Sardar Patel to persuade Gandhi and Nehru to meet Jinnah. He even met Sardar Patel personally. Jinnah agreed only if they met in Dalmia's house, though he remained sceptical about the outcome. "You hold a power over me, my friend. I shall agree to meet them at your house if you so desire, but remember those are the very people who wash their homes after I have walked inside them and rinse their plates with Ganga jal after I have eaten from them. How can there ever be a reconciliation?"[25]

The evening before the rendezvous, London Radio's airwaves crackled with the news that an Indian merchant was mediating to arrive at an amicable settlement between the Congress and the Muslim League. The next day, the newspapers carried an article that a Congress spokesperson had said that no significance needed to be attached to Dalmia's negotiations. This news byte scuttled Dalmia's efforts, and the proposed meeting never took place thereafter. Though the Congress spokesperson remained unnamed, many believe that it was Nehru's close aid. This event perhaps kindled the fires of heightened friction and confrontation between Dalmia and Nehru.

The pre-partition brutality was only a curtain raiser for the torture, killings and displacement unleashed by the horrific and largest mass migration in the history of humankind that the partition of 1947 entailed.

The fires of the partition stoked in Dalmia, seething anger against the dispensation and empathy for those displaced and devastated. He believed that this catastrophe created by human hands due to the selfish intent of a political few, was unpardonable.

---

[25] Ibid.

Accompanied by General Manmohan Singh of the Indian National Army, who was earlier a close associate of Subhash Chandra Bose, and his sixth wife, Dineshnandini, Dalmia extensively toured refugee camps, distributed relief material and tried to assuage people's grief. His speeches became increasingly strident against the Congress, especially targeting Nehru and blaming him for the mess that the country was in. The charlatan astrologer Haveli Ram was at play here as well, foretelling that Dalmia would become the future finance minister of India, rekindling the latent political aspirations of Dalmia, and egging him on in his anti-Nehru tirade.

Afraid of the backlash, Jaidayal and Shanti Prasad distanced themselves from Dalmia. Dalmia's newly acquired prize in 1946, *The Times of India*, published from Bombay (now Mumbai), became his mouthpiece for his censorious denunciation of Nehru. After many abortive attempts to make Dalmia see reason and wean him away from his suicidal mission, Jaidayal wrote to Dineshnandini to prevail upon her husband to either cease his crusade against Nehru or to initiate a family partition. They also requested that Dalmia publicly clarify that his stand against Nehru was not shared by his brother and son-in-law. Dalmia was beside himself with rage when his wife innocently forwarded their proposal to him, never forgiving her for the family partition that was to follow. Both Jaidayal and Shanti Prasad also resisted Dalmia's plans to start a Delhi edition of his paper, deeming it inopportune and foolhardy. Dalmia remained deaf to the voices of reason and to the entreaties of his family as he began a Delhi edition of *The Times,* along with a Hindi daily, *Nav Bharat Times,* and a weekly publication, *Dharmyug.*

With his hands full in trying to heal a country that was struggling to stand up after the destruction of the partition, the last thing that Nehru needed was to be unceremoniously hurled and abused in the public domain by a powerful industrialist and his newspaper. Dalmia's activities to him amounted to sedition and the man, his public enemy number one.

In May 1947, at a conference, the staunch Hindu Dalmia resolved to expiate the sins of his past life and purify himself by performing penance. He took a vow to dedicate his life, wealth, and spirit to the cause of the prevention of cow slaughter. Per his memoir, he vowed to eschew all grains in his diet and sustain himself only on fruits and milk until cow slaughter was banned. He made 10 Aurangazeb Road, the house he had acquired from Jinnah, as the head office for his anti-cow slaughter campaign. His campaign further threatened to destabilize the delicate state of the newly formed independent republic of India, where divisive issues of religious beliefs and food habits were damaging to the government. In one of his letters to his sister Vijaylakshmi Pandit, Nehru wrote, "Dalmia is proving to be the greatest thorn in my side. He makes crazy and frenzied speeches directed against cow-slaughter and the Congress. The crowds are listening..."[26]

American photographer Margaret Bourke writes that since Birla became the biggest businessman of India after independence, Dalmia made up his mind to be the business wizard for Pakistan. But since the investment backfired, Dalmia found a new cause in the anti-cow slaughter campaign.

As an interesting aside, it appears that Nathuram Godse, who had arrived in late January 1948 to assassinate Gandhi, had called up Dalmia from the Delhi Railway station. Dalmia believing the caller to be seeking charity had not taken the call. This proved later to be a blessing, for Dalmia's telephone number was written in Godse's small diary that later fell into CID's (Criminal Investigation Department) hands, but in their investigations, they were unable to link Dalmia to the assassin.

---

26 Ibid.

The denigration of the Congress and the personal attacks on Nehru became increasingly vitriolic by Dalmia. He began to question and castigate Nehru's beliefs and persona as well. Dalmia resented Nehru's socialist slant and his favouring the policies of the Soviet Union from where the Five-Year Plans for India had been adopted. Dalmia felt that Nehru's inclination towards Russia went against the grain of India's non-aligned stand. He called Nehru "an idealogue with blurred vision and bloated rhetoric."[27]

Nehru is reported to have said in a fit of rage, "He's an ugly man with an ugly face and an ugly mind and an ugly heart! Just because he owns a few newspapers, he claims to be an expert on foreign affairs."

In his memoirs[28] Dalmia does rue his misadventures, but the damage was irreparable by then.

It would be Feroze Gandhi's salvo in the parliament in 1955 that would seal Dalmia's fate and aspirations and give Nehru the opportunity to checkmate his most vociferous critic.

---

27 Ibid.

28 Dalmia, Seth Ramkrishna. *Some Notes and Reminiscences (A Guide to Bliss)*. Delhi: National Printing Works (The Times of India Press), 1959.

AN MP'S MAIDEN SPEECH, THE DEATH KNELL FOR PRIVATE INSURANCE

Late in the year 1955, investigations had revealed that a large amount of funds belonging to policyholders in an insurance company were missing. Since the parliament was not in session and the existing legislation inadequate to take punitive action, the President of India promulgated an ordinance on November 01, 1955 empowering the Insurance Act with greater authority. This included the power to attach property, hitherto available only to a court, in pursuance of any proceedings.

Later, when the parliament was convened, the Minister of Revenue and Civil Expenditure MC Shah, on December 06, 1955, moved the Insurance (Amendment) Bill in the Lok Sabha to replace the ordinance in force. Feroze Gandhi (elected by the people of Pratapgarh and Rae Bareli to the Lok Sabha in its first general elections held in early 1952) rose to speak after Shah, in support of the bill calling it "long overdue". In the allotted five hours to the house, Feroze Gandhi's sensational maiden speech took one hour and fifty minutes.

Opining that several players had mushroomed in the insurance industry owing to its attractiveness, the need for low capital and the ability to leverage the large premiums paid by the public, Feroze trained his guns on Bharat Insurance Company, a DJ group company.

He alleged that there had been a misappropriation of Rs 220 lakhs of pensioners' funds in Bharat Insurance, which had drawn the government's attention to this industry, as had its meteoric growth. Within a year of Dalmia's acquisition of this insurance company in 1936, it had declared a turnover of 25 crore rupees.

Peppering his speech liberally with drama and derision, Feroze began with Ramkrishna Dalmia's interviews given to the US press in 1949 in America, on his beginnings in speculation in silver and an astrologer's prediction of his riches and how Dalmia in his journey of speculation in various commodities had moved from boom to bust multiple times. Now, with his fingers in the insurance and banking industries, he was 'speculating' with the hard-earned public money.

The key allegations by Feroze Gandhi were the following:

1. Two textile mills, the Sir Shapoorji Broacha Mills Ltd (SSB) and Madhowji Dharamsi Manufacturing Co Ltd (MDM) had been purchased in 1946 by the DJ group, for a princely sum of 350 lakh rupees using funds belonging to Bharat Insurance Company.
2. Soon after the group's acquisition, these two mills purchased the shares of Bennett Coleman & Company Limited, a media company, far removed from the textile business. The rationale for this investment was questionable. Earlier, in October 1946, the directors of the DJ group had purchased a major shareholding of Bennett in the names of Jaidayal Dalmia, Shriyans Prasad Jain, and Shanti Prasad Jain for a price of 150 lakh rupees. Feroze hinted but didn't spell out that funds of Bharat Insurance had been used for these personal acquisitions as well.

3. Thereafter, the Dalmia and the Jains passed on the shares of Bennett to the two textile mills. The funds such a large acquisition by the mills didn't come from Bharat Insurance alone. The mills withdrew eighty-four lakh rupees from Gwalior Bank for the purchase of 15,000 preference shares of Bennett Coleman. "And what happened to the Gwalior Bank a few years later," Feroze exclaimed, "is probably known to Shri Deshmukh (the then finance minister). It was liquidated."[29]
4. Feroze ascribed the agility with which the directors of the group facilitated inter-company transfers as their modus operandi: "The Dalmia-Jains have a very sound method of operation. The method consists of this. Get hold of this company, get hold of that company, get hold of a dozen bogus companies.... the favourite method was to jumble up the accounts of several companies. That was started in October 1946 when they got these two new mills."[30]
5. Soon thereafter, the two mills transferred a substantial sum to the Dalmia Cement and Paper Marketing Company (DCPM) as a loan/advance besides a loan of 52 lakh rupees received from Bharat Bank (A bank owned by the DJ group) by one of the mills. The auditors of the mills, Ferguson and Company and Billimoria and Company, protested the blatant abuse of authority in transferring monies without an underlying consideration on three occasions. The amounts involved were about 200 lakh rupees. However, they were unable to stop such transactions and hence resigned.
6. In 1952, the Controller of Insurance objected to the large investments made by Bharat Insurance in the shares of Bennett

---

[29] Mukhopadhyay, Tarun Kumar. *Feroze Gandhi: A Crusader in Parliament*. Mumbai: Allied Publishers Ltd,1992.

[30] Ibid.

Coleman and directed the insurance company to recover the monies, the directors of Dalmia-Jain transferred (sold) assets of Bennett Coleman such as *The Times of India* Bombay building, and other buildings and godowns at exorbitant prices but didn't use this money to buy back the shares. Because of this questionable transaction, a sum of 100 lakh rupees remained due and unpaid to Bharat Insurance Company (and its policyholders). Feroze warned that if this sum wasn't recovered expeditiously from Dalmia-Jain, it would be lost forever. He further requested that the government direct the insurance company to invest the proposed recoveries at handsome rates for the benefit of their policyholders.

7. Citing other murky dealings of the directors of the group, Feroze quoted from the newspaper *Bombay Gazette* (dated January 02, 1955), which had published the award of an adjudication. The Employees Union of Bennett Coleman had alleged that the company had paid several lakhs in advertisement commission to a particular unnamed entity controlled by Dalmia. The adjudicator found that while Bennett and Coleman had provided the names of all other recipients of advertisement commission, this company's name was withheld. Further, the amount of commission paid was far in excess that paid in prior years. Bennett and Coleman had responded, advising that revealing the recipient's name would be prejudicial to the company's interests and if the court were to disallow the same as expenses, the amount would be added back to the gross profits of Bennett for the particular year and taxed accordingly.

8. Feroze next turned his attention to the aviation and automotive ventures of the group. He spoke of how, Allenberry, a private

concern of the group, had become privy to the decision taken by the US government to dispose the large number of spare parts and a fleet of vehicles at the end of the war, in India and wished to bid for the business. The Director General of Disposals wanted over 550 lakh rupees for the entire stock and was keen to close the deal early and preferably with a single buyer. However, it being a private company, Allenberry didn't have the financial muscle, nor could it raise public money to fund this transaction. In 1946, the DJ group started a company named Dalmia-Jain Airways. Dalmia Jain Airways had a capital of 350 lakh rupees raised from 25,000 shareholders. But the company never owned an aircraft and never ran an airline. Allenberry and Dalmia-Jain Airways started a joint venture to bid for the opportunity on offer and subsequently sold the refurbished vehicles for a substantial profit. In Allenberry, Bharat Insurance held 30,000 preference shares. Feroze drew upon Ramkrishna Dalmia's speech in March 1947, as the Chairman of Allenberry where, while advising the success of the joint venture Dalmia had said, "During the past four months, by a 10 per cent sale of your stock, your company (Allenberry) has been able to move in 25 per cent of our investment... Your partners (Dalmia-Jain Airways) will participate in the quick return which your company's business will bring and I hope they will be able to give dividends to the shareholders before any other Airways company will contemplate to do so."[31]

By this, argued Feroze, 60 lakh rupees worth of disposal sales would yield 150 lakh rupees and thus when the entire stock of goods worth five crore eighty-six lakh thirty-two thousand

---

[31] Ibid.

and five hundred rupees were completed (the value of the total stock acquired from the Director General of Disposals), what would be the yield? "I leave it to the Finance Minister to calculate. There are too many zeroes." However subsequently, the joint venture was suddenly dissolved one day and an amount of three crore ten lakh forty-seven thousand three hundred and forty-five rupees was shown as a loan (due from) Allenberry and the 25,000 shareholders of Dalmia-Jain Airways were left holding receipts for this amount and never got any return from their investment (shareholding) in the public company.

9. Further, Feroze's investigations had revealed that besides Bharat Insurance holding 30,000 shares of Allenberry, two trusts – Yogiraj Trust (registered on May 07, 1949) and Bhriguraj Trust (registered on May 09, 1949) – had become ordinary shareholders of Allenberry, each holding shares worth 8 lakh rupees despite having a paltry capital of 10,000 rupees only. Feroze questioned on how the trusts garnered the funds to acquire such a large holding in Allenberry, marginalising Bharat Insurance as a shareholder.

10. Bharat Insurance had also invested in preference shares in another Dalmia-Jain company, the Lahore Electric Supply Co Ltd (LES), where the directors of LES too held substantial shareholding (again allegedly financed by Bharat Insurance). The license of LES, however, wasn't renewed on account of partition and the Punjab government paid 100 lakh rupees as compensation. LES also disposed its assets for 70 lakh rupees. However, Bharat Insurance received nothing from these funds totalling 170 lakh rupees.

11. Feroze also observed that many of the group's financially sound companies were dissolved and reborn as new companies. DCPM, the clearing house of the entire Dalmia-Jain group with dealings of about 7 to 8 crore rupees was liquidated and turned to a new company, Delhi Glass Works Ltd. Dalmia-Jain Airways and Dalmia-Jain Aviation were dissolved and a new company Asia Udyog Ltd was started in their place.
12. When public entities were suddenly liquidated, they prompted existing shareholders to panic and sell out at low prices, allowing the members of the group to buy these shares cheaply in the market. He referred to the instance of Bharat Bank. When disturbing news of the bank were published in the papers, there was a rush in the stock market to sell its shares. Shares valued at Rs 2/8 (rupees two and eight annas) were picked up by SP Jain for four to six annas.[32] Similarly, Dalmia-Jain Airways shares worth rupees ten were purchased by Dalmia and Jain for about Rs 2 and Rs 2/8.

Feroze Gandhi finally posed the question of what the government was going to do with these atrocities committed by the Dalmia-Jain group. The amount of 2 crore rupees recovered thus far from Bharat Insurance Company, he felt, was inadequate. Also, on account of legal opinions and constitutional roadblocks, this recovery had taken two and a half years. In his estimate, the

---

[32] An anna was a currency unit formerly used in British India, equal to 1/16 of a rupee. It was subdivided into four (old) paisa or twelve pies (thus, there were 192 pies in a rupee). When the rupee was decimalised and subdivided into 100 (new) paise, one anna was therefore equivalent to 6.25 paise (100 divided by 16). The anna was demonetised as a currency unit when India decimalised its currency in 1957, followed by Pakistan in 1961.

entire combined dues of the shareholders of Bharat Bank, LES, and Dalmia-Jain Airways would be about 8 crore rupees. He felt that the enquiries against the group thus far had been disjointed and prolonged. He urged the government to take concerted steps to recover all monies due.

Though rabble rousing, Feroze's speech was met with some degree of resistance on the floor of the house, principally in that his dwelling on the other businesses of Dalmia-Jain had little bearing on the Insurance (Amendment) Bill under discussion. Nevertheless, he was allowed to finish his speech and applauded for his diligent investigation by some members who took the floor after him.

While ensuring that his exposition engaged and educated the house, Feroze had to be careful with his comments as there were several cases pending, involving the insurance company and the embezzlement of government securities and other matters in different courts. Thus, despite being prodded by the deputy speaker and the others on the exact relationship between Bharat Insurance Company and the other companies of the Dalmia-Jain group and how explicitly had the funds been misappropriated, he was unable to provide details. However, he was unequivocal in his demand for nationalization of the insurance business as expeditiously as possible, citing the following as ills that had infected the entire industry:

a. Sixty-six insurers hadn't submitted their accounts and returns as on July 07, 1955, to the Controller of Insurance; twenty-three companies had not submitted their returns of valuations for the year 1954, even by October 1955.

b. Insurance companies spent a huge amount on collection charges. In 1954, of the premiums collected by the insurance sector of nearly 54 crore rupees, 15.5 crore rupees had been spent in collecting (both commission and collection charges for delays/defaults) the premiums!

c. The claim by the insurance companies that they had been very successful in mobilizing the small savings of the country was incorrect as between the years 1951-52 and 1955-56, the 'Small Savings Scheme' run by the government had garnered more than the premiums collected by the insurance companies. And this was achieved without spending anywhere close to the 15.5 crore rupees by the private insurance companies in garnering premiums.

d. The 'Indian Insurance Yearbook' revealed that the lapse ratio[33] of policies for private insurers was between thirty to fifty per cent. In contrast, the Empire of India Insurance Company that had been taken over by the government, the lapse ratio was only fourteen per cent.

Despite mixed reactions within the lower house, outside the Lok Sabha, Feroze's maiden speech was lapped up by the newspapers and strengthened the cause of those against the private sector. The protagonists of the public sector and nationalization received a fillip with the speech.

Such was the impact of Feroze's speech that only a month later, in January 1956, the president promulgated the Life Insurance (Emergency Promulgation) Ordinance by which the Central Government was to manage all life insurance businesses in the country. In one fell swoop, all 245 insurance companies

---

[33] A lapse ratio, or expiration ratio, is a measure of the number of policies issued by an insurance company that are not renewed compared to the number of policies that were active at the beginning of that same period. The ratio serves as an important indicator in the insurance industry because it reveals how efficient a company is at retaining its customers and earnings.

and provident societies then doing business in the country were nationalized. It was followed by the Life Insurance Corporation bill on May 23, 1956. The organizational structure of the corporation was deliberated over in the next three months and then the Life Insurance Corporation of India (LIC) was established on September 01, 1956. HM Patel, secretary to the government in the Ministry of Finance (who plays a significant role in our narrative on Mundhra) became the Chairman. On the same day, TT Krishnamachari (TTK) took over the mantle of the finance minister of India as Deshmukh had resigned from the government. TTK's involvement in the Mundhra scandal too has been chronicled later.

After the fated day of December 06, 1955, many other unethical practices of private insurers were written about and discussed – such as the investment of an insurance company of the monies of policyholders in speculating in shares in the secondary market, without informing brokers about the name of the buyer. If the share price went up, the profits were booked in the names of the directors and proprietors of the insurance company, and if the share price fell, the losses were entered in the name of the insurance company.

The nationalization was resisted by private businesses as well. Since life insurance companies invested policyholders' funds in various companies, nationalization meant that the central government would now become a majority shareholder via the LIC to the extent of twelve to fifteen per cent of their companies. At the time of nationalization, all the large industrial houses were running and controlling their own insurance and banking businesses[34] handling about 55 crore rupees of premiums paid by lakhs of persons. The names of a few prominent houses are provided below:

---

[34] Mukhopadhyay, Tarun Kumar. *Feroze Gandhi: A Crusader in Parliament*. Mumbai: Allied Publishers Ltd,1992.

NAMES OF INDUSTRIALISTS	NAME OF INSURANCE COMPANIES	NAME OF BANKS
Birlas	Ruby General Insurance, New Atlantic, Bombay Life	United Commercial Bank
Singhanias	National Insurance, National Fire and General Insurance, Free India General Insurance	Hindustan Commercial Bank
Tatas	New India Insurance Company	Central Bank of India
Goenkas	Hercules Standard General	Hind Bank
Tulsidas Kilachand	New Great Insurance Company	Bank of Baroda
Dalmia-Jain	Bharat Insurance Company	Bharat Bank, Punjab National bank

THE COMMISSION OF INQUIRY, THE ROADBLOCKS AND WAS THERE A SPLIT?

Feroze's revelations in the parliament provided Nehru the perfect opportunity. On December 11, 1956, a notification of the Ministry of Finance (Department of Economic Affairs) was published in the Gazette of India by the central government under provisions of Section 3 of the Commission of Inquiry Act 1952 (COI Act).

The gazette mentioned the companies under the DJ group, names of persons in control and the intent of the COI to examine the possible misuse of monies invested by the public in the shares of these companies. Through this proclamation, the central government established a Commission of Inquiry (COI) and appointed the COI members within three months of formation of the LIC.

This included Justice SR Tendolkar, judge of the High Court of Bombay as chairperson, NR Mody of Messrs AF Ferguson and Co chartered accountants, and SC Chaudhuri, Commissioner of Income Tax. Justice Tendolkar resigned on December 19, 1957, due to ill health and succumbed to his illness in March 1958. Despite his appointment as chairman on August 20, 1958, Justice Vivian Bose effectively took charge only on September 18, 1958, due to his prior engagements with another enquiry (possibly the Mundhra investigations under the Bose Board, which we shall discuss later).

COI's mandate was to inquire into and report on the administration of nine companies on the nature and extent of the control exercised over them, direct or indirect, by Ramkrishna Dalmia, Jaidayal Dalmia (brother), Shanti Prasad Jain (son-in-law), Shriyans Prasad Jain (Shanti Prasad Jain's brother), their relatives, employees, and connected persons. Later, a tenth company was added on November 14, 1958: Dalmia Dadri Cement Ltd.

The companies under investigation were:

1. Dalmia Jain Airways Limited;
2. Dalmia Jain Aviation Limited (later Asia Udyog Limited);
3. Lahore Electric Supply Company Limited (later South Asia Industries Limited) - (LES);
4. Sir Shapoorji Broacha Mills Limited (SSB);
5. Madhowji Dharamsi Manufacturing Company Limited (MDM);
6. Allenberry and Company Limited;
7. Bharat Union Agencies Limited;
8. Dalmia Cement and Paper Marketing Company Limited (later Delhi Glass Works Limited) - DCPM;
9. Vastra Vyavasaya Limited;
10. Dalmia Dadri Cement Limited.

Though the involvement of Bharat Insurance was dealt by the COI in the transactions with the above ten entities, Bharat Insurance itself wasn't under scrutiny as it was sub judice and at the courts. The case of embezzlement of funds from Bharat Insurance through Bharat Union Agencies Ltd appears separately under the chapter: 'No Assurance in Insurance'.

The COI faced heavy weather from the word go, prompted in part by the procedures and legalese, in part by the onerous process of establishing the shape-shifting documentary evidence and in part because of the intransigence of those under investigation.

On January 10, 1957, the COI issued notices to the persons and companies involved, advising that a preliminary meeting of the COI would be held on January 28, 1957. On the same day, a notice was issued to the special police establishment to produce the record seized by the police in November 1953 during a search.

On January 20, 1957, the council for Shanti Prasad Jain and Jaidayal Dalmia informed that their clients and other parties preferred to take proceedings in the High Court by February 15, 1957 as they challenged the appointment of the COI and thus the validity of its notification.

Since Shanti Prasad and Jaidayal Dalmia had distanced themselves from Ramkrishna Dalmia, on February 15, three separate petitions were filed in the Bombay High Court, challenging the appointment of the COI on various grounds. The first of these petitions was filed by Ramkrishna Dalmia, the second by Shriyans Prasad Jain and Shanti Prasad Jain, and the third by Jaidayal Dalmia and Shanti Prasad Jain. The court dismissed the petitions on April 29, 1957, but on May 10, 1957, allowed appeals to be filed, which the petitioners did immediately to the Supreme Court.

On May 22, 1957, the Supreme Court issued an order staying proceedings of the COI. The work of the COI came virtually to a standstill for nearly a year. On March 28, 1958, the Supreme Court broadly upheld the ruling of the High Court, barring a few changes.

Barely had the COI resumed work with a few public hearings at which witnesses were examined and cross-examined, that another writ petition was filed on June 25, 1959, in the Punjab High Court by Ramkrishna Dalmia and Allenberry and Company. This prevented the COI from holding public inquiries until October 08, 1959, when the petition was dismissed. The petitioners then filed an appeal in the Supreme Court, which was dismissed on January 05, 1960. These continuous interruptions by various courts retarded the progress of the COI by over twenty-two months.

Numerous applications were made to the COI by Ramkrishna Dalmia and others between April and June 1960, raising various objections. These were dismissed. The order of the COI based on their findings was passed on June 16, 1960. On August 24, 1960, Ramkrishna Dalmia and others filed writ petitions in the Punjab High Court against the order. These petitions were also dismissed on March 06, 1962. During the pendency of these petitions, another petition was filed by Ramkrishna Dalmia on February 12, 1962, which was also dismissed in May 1962. A subsequent petition for special leave was filed by Dalmia in July '62, which was also subsequently dismissed. In all the writ petitions, the Union of India was a party, and contested the petitions. The COI took a stand that it would not file affidavits but would abide by the decisions of the court.

The COI noted that there were no fewer than twenty-nine applications and petitions made to it, of which Ramkrishna Dalmia had filed thirteen. Efforts by Ramkrishna Dalmia and other persons and companies under his control to stay the COI proceedings in hopes to scuttle the inquiry persisted till as late as May 1962. The trigger in Dalmia's relenting from his continuous case filings was perhaps due to the Supreme Court indicting him on April 05, 1962, in the Bharat Insurance case.

No other Commission of Inquiry had to meet so many legal objections and overcome impediments calculated to defeat the inquiry. The objections included the validity of the commission, and even the appointments of the chairman Vivian Bose, other members, and the solicitor to the COI, NK Petigara!

Interestingly, when the COI was appointed, there were no rules of procedure framed by the central government other than those relating to the appointment and functions of assessors and to the service of summons. The COI was left with no alternative but to frame certain rules to regulate its procedure until on May 07, 1960, the central government published rules called the Central Commission of Inquiry (Procedure) Rules 1960.

Though the COI Act had empowered the COI with drastic powers such as the search and seizure of documents, the COI was reluctant to use them. When their efforts to invite persons to record their statements voluntarily failed, as did their 380 notices requesting answers to questions without having to appear, the COI was left with no alternative but to summon several persons as witnesses and require them to testify under oath. Only ten responded. Finally, and reluctantly, the COI exercised their powers of search and seizure in one case on March 17, 1960. That they waited for this draconian step since 1957 indicated the restraint of the COI, notwithstanding perhaps any political pressure that they may have had to face.

The question of public hearings was deferred to the second stage of the inquiry. In the first stage of inquiry, only a statement in writing was recorded in private by a COI official, without an oath. A shortlist was then prepared of persons called to depose on oath at the second stage. However, as the main persons, i.e. Ramkrishna Dalmia, Jaidayal Dalmia, and Shanti Prasad Jain refused examination under oath in private, the COI was forced to summon them and others as witnesses and be examined under oath. This destroyed the private nature of the questioning and made the examination analogous to that of a public trial, a part of which was held in camera. By their own obduracy, Dalmia-Jain had thrown open the entire proceedings to public scrutiny and the attendant exposure.

It was decided that the period of investigations would span ten years, starting from 1945. When the records of the company were called for, they could not be produced in the case of Dalmia Jain Airways, MDM, SSB, DCPM, and Vastra Vyavasaya Limited. Nor were the joint venture books of Allenberry available. The plea was that they were at Dhaka (the erstwhile capital of East Pakistan, now Bangladesh). The COI believed that other records were destroyed deliberately by the persons in control to thwart enquiry proceedings. Persons who could have explained matters on account of the intimate association deliberately withheld all relevant information.

When the COI drew up the list of accusations or charges, they decided to name them more benignly as "statement of matters." Between December 11, 1959, and May 28, 1960, statements of matters were issued to seventy persons and companies concerned in the inquiry.

Ramkrishna Dalmia did not reply to any of the statements of matters. Nor did he produce evidence, on the grounds that the COI had no power to ask him to file a return statement. Others, some of whom held responsible positions in the companies and within the DJ group, did not reply as well.

Because of the repeated petitions before the High courts, the appeals before the Supreme Court and applications before the COI itself, the COI often could not proceed because the matter was sub judice, even though there was no order of stay.

The COI determined that the DJ group and its constituent companies were controlled by five persons: Ramkrishna Dalmia, the senior most member with the most prominent voice in all matters relating to all the ten companies under investigation; his brother Jaidayal, son-in-law Shanti Prasad Jain, and Shanti Prasad's brother Shriyans Prasad and his nephew Shital Prasad Jain. Ramkrishna

Dalmia, Jaidayal Dalmia, and Shanti Prasad Jain were significant in their actions as a "group" from the year 1946. Shriyans Prasad and Shital Prasad Jain were not in the inner circle, but assisted them in several transactions.

Dalmia-Jain functioned as a group till May 31, 1948. It was contended by Shanti Prasad and Jaidayal that the group was dissolved by a mutual decision by its members on or about April 20, 1948. The COI's inquiry found the contention of dissolution on May 31, 1948 to be untrue. The group did not form a joint Hindu family because Shanti Prasad Jain as a son-in-law could not have been a member. But by a family arrangement or some other agreement, the three members of the group constituted themselves into tenants-in-common[35] of all group property. The property was pooled even though parts of it stood or were acquired in individual names. The income from this common property was also pooled and then distributed among the three, after meeting certain specific liabilities. The property consisted of cash, bank balances, shares in limited liability companies and in at least one case, an item of immovable property. The total value ran into crores of rupees. The companies in which the group held shares and/or which they controlled, numbered more than sixty. However, the COI did not investigate any company outside the ten that had been determined.

The COI accepted the evidence that the companies were divided between the three for convenience of management, and that in theory, though the control resided "as a group", it was normally exercised by what the Commission described as the "member in

---

[35] Tenancy in Common (TIC) is a legal arrangement in which two or more parties share ownership rights in a real estate property or parcel of land. Each independent owner may control an equal or different percentage of the total property, whether commercial or residential. The parties are known as tenants-in-common.

charge". This arrangement was flexible; in some cases, one or more of the others were associated with the management and control in varying degrees.

Since material evidence had been deliberately withheld and most of the efforts of the inquiry were successively foiled, the COI could not decide conclusively a) If there had indeed been a dissolution of the group and b) The effective date of such a dissolution.

Neither Shanti Prasad Jain nor Jaidayal Dalmia alleged or proved that a dissolution happened at any later date, sticking on to May 31, 1948 as the date of effective dissolution. Therefore, the date of May 31, 1948, became meaningless, as did the contention of Shanti Prasad and Jaidayal that the group was a loose association of persons who had no common property, except the Lauriya farm, and that it was not bound by any legal tie.

THE LAURIYA FARM

The Lauriya farm became important to the COI as it was the only piece of tangible asset with transactions purportedly on the date of the split. It was also presented by Shanti Prasad as evidence that the farm had been transferred to him by the other owners on May 31, 1948. The COI observed that "all the rest was intangible and notional; a mere decision taken in April 1948 to have nothing to do with each other's business as from May 31, 1948, a decision that was not implemented on that day, but which was carried through in a leisurely way after May 31, 1948, at different stages and on different dates."

The farm was bought in Shanti Prasad Jain's name (the title deeds were in his name), but by his own admission, both Ramkrishna Dalmia and Jaidayal Dalmia had paid for its acquisition and thus held "share title and interest" in it. Shanti Prasad Jain was thus a *benamidar*,[36] for the beneficial interest of the other two. The books of accounts indicated that Ramkrishna Dalmia had paid Rs 1.5 lakhs for the shares, while Jaidayal and Shanti Prasad had paid Rs 1.35 lakhs each. However, no legal documents or the signing of the list of shares existed between Shanti Prasad, Ramkrishna, and Jaidayal; the only evidence were the entries in the respective books of accounts of the three parties.

Regrettably, the books of accounts were not regularly maintained. They were withheld and not brought to light till the very last stages; they were manipulated, and witnesses called to prove the entries in them gave demonstrably false evidence. The accounts indicated that the farm was sold by Ramkrishna and Jaidayal Dalmia to Shanti Prasad Jain. However, there was no evidence to indicate that this transfer had taken place on May 31, 1948, despite the group having agreed to a split in the family assets nearly a month back. Rather, the COI discovered that blank spaces in the books of accounts had been hastily entered under the date of May 31, 1948, on a retrospective basis. Furthermore, no one in Dalmianagar was aware of any transfer of ownership of Lauriya farms. The books of accounts of the farm closed on June 30, and entries for credit of profits from the farm for the year ended June 1948 were made after March 1949 to three owners, once the amount was known in February 1949 along with the intimation for the sale. Accordingly, in the books of Jaidayal and Shanti Prasad, entries for both apportionment of profits as well as the transfer of shares (sale) was recorded in Jaidayal's books on September 30 and in Shanti Prasad's books on October 03. The sale entries were thereafter erased and entries made in the respective books antedated to

36 A term used in benami transaction (denoting a purchase of property that is conducted in such a way as to conceal the identity of the true buyer or transferor).

May 31, 1948 to indicate that the entries of September 30 and October 31 had been errors. It was clear to the COI that on some unknown date *after* March 1949, the decision to antedate the sale and manipulate the books was taken, to make it appear that the entries had been made on May 31, 1948, or soon thereafter.

The COI also came to know that certain entries were made in the books of Jaidayal Dalmia as late as 1951, consequent on the orders of the Income Tax Investigation Commission (ITIC). This was after the income tax officer had signed the page on March 07, 1950. It became clear to COI that if entries to the books could be made after the date of an IT investigating officer signing, any other entry could be changed. The books of all three persons were replete with erasures, frequent changes of entries, reversal of entries, blank pages, and blank spaces (enabling subsequent interpolations), corrections, cancellations, etc., which brought their validity into question. The COI also found evidence that there were multiple sets of books maintained either in the names of individuals or companies and assets that were not disclosed.

The ITIC, opined the COI, was instrumental in hastening the split in the group. An IT order for Jaidayal Dalmia, for the accounting year September 30, 1952, showed that the ITIC computed the concerned assets of the DJ group through concealed shares in limited companies to the order of Rs 419.73 lakhs. It was admitted before the ITIC that these concealed assets were joint property until the division in 1948. Though Jaidayal Dalmia advised his share of the value of the shares at Rs 132.41 lakhs and provided a list, the ITIC was unable to obtain the share ownership and the tax liability between Shanti Prasad Jain and Ramkrishna Dalmia.

Shanti Prasad raised the issue of partition, and he said that the group had no joint property or assets except the Lauriya farm.

However, various exhibits and evidence executed by the three indicated the contrary. Incidentally, Shriyans Prasad Jain, who appeared as a witness before the COI, advised that even in April 1948, the three had agreed to set the IT liability in the proportion of 50:25:25 to be borne by Ramkrishna, Jaidayal, and Shanti Prasad Jain respectively. On September 21, 1952, a document signed by these three signatories accepting joint liability in respect of Rs 96.52 lakhs which was outstanding under the ITIC order, agreed to divide that liability between themselves as follows: Ramkrishna Dalmia, Rs 48.34 lakhs, Jaidayal Dalmia Rs 24 lakhs and Shanti Prasad Jain Rs 24.18 lakhs. The proportions were very nearly 50:25:25.

While Ramkrishna Dalmia's internecine war with Jawaharlal Nehru did prompt Shanti Prasad and Jaidayal to distance themselves and hasten the split, as has been discussed earlier, another reason for the split was on account of the multiple marriages of Ramkrishna Dalmia and the attendant complications of inheritance, which was resisted by Shanti Prasad and Jaidayal.

The COI also concluded that the three of them had joint assets over and above Lauriya farm and that the shares held by them in joint stock companies were joint property and not individual property. Though Ramkrishna Dalmia commenced and carried on business at various places, incorporating various joint stock companies and later, acquiring the management of several companies, he "out of love and affection for Jaidayal and Shanti Prasad associated them with the management of the said companies which continued to be carried on under the guidance of Ramkrishna Dalmia." Importantly, the recitals further indicated that Ramkrishna Dalmia financed the acquisition of the companies, and the others were only associated with the management. There was no reference to the capital subscribed by the others; nor was there anything to indicate that they had anything to do with the acquisitions.

While the original property was paid for and acquired by Ramkrishna, in 1946 he gave his brother (Jaidayal) and son-in-law (Shanti Prasad) defined shares in the income and apparently in the capital as well. Hence, whatever the truth of the recital about the termination of the arrangement by mutual consent, there was a clear admission that there were joint assets other than the Lauriya farm at any rate up to June 1948, as also joint liabilities other than income tax.

Finally, the COI concluded that:

a. There was no clear evidence of the partition of the group as on May 31, 1948.
b. After 1949, Ramkrishna alone controlled and managed certain companies and neither Shanti Prasad nor Jaidayal had any role to play in their control and/or management.
c. The COI also accepted the evidence that proved that Ramkrishna Dalmia was in effective control of all the ten companies under investigation both before and after May 31, 1948, and hence was responsible for all the malpractices that the COI discovered in these ten companies.
d. From all the direct and circumstantial evidence discovered, the malfeasances couldn't have occurred without Ramkrishna Dalmia's knowledge, connivance, and directions.

The others were implicated only when directly linked to actions discovered or when they were director(s) at the time that a malpractice occurred.

HOW CONTROL WAS ABUSED

The DJ group had a labyrinth of companies and used them for complex inter-company transactions. Many of these were liquidated and appeared in new avatars as well. Therefore, an overview of the kinds of perpetrations committed is necessary before we begin with the wrongdoings in individual companies. We will only examine a few major companies here as representatives of the ills that prevailed in the ten companies inspected by the COI.

The investigations of the COI disclosed that funds of public limited companies, banks, and insurance companies were diverted for buying shares and gaining control of other companies that had large, accumulated resources and substantial liquid resources. The Lahore Electric Supply Co Ltd (LES), the Sir Shapoorji Broacha Mills Ltd (SSB), and the Madhowji Dharamsi Manufacturing Co Ltd (MDM) were prime examples of target companies so acquired. After acquisition, the funds were used for the benefit of the DJ group or Ramkrishna Dalmia or for companies in which Ramkrishna Dalmia was interested. The various methods of exploitation were as follows:

LOANS AND ADVANCES

Companies where the public had invested their monies were made to give loans and advances without security and at lower rates of interest to the companies in which the group or Ramkrishna Dalmia were interested, even if the financials of the borrowing companies were unsound. Most of the loans remained unpaid and were shown to have been realised by means of book adjustments.

Loans were also given to Ramkrishna Dalmia personally. His dues to the public companies increased from Rs 17.30 lakhs in 1948 to Rs 152 lakhs in 1951. Additionally, his personal expenses were paid by Dalmia Cement and Paper Marketing Company Limited (DCPM), though he was neither a director nor an officer of DCPM in those years. The total of these payments between 1948-51 was Rs 4.62 lakhs. DCPM's role will be discussed later.

Loans were also made by DCPM to companies that are said to have gone to Ramkrishna upon the purported dissolution of the group. The *maximum* amounts outstanding against some of these companies at various points in time post the alleged dissolution were as follows:

a. Rashtriya Financial Corporation, Rs 288 lakhs (as on February 28, 1951)
b. Allenberry and Co Ltd, Rs 108 lakhs (as on February 29, 1949)
c. Bennett Coleman and Co Ltd, (eventually went to Shanti Prasad Jain), Rs 94.41 lakhs (as on October 30, 1951)

It is to be noted that Jaidayal Dalmia too benefitted from personal loans from DCPM for Rs 30.94 lakhs (as on the financial year-end 1948 for DCPM). Loans were provided to Jaidayal's company Vyapari Ltd too (Rs 103 lakhs outstanding as on February 28, 1951). Though Shanti Prasad Jain did not personally secure any loans from DCPM, his companies Ashok Agencies (Rs 200 lakhs outstanding as on February 28, 1951, and Ashok Marketing (Rs 87.7 lakhs outstanding as on February 28, 1950) were indebted to DCPM. It is important to underscore here that DCPM's source of funds for such lending was its own borrowings from public companies, including banks and insurance companies owned by the group. Hence, DCPM has been often referred to as a "clearing house" for the group in the way it facilitated the movement of funds from public companies to the private ones.

IMPROPER TRANSFER OF ASSETS

The assets of one company were transferred to another by way of mere book entries, with the object of benefiting the DJ Group or Ramkrishna Dalmia and to the detriment of the investing public. Intercompany investments/transactions included various forms of abuse:

a. Subscriptions to share capital were recorded to be made in cash, even when no cash was received.

b. Similarly, payments for the purchases and receipt for sales purportedly in cash were only book entries, debiting or crediting the respective accounts.

c. Shares were not registered in the name of the beneficial individuals (those deriving benefit from the shares).

d. Shares purchased and sold in the normal course of business; were at manipulated rates to benefit the DJ group or Ramkrishna Dalmia, and/or his companies. In most cases, these shares either did not yield any dividend to the public, or they were transferred to companies and persons within the group just before the declaration of dividend to benefit the transferee.

LIQUIDATIONS

In the words of the COI, "This was another device. After the public companies were squeezed dry, the husks were discarded and destroyed." An erstwhile profitable venture would be drained of its resources and be brought to voluntary liquidation. A willing liquidator would be appointed who would get the scheme of arrangement sanctioned by the courts. All the assets, records, and books would then be handed over to a concern having puppet directors orchestrated by Ramkrishna Dalmia. This transferee company would then proceed to destroy the books and records, so that all traces of the frauds and manipulations were erased. The COI examined the following companies in detail, which were liquidated (names in brackets are the names of the transferee company and the date of the transfer):

a. Dalmia Jain Airways – DJ Airways (Dalmia Jain Aviation, February 10, 1953)

b. SSB and MDM (South Asia Industries, December 31, 1951)

c. DCPM (Delhi Glass Works Ltd, February 18, 1953)

d. Vastra Vyavasaya Ltd (Bharat Union Agencies Ltd, April 11, 1953)

The COI found their attempts to obtain assistance from some of the concerned liquidators frustrating. These individuals did not cooperate and tried to thwart the investigations. With the intransigence of the liquidators, the COI redoubled efforts to establish if the liquidations of the five companies mentioned above were bona fide. They collected the evidence of nineteen other companies that were taken into voluntary liquidation by the group from 1951 to 1956. These were non-scheduled companies and outside the remit of the ten under investigation, but their similar pattern became relevant under sections 14 and 15 of the Evidence Act to establish bad faith, intention, and design. These included the Gwalior Bank Ltd (alluded to by Feroze Gandhi in his maiden parliamentary speech). The COI also discovered that of these nineteen companies, the books of account and records of nine companies (including Gwalior Bank) were destroyed within a period of four years from 1953, and concluded that the liquidations had been orchestrated.

THE LAW, COURTS, AND ARBITRATORS

The COI discovered that Ramkrishna Dalmia had exploited the weaknesses in the safeguards of the law even as procedure was followed in all cases. The assumption that there is an intelligent and alert body of shareholders able to look after their own interests was thwarted by the DJ group. Registered offices of some companies were situated in inaccessible places such as South Asia Industries (formerly LES) located in Gurgaon, "a small out of the way place about 18 miles from Delhi, and only a branch office was maintained at Delhi." When COI ordered a search at the Gurgaon registered office, they were advised that all the records were in Delhi!

It was not possible for shareholders to present a united front to protect their own cause as they were scattered. The so-called General Meetings and Extraordinary General Meetings of the shareholders were usually a farce. The COI found that in most cases, a small coterie comprising those close to Ramkrishna Dalmia with sometimes a small minority of independent shareholders easily outvoted the public shareholders and did as they pleased. The independent liquidators were mere instruments in the hands of those in control. In exchange for abnormally high remuneration paid to them, they did little to safeguard the interests of the general body of the shareholders. The COI also opined that courts excluding those in the large towns of Calcutta and Bombay weren't equipped with personnel, well-versed in Company Law to stop malpractices, nor had adequate machinery to handle liquidations. It was thus impossible for them to function effectively, unearth flaws, and handle the frauds.

In the liquidation proceedings of DJ Airways, a few shareholders did protest. However, they were influenced or paid off and eventually withdrew their objections and approved the scheme.

REGISTRARS

Registrars of companies were found to be lacking, especially noted by the COI in the case of DJ Airways.

AUDITORS

Auditors were found to be negligent or complicit by the COI. An auditor of some of the scheduled companies, PS Sodhbans was named as dishonest in the manner that the audits for DJ Airways and LES were dispensed with. In the DJ Airways Joint Venture (JV) with Allenberry, the auditors never examined the original/real account books and vouchers available at the branches, and limited their audit based on the sparse information available in the books at the headquarters. What was being audited was clerical accuracy and not veracity of transactions.

SELLING AND MANAGING AGENCIES

Private concerns where the group or Ramkrishna Dalmia owned and derived benefit from were appointed as selling and managing agents of the public companies. These agents got their remuneration at high rates, reducing profits and thus depleting the returns to the shareholders. What was worse was the blatant abuse and extraction from public companies via these agencies. In the instances of SSB, MDM managing agents were not necessary. Yet the managing agencies were appointed with long-term contracts for twenty years. The modus operandi of their premature termination and compensation paid has been discussed later in the chapter

"Ru(i)n of the Mill(s)". The managing agents were compensated from the two mills a sum of Rs 119.90 lakhs. There was a similar pattern in the case of DCPM, appointed as the selling agent for the two mills, which was compensated Rs 46.90 lakhs. This has also been discussed in the same chapter. In the case of Dalmia Dadri Cement, Dalmia Jain (Jind State) Co was appointed managing agents. In 1952, a breach in the contract period of nineteen years resulted in a sum of Rs 6 lakhs being paid as compensation.

Interestingly, long-term contracts were structured for employment as well! Shriyans Prasad Jain, Shanti Prasad's elder brother was appointed in DCPM at a remuneration of Rs 4,000 per month, which together with his perquisites that averaged Rs 5,400 per month was a handsome figure of Rs 9,400 a month (Applying our multiplier of 92, this translated to a mensem of Rs 864,800!). He was appointed to this position in 1943 when he was thirty-six years old, for a period of twenty-five years. The COI found this unusual when "even in government service a man of 36 would never be appointed for a term of 25 years" for this would be beyond the superannuation age of sixty. On February 07, 1950, there was a breach, and he was paid Rs 7 lakhs as compensation by a company that had been unable to pay its ordinary shareholders any dividends since 1941 and its preferred shareholders since 1943. The pattern of the dates of the breaches in all these cases, in February and October 1950 and in 1952 was strange and involved a total compensation of Rs 179.80 lakhs in these two years – a sum that the public companies could only afford at a grievous cost to their shareholders. Though DCPM was privately and almost entirely owned by Ramkrishna Dalmia, it got its funds from the public companies. The COI also frowned that not only the business owners of the group but also their relatives (such as Shriyans Prasad Jain) were siphoning money off the public companies acquired by the group.

MANIPULATIONS

The COI discovered several instances where the financials were manipulated. These have been discussed in individual instances dealt with later.

DIFFERENT FINANCIAL YEARS

Full advantage was taken of companies having different financial years to manipulate inter-company loans, transfers, and investments. The same blocks of shares were moved from company to company to give a false appearancc of prosperity to companies that were not doing well and to enable manipulation of the profits and losses for the year. These too have been detailed under individual companies discussed later.

NON-DECLARATION OF DIVIDENDS

Another abuse of control was not to declare dividends although the public companies concerned made profits. This would depress the value of the shares and enable Ramkrishna Dalmia to purchase the shares at reduced rates. Once he had acquired enough shares, then dividends would be declared, and Ramkrishna Dalmia would reap the benefits. The COI found this to have happened for all the ten companies investigated, except for Allenberry and LES.

PRIVATIZATION OF PUBLIC LIMITED COMPANIES

Dalmia Jain Aviation (DJ Aviation) was converted to a private limited company on April 26, 1952; DCPM on April 10, 1952; and LES on December 05, 1952. This was done to take advantage of the less stringent provisions of the Companies Act for private companies.

AVOIDANCE OF INCOME TAX LIABILITY

This was done using the following ways:

a. By suppressing taxable profits by manipulation of accounts.

b. By extinguishing reserves and accumulating profits before taking the companies into liquidation.

c. By introducing secret profits under cover of share money by allotting shares to non-existent persons.

d. By transferring the assets and liabilities of companies that were taken into liquidation, while their income tax liabilities for the periods up to the dates of liquidation were yet to be determined/assessed. Such a transfer was made to other Ramkrishna Dalmia concerns under the scheme of arrangement under the Indian Companies Act, 1913 (under provisions of section 153/153A or 208C). When the arrears/dues were finally calculated, there were no assets left in the company under liquidation to recover from. Even if the transferee company holding the relevant assets could be treated by law as the successor and be bound to satisfy the liabilities of the company under liquidation, the recovery provisions of the Income-tax Act were not applicable to the transferee company.

We will find several instances where one or more of the above infractions occurred in our subsequent narrative.

AERONAUTICS OR AUTOMOTIVES? - THE JV PERIOD

Allenberry and Co Ltd, a profitable English company with substantial assets and reserves, was taken over by the DJ group around April 1945, and in gradual stages became a Ramkrishna Dalmia concern by March 27, 1950. Initially, Shanti Prasad Jain, VH Dalmia (son of Jaidayal) and paid employees HD Bishnoi, and R Bajoria were appointed the directors of the company. Ramkrishna Dalmia though not a director, provided consultancy and had a predominant role in the management, while Shanti Prasad effectively ran the company, as VH Dalmia was only twenty-one years old.

At a shareholder meeting on April 15, 1945, the registered office of the company was shifted from Calcutta to Dalmianagar in Bihar and the inexperienced VH Dalmia was appointed managing director. The share capital was also augmented from 7 lakh rupees to 5 crores and shareholders were awarded bonus shares[37] 3:1 on February 28, 1946. Thus, the process of extraction from reserves had already begun almost immediately after the takeover. For these significant decisions, only six shareholders were present in person

---

37 A bonus issue, also known as a scrip issue or a capitalization issue, is an offer of free additional shares to existing shareholders. A bonus issue of shares is funded by a company's earnings or share reserves.

and seven by proxy. The chairman of the meeting VH Dalmia and all twelve others were interested parties in the DJ group. The group's shareholding from 78 per cent at the time of the takeover increased to a little over 81 per cent in September 1946, and remained at this level till March 27, 1950.

Between March 27, 1950, and January 10, 1952, the entire shareholding (1,60,000 shares) was acquired by two trusts – The Yogiraj Charity Trust and the Bhriguraj Charity Trust. As the founder trustee, Ramkrishna Dalmia had absolute control of these trusts. Therefore, from March 27, 1950 onwards, Ramkrishna had 100 per cent of the shareholdings of Allenberry through these two trusts. We have already seen the questions raised by Feroze Gandhi in the parliament about how such a large shareholding was acquired by these trusts, which had paltry capital.

During WWII, India had provided a major base of operations for the United States to deploy their forces in the China-Burma-India theatre of the war. After the hostilities had ceased, American troops withdrew, leaving behind their jeeps, weapon carriers, and command cars. Keen to expedite the disposal of this stock of surplus vehicles and stores as part of their winding up of affairs in the subcontinent, the US government sought to dispose these stocks, offering a bulk discount to a buyer who would take the entire lot at an early date. The Director General (DG) of Disposals had determined a price of over Rs 550 lakhs for the entire business.

Allenberry, which handled the US Army aviation department contracts for servicing and conditioning of their vehicles, learnt of the deal even before the war ended and positioned themselves as bidders quickly. The DJ group was anxious to corner the market because of the high demand for motor vehicles and stores, and poor supply of the same. This gap would only increase since new vehicles and stores would not reach this country for a long time after the cessation of hostilities. Thus, refurbishments and sales of these vehicles presented a profitable opportunity.

Initially, Allenberry had wanted to only take a part of the motor vehicles business, which was valued at about Rs 242 lakhs (raised later to Rs 271 lakhs). However, when they were offered the entire deal, including the balance motor vehicle supplies valued at Rs 250 lakhs, the stores business (for Rs 50 lakhs) and an R-3A part (a unit used for reconditioning the vehicles valued at Rs 15 lakhs), the group realized that despite having the organization and technical staff necessary for the transaction, they did not have the financial muscle to afford the total sum of over Rs 550 lakhs. (Interestingly, the COI could never find the R-3A plant recorded as an asset in the books of the JV.) It was then that Allenberry advised the DG disposals of its intention to partner with DJ Airways, and sought permission from the controller of capital issues for the raising of additional capital by DJ Airways. This presented no difficulty; as the DG Disposals simply made a telephonic call to the examiner of capital issues, who in the same call assured of the necessary permissions.

Allenberry's bankers revealed that Allenberry's balance sheet would allow raising only Rs 150 lakhs; therefore, another Rs 400 lakhs plus was needed. Thus, Allenberry's contention before the COI that they would have been able to purchase the initial lot of vehicles valued at Rs 242 lakhs without the assistance of DJ Airways was incorrect, let alone the amended deal requiring more than double the investment.

The group argued with the COI that DJ Airways was formed to run an aviation business and that the idea of taking it on as a financing partner for Allenberry for the disposal goods business arose at a later stage. The COI, however, determined that though it was true that the application to float the public limited company (DJ Airways) was made on May 03, 1946, the group had indeed inspected the surplus vehicles at the Moran depot *before* this date; the group had insider information on the opportunity and the Memorandum of Association of DJ Airways had other objects in addition to the aviation business. DJ Airways' formation was thus pre-meditated and was created solely for the purpose of raising public funds to finance the shortfall in the purchase price of the disposable business.

In the words of the COI, "As a matter of fact, there was never any intention to do any serious air business and the only reason the company was floated in this form was because aviation was very much in the public eye at that time and there was a big demand for shares in airways companies." DJ Airways never got a scheduled airline licence. Only a provisional licence (which was never renewed) was issued; and it was confined to the operation of a cargo service for the carriage of goods between Delhi and Srinagar. It had a fleet of six refurbished Dakota aircraft costing about Rs 7.0 lakhs only. The aviation losses during the period of the joint venture (August 26, 1946, to June 30, 1948) amounted to a little over Rs 16.5 lakhs.

The speed of the sequence of events was also mind-boggling. DJ Airways was formed on July 09, 1946. On July 11, 1946, the opportunity to increase Allenberry's initial commitment came through by way of an offer of the balance vehicles, stores business, and the R-3A plant. The same day, a board meeting was convened for DJ Airways, where the resolution to form the JV with Allenberry was taken, provided DJ Airways was able to raise additional capital which required the approval of the Examiner of Capital Issues. The same afternoon, DG Disposals was approached who made the telephone call mentioned earlier.

According to the arrangement of the JV, Allenberry was supposed to be the working partner and DJ Airways the financing partner, and on July 12, 1946, an application was made to the Examiner of Capital Issues seeking permission for an issue of capital amounting to Rs 310 lakhs for DJ Airways. On the same day, sale notes were procured as well for the business on offer in the name of the JV! Yet, there was no evidence of a partnership deed with Allenberry, nothing to suggest the terms on which the money would be given or how much each partner would contribute, nor how would the profits and losses be shared. The application to raise Rs 310 lakhs of public monies included Rs 242 lakhs of capital commitments and Rs 68 lakhs as working capital commitment by DJ Airways.

At this juncture, Ramkrishna Dalmia intervened with the desire to purchase the remaining Rs 250 lakhs worth of balance vehicles on August 02, 1946. He was not a director of either company (Allenberry or DJ Airways), nor had he been put forward as a promoter. Though Dalmia Jain and company were proposed as managing agents on July 12, 1946, the agreement was not made till August 28, 1946. Hence, when he committed DJ Airways for the further purchase, he had no locus standi. Again, there was no resolution from the board of directors of either company, nor did he hold a power of attorney from DJ Airways. And there still was no partnership agreement. Although Allenberry could have raised Rs 150 lakhs or so on its own, it made no attempt to do so. All it did was make an initial payment of Rs 82 lakhs on July 11, 1946, which it quickly recouped from the funds of DJ Airways on July 26, 1946.

Control of the public company DJ Airways and marginalization of the subscribing public was achieved in several ways.

The first was through shareholding. The initial public shareholding of 91.3 per cent (amounting to a little over Rs 319 lakhs) reduced to 43.6 per cent in December 1952, with the DJ group and their employees, relatives and concerns correspondingly increasing their ownership from 8.7 to 56.4 per cent. Notwithstanding that the majority holding until December 1952 was by the public, they were scattered and unable to present a united front, allowing the DJ group to exercise control.

There was more. Of the first 121 names in the register of subscribers, not less than 114 to whom share certificates were issued were fictitious. It was unusual that they had paid for the share subscription by way of cash into Bharat Bank (A DJ group entity) a total sum of Rs 16 lakhs (1,60,000 shares each with a face value of Rs 10). The subscription money was all received within a very short period (between July 11, 1946, and July 17, 1946). Of these 1,60,000 shares, 1,58,850 shares were transferred by these 114 persons in apparently widely scattered localities to only four persons and two concerns (both Ramkrishna Dalmia concerns) and the majority of the transfers were affected in one day. One of the four individuals was VS Chordia, an employee, and a brother-in-law of Ramkrishna Dalmia. These two concerns and VS Chordia between them accounted for Rs 15.76 lakh worth of shares (of the total of Rs 16 lakhs) with the entire transfer effected on a single day, i.e. July 04, 1950.

The shares were brought at low prices ranging between rupees 1/9 annas and rupee 1/10 (for shares with a face value of rupees 10) at a 50 per cent discount to market prices. The price quoted on the Delhi Stock Exchange for DJ Airways shares on July 03, 1950, was rupees 2/2 annas.

And how did these two concerns, each of which had a paid-up capital of rupees 1,000 only, afford the acquisition? For each concern had borrowed only Rs 98,000 from the Bharat bank on the security of shares of DJ Airways, which was clearly inadequate.

The COI concluded that the issue of the Rs 16 lakhs worth of shares in these fictitious names was fraudulent and surmised that this was a manoeuvre to bring the secret profits (black money) of the DJ group into circulation and convert it into "white money".

The second method to drain money from public companies was to get their own concerns appointed as underwriters[38] and managing agents, and then have them charge large sums as commission.

Of the two applications made to the examiner of capital issues for raising a total sum of Rs 350 lakhs of share capital by DJ Airways, the first on May 03, 1946, was for Rs 40 lakhs, for which Dalmia Jain and company (Dalmia Jain), a company owned and controlled by Ramkrishna Dalmia, was appointed as underwriters. The second, made on July 12, 1946, for Rs 310 lakhs, while not naming an underwriter, provided for "brokerage and underwriting commission to be paid to bona fide brokers," and proposed Dalmia Jain as managing agents, i.e. a role reversal within a two-month period. Yet there was no documentation supporting this change of engagement for Dalmia Jain.

On August 24, 1946, an underwriting agreement was made with DCPM, a DJ group company. DCPM were to be paid Rs 7.87 lakhs as commission for underwriting Rs 345 lakhs worth of shares. Two days later, in the prospectus issued, the directors said in the prospectus that the full amount of the issued capital of Rs 350 lakhs had *already been received*. The account of DJ Airways with Bharat bank at Delhi reflected that Rs 195.86 lakhs had been received before August 26, 1946, while the rest had been received earlier at

---

[38] In the context of share issuance, an underwriter is a person or institution that takes the risk of non-subscription of shares by the public by committing to buying a certain number of shares or securities from a company usually as part of an initial public offering (IPO). The underwriter then sells them to the public/institutions at a later date. The underwriting service involves a fee payable by the issuer of shares to the underwriter for the risk taken by the latter.

other places such as Bombay and Calcutta but had not yet been remitted to Delhi. Therefore, DCPM ran no risk in underwriting the Rs 345 lakhs, (as the subscriptions to the share issue had already been received), and the DJ group had merely gifted themselves a risk-free sum of Rs 7.87 lakhs from public subscriptions collected. The COI surmised that the manoeuvre for DCPM's appointment was to make Dalmia Jain and company the managing agents, as it would be strange for both the underwriters and the managing agents to be the same entity.

The third device was the managing agency. The terms for Dalmia Jain's engagement as a managing agent set out in the prospectus, included an office allowance of Rs 7,500 a month and a commission of 10 per cent on the net profit of the company. They would continue as managing agents for a period of twenty years from July 09, 1946, the date on which DJ Airways was incorporated.

The books of DJ Airways were destroyed when it was discovered that an investigation into the affairs of DJ Airways was afoot. The books of the joint venture were kept by Allenberry, along with their own books. However, except for those that were seized by the Special Police Establishment, the COI wasn't allowed to access to the rest. From material available, the COI discovered that the books were manipulated.

Ironically, all the assets (the joint venture stock) acquired from public money via the instrument of DJ Airways were kept in Allenberry's physical possession, including the vehicles, stores, and the plant. It was also in control of all the sales. Whenever it sold a disposal vehicle, it debited the sale amount to the customer's account. The money received went into Allenberry's general account rather than into a separate partnership account. Nor were they segregated from Allenberry's own funds. Hence, Allenberry had the use of the money until it chose to hand it over to somebody else. All that DJ

Airways received were credit entries in Allenberry's books.

In the case of 2323 vehicles, which Allenberry sold from this stock to various retail customers between February 28, 1947, and December 31, 1947, on behalf of the JV, Allenberry recorded these as sales on behalf of DCPM, and made out a statement in favour of DCPM for Rs 102.63 lakhs. This sleight was done on December 18, 1948, but antedated to December 31, 1947, as the DJ group realised that while Allenberry and DJ Airways had made profits, DCPM had run into losses. Routing this transaction to DCPM reduced the profits of the JV to the detriment of the public shareholders of DJ Airways, but benefitted Ramkrishna Dalmia and his concerns and robbed the government to the extent of Rs 3.52 lakhs in tax payments. Shanti Prasad Jain who was a director in the three companies – namely, DJ Airways, Allenberry and DCPM – and Jaidayal Dalmia, who was a director in two of these three companies (excluding Allenberry) on February 28, 1947, denied all knowledge and responsibility for these transactions because of the dissolution of the DJ group on May 31, 1948, earlier than the date of passing the antedated entries in December 1948.

Incidentally, the COI found similar transgressions by Allenberry for its Drum and Pipeline business in a transfer of Rs 52 lakhs to DCPM.

The JV between DJ Airways and Allenberry lasted from August 1946 up to June 30, 1948, when it was terminated. Total sales during this period were recorded as Rs 463.83 lakhs (excluding sales routed via DCPM of the 2323 vehicles discussed above of Rs 102.63 lakhs). With the cost of vehicles transferred from the JV to DCPM of Rs 47.20 lakhs (see table below) the profit transferred in DCPM's book was substantial as was the quantum of tax evasion.

As on June 30, 1948, the stock of vehicles and spare parts left over in the JV amounted to Rs 246.59 lakhs as under. The closing stock was however adjusted (inflated) on July 01, 1948, in the books of Allenberry by a sum of Rs 30.31 lakhs to Rs 276.90 lakhs allegedly due to a "wrong entry" by Allenberry's Lucknow branch, which increased Allenberry's profits by this sum of rupees 30 odd lakhs as well.

DETAILS	RS (IN LAKHS)	RS (IN LAKHS)
Total purchase price - the purchase price of vehicles was increased resulting in the increase of the acquisition price from Rs 550 lakhs		571.33
Less: Cost of sales (a)	277.54	
Less: Cost of vehicles purportedly transferred to DCPM (b)	47.20	
Total Cost (a + b)		324.74
Closing Stock		246.59*

*Revised upward to Rs 276.90 as mentioned.

A method of depriving DJ Airways of its correct share of profits was inflating the cost of sales and expenses chargeable against the sales in the joint venture. From the table above, the cost of sales of Rs 277 lakhs on sales of Rs 464 lakhs amounted to 59.7 per cent. If one were to add the selling expenses additionally of Rs 141 lakhs, or another, 30.3 per cent, the margin in this business for the JV was barely 10 per cent.

And this was one of the justifications provided by the group that the disposal business wasn't attractive and hence the JV was being disbanded.

Surprisingly, the COI found the post-demerged performance of the business (between July 01, 1948, to October 31, 1953) far rosier, as under:

DETAILS	RS (IN LAKHS)	RS (IN LAKHS)	(PER CENT OF SALES)
Sales		606.11	
Less: Cost of sales*	276.90		45.6
Less: Selling expenses	190.32		31.4
Total Cost		467.22	77.0
Profit (Rs lakhs)		138.89	23.0

*Accepting "error of Allenberry's Lucknow office" mentioned earlier.

As evident, the post-JV profit margin was almost two-and-a-half times higher than the JV period.

The COI estimated this difference of profit of about 13 per cent on sales (during the JV period), together with the Rs 14.97 lakh profit fraudulently diverted to DCPM on the 2,323 vehicles, to be the suppressed total profits to the tune of over Rs 75 lakhs.

The books of accounts of the joint venture were not produced before the COI with the excuse that they were in Dacca (now Dhaka in Bangladesh). COI's offer to depute an officer to accompany an Allenberry staff to proceed to Dacca to examine the books at their cost was not accepted.

It was clear to the COI that the disposal business was a very profitable venture and the group deliberately manipulated to keep profits low during the JV period. When the financing partner DJ Airways was no longer necessary (because sales were rolling in by then), the JV was disbanded less than two years from its start, just when the shareholders of the public company would begin to get a return on the investment. The pretext was that of safeguarding DJ Airway's interest by declaring the disposal business unprofitable. DJ Airways went into voluntary liquidation on June 13, 1952, without a single rupee of dividend being paid to its shareholders.

AERONAUTICS OR AUTOMOTIVES? - POST JV PERIOD

DJ Aviation was floated, supposedly to take over the aviation business of DJ Airways. As with DJ Airways, the COI concluded that "it was orchestrated by Ramkrishna Dalmia in the background with a set of dummy directors in the front, with no financial stake in the concern."

Though the application for the new company was made to the Controller of Capital Issues (CCI) on October 13, 1947, there was an objection to the name proposed (Dalmia Jain Air Ltd). An extension was sought from the CCI till February 28, 1949. The JV in the interim had already been terminated with effect from June 30, 1948. Hence, only the air business remained in DJ Airways. So, where was the need for the new company? Especially when the aviation business in DJ Airways' hands was a complete failure and was being run at a loss with no hope of revival?

Further, the first and only temporary license issued to DJ Airways had expired by then. No attempts had been made to get a fresh one, not even a temporary license. DJ Aviation was originally floated as a public limited company but was converted to a private company on April 26, 1952. Incidentally, this was just ten days after DCPM had similarly been changed from a public to a private limited company.

The initial capital of Rs 1 crore of DJ Aviation was subscribed as under:

a. Rs 75,00,000 equity shares and Rs 25,000 preference shares by DJ Airways;
b. Rs 24,75,00 preference shares by Bharat Insurance.

At that time, DJ Airways was a public limited company with 85 per cent shares held by the investing public, while in Bharat Insurance, its shareholders and policyholders had a substantial stake. Public monies were thus "invested" in a questionable venture. More startling was the nature of the investment and the manner of recording in the books of DJ Aviation:

a. Of the Rs 75.25 lakhs due from DJ Airways towards the equity/preference subscription, only Rs 10,000 was received in cash. Of the balance Rs 75.15 lakhs due, a sum of Rs 75.13 lakhs was transferred to the account of DCPM as the latter's indebtedness. (The balance of Rs 2,036 had already been adjusted as Preliminary Expenses.)
b. The entire amount of Rs 24.75 lakhs due from Bharat Insurance was debited to DCPM's account.

Both DJ Airways and Bharat Insurance drew *hundies*[39] (Bills of Exchange) on DCPM in favour of DJ Aviation. But DJ Aviation did not realize these hundies in cash. Instead, it debited the account of DCPM in its books with the amount of the hundies i.e. Rs 99.88 lakhs and took no security for the debt. Yet the capital of DJ Aviation was shown as fully paid up to the extent of Rs 1 crore!

As on February 28, 1949, DCPM owed DJ Airways Rs 60.21 lakhs and Bharat Insurance a sum of Rs 33.33 lakhs (total Rs

---

39 An unconditional order in writing made by a person directing another to pay a certain sum of money to a person named in the order.

93.54 lakhs). Both these sums were repayable on demand, and both carried interest, albeit at very low rates of 4-4.5 per cent per annum compared to 6-8 per cent being charged by the group's own Bharat Bank.

The elaborate arrangement was a ploy to give indirect financial assistance to DCPM in respect of Rs 99.88 lakhs, to offset these debts it owed DJ Airways and Bharat Insurance.

In the books of DJ Airways and Bharat Insurance, the indebtedness of DCPM to them was wiped out and was substituted by the investment in shares of DJ Aviation, a company that had no assets against its supposedly paid-up capital of Rs 1 crore, except the unsecured indebtedness of DCPM. Over time, this indebtedness of DCPM was transferred as "investments" in shares of other group companies, such as Jaipur Udyog, LES, and later Bennett Coleman. Not one of these shares, "purchased" by DJ Aviation, was held by it in its own name, and not a single dividend was received on any of them during these three years (between July 1950 to July 1952), except Rs 55,017 from LES.

Though DJ Airways was the owner of Rs 75.25 lakhs worth of shares in DJ Aviation, they were never entered as shareholders in the register of shareholders. Instead, their shares were held benami by thirteen persons, all of whom were either relatives or employees of the DJ group or its concerns.

Returning to the question of DCPM's liability to DJ Airways of Rs 60.21 lakhs, how did this arise?

It may be recalled that when the JV was terminated on June 30, 1948, stocks of nearly Rs 277 lakhs were transferred to the books of Allenberry. Allenberry was due to pay for this in instalments to DJ Airways, plus interest at the benign rate of 3 per cent per annum. A sum of Rs 1 crore was payable by June 30, 1949, another Rs 1 crore by June 30, 1950, and the balance by June 30, 1951.

On February 05, 1949, DJ Airways in its books transferred a sum of Rs 60 lakhs along with accrued interest (being part of the dues from Allenberry from the first tranche) to the account of DCPM. A good debt by a profitable entity (Allenberry) had been converted to a debt from "a man of straw"[40] (DCPM) by the simple stroke of a pen. This debt, as on May 31, 1949, in DJ Airways books had reduced to Rs 52.32 lakhs. It was unclear to the COI if DCPM had repaid a part over the intervening three months or if there were further book adjustments. Since the liability of DJ Airways to pay DJ Aviation for the shares issued for Rs 75.13 lakhs had been transferred to DCPM, DCPM became a creditor (lender) in DJ Airways books to the extent of Rs 22.81 lakhs (Rs 75.13 lakhs less Rs 52.32 lakhs).

DJ Airways then, on May 31, 1949 (within three months of subscribing for them) transferred Rs 40 lakhs to DCPM in the shape of DJ Aviation shares and DCPM thus again became indebted to DJ Airways: but this time only to the extent of Rs 17.19 lakhs (Rs 40 lakhs less Rs 22.81 lakhs). The transfer of these shares was done at cost; hence, DJ Airways (and its shareholders) didn't gain anything in the transaction. The term "at cost" is misleading too because DCPM was to pay DJ Airways for this amount in annual instalments spread over 17 years without interest! It was estimated by COI that the shares were transferred to DCPM at about 50 per cent loss to the investors in DJ Airways, (in terms of the amount and timeline of the receipts of monies against these).

These series of accounting entries and complicated manoeuvres with very little actual consideration (cash) were to be affected before June 30, 1949 (the date on which DJ Airways' balance sheet

---

40 A person undertaking a financial commitment without adequate means. Also used to refer to a person regarded as having no substance or integrity.

had to be drawn up in order that the shareholders of DJ Airways could be told that (a) Allenberry had paid a substantial part of the instalment of Rs 100 lakhs due from it under the agreement and (b) that DCPM's liability to DJ Airways had been reduced by more than Rs 35.5 lakhs. Also, by transferring Rs 40 lakh worth of shares of DJ Aviation to DCPM, DJ Airways' shareholding in DJ Aviation dropped to Rs 35.25 lakhs or 35.25 per cent. Any holding greater or equal to 40 per cent would have required DJ Airways to declare DJ Aviation as a subsidiary and would have been obliged to attach the balance sheets of its subsidiary with its own financials and thus would have needed to disclose the true assets of the subsidiary to the shareholders of DJ Airways.

The purpose of creating DJ Aviation was to transfer the dues of the DJ Group companies (principally DCPM) payable to DJ Airways and allow DCPM the continued use of funds (for a period of 17 years without interest) that should have been refunded to DJ Airways.

The COI determined that all the manoeuvres had resulted in a loss of Rs 3.41 lakhs to the shareholders of DJ Airways. The gains had all gone to the group companies; principally Allenberry and DCPM.

After the termination of the JV, Ramkrishna Dalmia exploited the funds of public company DJ Airways for the benefit of the concerns under his control. The accounting year of DCPM ended on February 28, while that of DJ Airways was June 30 and that of Allenberry was December 31. The COI realized that accounting years were purposely kept different to enable manipulations accordingly. The incidences of the transactions with SSB and MDM shares, discussed below, proved just this.

On July 01, 1949, at the start of the accounting year of DJ Airways had the following receivables:

a. From DCPM, Rs 15.44 lakhs;
b. From Allenberry, Rs 247.20 lakhs. (Including the Rs 40 lakhs unpaid from the first instalment due by June 30, 1949.)

By the end of July 1949, the Rs 40 lakhs of indebtedness (unpaid/overdue) by Allenberry was extinguished by simply transferring the liability to DCPM. Along with interest calculated on these dues, DCPM's dues to DJ Airways as on February 28, 1950 stood at Rs 67.83 lakhs.

DCPM, which, in this manner had become the receptacle to park the various indebtedness of the group, had now a total indebtedness of nearly Rs 6 crores against its paid-up capital of only Rs 50 lakhs. This would rise to Rs 7.5 crores within the next year (see next chapter).

In March 1950, DJ Airways was directed to buy shares worth Rs 43.60 lakhs of SSB and Rs 21.60 lakhs of MDM shares from DCPM, reducing DCPM's indebtedness to DJ Airways to Rs 2.63 lakhs. The transaction was done post-February 1950, as DCPM was still a public company in February, and Ramkrishna Dalmia didn't want to tell the shareholders that DCPM had parted with valuable shares. On the other hand, the shareholders of DJ Airways were shown these valuable shares in the balance sheet of DJ Airways on June 30, 1950, and a reduced liability from DCPM in the books of DJ Airways. However, the transaction was reversed exactly at the same price on February 28, 1951, just before DCPM's financial closing the next year!

On June 30, 1951, after the SSB/MDM shares had been given back to DCPM they paid a dividend of Rs 3.26 lakhs, which DCPM received. The calculated yield was 5 per cent, whereas the interest that DCPM promised to pay was only 4.5 per cent. These facts make it evident that SSB and MDM shares were not acquired for bona fide investment purposes. In the investment book of DJ Airways, these shares were never transferred in their name, nor did DCPM pay DJ Airways for the retransfer of shares till DJ Airways went into liquidation.

A similar artifice was employed when the payment to DJ Airways for Allenberry's next tranche of Rs 1 crore fell due on June 30, 1950, along with interest. On June 29, 1950, Rs 74 lakhs were transferred in DJ Airways' books to reflect as a debt from DCPM rather than Allenberry.

DJ Airways acquired Rs 74 lakhs worth of Jaipur Udyog shares on June 30, 1950 (the last day of DJ Airways financial year) and it paid for the acquisition by drawing a hundi on DCPM for Rs 74 lakhs. This manoeuvre naturally wiped out DCPM's obligation regarding the Rs 74 lakhs that it had taken over on that day from Allenberry. At the same time, the shareholders of DJ Airways were told that their company had acquired a nice bundle of Jaipur Udyog shares among its assets, which was untrue.

Jaipur Udyog was a private limited company controlled by Ramkrishna Dalmia and its shares were not quoted on the stock exchange and so not readily marketable. Also, it was a new concern, and its factory was still under construction, so it was unlikely to pay dividends soon (nor did it pay any during the time that DJ Airways held the shares). They were acquired on June 30, 1950, and then passed onto DCPM on August 05, 1951, supposedly at the same rate; another instance of a familiar pattern, as no dividend was paid. DJ Airways lost Rs 3.61 lakhs of interest at 4.5 per cent during these thirteen months. The Rs 74 lakhs expended in the purchase amounted to over 49 per cent of the ordinary paid-up capital of Jaipur Udyog and to 33 per cent of its entire paid-up capital. While this would ordinarily have given DJ Airways the right to have a nominee director on the board of Jaipur Udyog, it was not given this right. The shares stood either in the names of close relatives of Ramkrishna Dalmia or in the names of employees of Dalmia concerns. As with the SSB and the MDM retransfer, DCPM was given time to repay the debt to DJ Airways, but in far lenient and shocking terms (discussed below).

This game or round robin was running out of steam and there was increasing disquiet among the shareholders of DJ Airways when they became aware of the pattern.

By June 30, 1951, when the final dues were to be paid to DJ Airways along with interest, Allenberry was in default for a sum of Rs 135.25 lakhs, along with interest at 4.5 per cent. At this point, DJ Airways held Rs 74 lakhs of shares of Jaipur Udyog and shares for Rs 35.25 lakhs in DJ Aviation (it may be recalled that a sum of Rs 40 lakhs had been transferred of the initial Rs 75.25 lakhs of subscription to DCPM). The sum total of these 'assets' on DJ Airways books amounted to Rs 244.25 lakhs.

To milk these assets away from DJ Airways and relieve Allenberry and DCPM of their obligations to DJ Airways, Ramkrishna Dalmia transferred these assets to DCPM under an agreement between DJ Airways and DCPM, by which the repayment for these by DCPM would commence five years hence, i.e. to start in October 1956 and then repaid without interest in instalments spread over 19 years! DCPM's own debt outstanding on June 30, 1951 to DJ Airways for about Rs 99.53 lakhs which carried an interest at 4.5 per cent was allowed to be repaid first in four annual instalments from October 1952 to October 1956, after which the repayment for the freshly minted debt of Rs 244.25 lakhs was to commence. However, all this was on paper, for DCPM (just like Allenberry) didn't have any intention of ever repaying this debt.

The agreement to transfer dues payable to DJ Airways' to DCPM's books was not disclosed to the shareholders of DJ Airways and the extended 19 years repayment without interest meant that there was nearly a 50 per cent erosion in the value of receivables (assets) of DJ Airways (or a sum of over Rs 128 lakhs, the net present value of the debt determined by COI using a 4.5 per cent discount rate for 19 years). The sum of Rs 128 lakhs represented a 36 per cent of the total paid up capital of DJ Airways and hence a direct erosion of shareholder value.

From records available as of Aug 05, 1951, the COI determined that Ramkrishna Dalmia owned 44 per cent of preference shares of DCPM (22 per cent directly and 22 per cent through Govan Brothers in which he owned 100 per cent), 37 per cent of equity shares and 72 per cent of deferred shares.[41] His intentions to protect DCPM were clear.

Between March 1949 and November 1951, there were a series of complaints about the way in which the affairs of DJ Airways were being managed, the most serious of these being the Rs 310 lakhs, representing 90 per cent of DJ Airways' capital having been advanced to Allenberry. At a shareholder meeting on March 30, 1950, a resolution was moved to prohibit any further investments and to refund one-fourth of the sum from the Allenberry repayments to the shareholders or invest the same only in government securities. Though this resolution was disallowed, and the audited accounts were passed (as only 29 per cent of the votes opposed the ratification of accounts), shareholder resistance was clearly growing.

In the following year, the fourth and last balance sheet of DJ Airways, as on June 30, 1950, was considered at a shareholders

---

41 A deferred share is a share that does not have any rights to the assets of a company undergoing bankruptcy until all common (equity) and preferred shareholders are paid. It may also be a share issued to company founders that restricts their receipt of dividends until dividends have been distributed to all other classes of shareholders.

meeting held on June 20, 1951. Ramkrishna Dalmia presided. Some of the shareholders expressed concern over the amount due from Allenberry and about the investments in sister companies. This was followed by a complaint made to the finance minister on November 20, 1951. This complaint was forwarded to the registrar of companies and inspectors were appointed under the Companies Act to enquire into the affairs of DJ Airways. They were thwarted in their task. The books of DJ Airways were withheld and later destroyed so that the inspectors only saw a part of them.

Shareholder pushback and agitation alarmed Ramkrishna Dalmia and his associates, and they prepared to wind up DJ Airways and denude it of the bulk of its assets to prevent them from falling into the hands of the shareholders of DJ Airways in liquidation.

The steps included the gradual transfer of Allenberry's indebtedness to DJ Airways to DCPM until on April 10, 1952, DCPM owed DJ Airways Rs 343 lakhs (Rs 244 lakhs plus DCPM's dues of Rs 99 lakhs discussed earlier) representing 98 per cent of DJ Airways capital on extended repayment terms. On the same day, DCPM was converted from a public to a private limited company.

Just three days later, on April 13, 1952, Ramkrishna Dalmia issued a circular to the shareholders of DJ Airways, asking them not to sell their shares and adumbrated a scheme for voluntary liquidation of the company. The next day, certain shareholders petitioned the court for a compulsory winding up of the company in a bid to protect the assets and requested for termination of the managing agency agreement. On April 22, 1952, Ramkrishna Dalmia issued a second circular and again outlined the scheme that was later adopted in the voluntary liquidation. Four days later, on April 26, 1952, DJ Aviation was converted from a public to a private limited company. In the interim, Ramkrishna Dalmia started buying up DJ Airways shares. Between April 13, 1952, and December 1952, he bought 12 lakhs through Bharat Union Agencies. In his circular of April 22, he also asked for proxies. Therefore, it was clear that he began buying up shares and collecting proxies in anticipation of the scheme that he had outlined for liquidation. On May 14, 1952, notices were sent to the shareholders of DJ Airways about the proposal to take it into voluntary liquidation. The meeting for this was held on June 13, 1952. In the meantime, the government ordered an investigation into the affairs of DJ Airways and appointed inspectors on June 7, 1952, under the Indian Companies Act just six days before the meeting. At the shareholders' meeting, important information was withheld, including the transfer of almost all assets under 19-year repayment terms to DCPM and the fact that the government had ordered an investigation. All that they were shown was the balance sheet as of June 30, 1950, which, by then, was two years old. DJ Airways was taken into voluntary liquidation at this meeting on June 13, 1952. One of the key differences between voluntary and compulsory liquidation was that, in the former, the company in liquidation chose the liquidator, rather than the court.

CP Lal was appointed a voluntary liquidator at a consolidated (and princely!) remuneration of Rs 52,500. He knew about the allegations made by the shareholders in their petitions filed in the court on April 14, 1952, but took no steps to look into the truth. Although he knew that the scheme of amalgamation was proposed by only 5 out of 20,000 shareholders of DJ Airways, he didn't consider it necessary to find out who they were, nor did he ascertain how many shares they held. He did not even evaluate whether DJ Aviation would be able to carry on the business of DJ Airways.

He did not disclose any of the material facts either to the court or to the shareholders. Despite being aware of the serious allegations by some of the shareholders against management malpractices, he didn't take it to the court, precluding the court from ordering a compulsory winding up or directing a search and enquiry before permitting a voluntary winding up. He obstructed the work of the inspectors appointed to investigate the affairs of DJ Airways and continued doing so for almost four-and-a-half months. From his conduct, COI concluded, "that from the very first to the last, he was working hand in glove with R Dalmia."

On November 16, 1952, five of the shareholders of DJ Airways wrote to the liquidator that DJ Aviation had agreed to take over all the existing assets and liabilities of DJ Airways under a scheme that they wanted CP Lal to present to the court. Accordingly, on January 05, 1953, Lal presented a petition to the court of the District Judge, Delhi, for a scheme under Section 153 and. 153-A of the Companies Act. The scheme was passed by the court on February 10, 1953 as they were in the dark about material facts, which had been suppressed.

One of the purposes this bizarre scheme of takeover by DJ Aviation and liquidation of DJ Airways was to enable destruction of the books of the latter. The COI found that CP Lal was a party to this as well.

The destruction of the books was necessary to obliterate all the trail of frauds, manipulations, and irregularities. Also, the inspectors said in their report that they had discovered several frauds and irregularities but needed the books to substantiate. Civil and criminal proceedings might well have followed.

Third, destruction put the books firmly out of the reach of the income-tax authorities and thus reduced penalties and monetary liabilities on Ramkrishna Dalmia and his ilk.

THE DCPM CESSPOOL: BORROWINGS AND ADVANCES

Dalmia Cement and Paper Marketing Company Limited (DCPM) was incorporated as "The Indian Cement and Paper Marketing Co Ltd" in October 1937 with an authorized capital[42] of Rs 1 crore. The paid-up capital was Rs 50 lakhs. On May 27, 1938, the company's name was changed to DCPM. The first directors were Shanti Prasad Jain and VD Agarwal.

DCPM played a very important and dominant role among the companies under the control of the DJ group and Ramkrishna Dalmia, including those being investigated by the COI. All questionable transactions of the group were routed through DCPM in one manner or another.

Through common control, DCPM was used as a "Financial Agency" to:

a. Borrow large sums of money from banks, insurance companies and other public companies with or without security.

---

42 Authorised Share Capital is the maximum amount of capital for which shares can be issued by the company to shareholders. It is mentioned in the Memorandum of Association of the Company. Paid up Share Capital, on the other hand, is the amount of money for which shares of the Company were issued to the shareholders and payment was made by the shareholders. At any point of time, paid-up capital will be less than or equal to authorised share capital.

b. Divert such borrowed funds to one or more of the several companies in the group or Ramkrishna Dalmia companies or to one or more members of the group.

c. Invest in shares of sister companies and/or,

d. Acquire or retain control by the group (and later by Ramkrishna Dalmia) over such companies.

DCPM frequently acted as a broker or agent for buying and selling shares/securities for the companies. Its role as underwriters for the public entity DJ Airways, and receiving wrongfully Rs 7.87 lakhs as commission has already been discussed.

DCPM also acted as selling agents for SSB, and MDM, the two textile companies, Rohtas Industries Ltd, SKG Sugar Ltd, and Dalmia Cement, etc. For SSB and MDM, DCPM extracted Rs 46.90 lakhs as compensation for a purported breach of the selling agency agreements.

Interlocking of control and funds also enabled the control and manipulation of profits from different companies, thereby reducing the overall tax liability. We have already seen an example of this where the profits of the Allenberry and DJ Airways JV and Allenberry's other businesses were diverted to DCPM to be set off against its losses.

After using DCPM for various transgressions, Ramkrishna Dalmia – who was then in full control of DCPM and its sole beneficiary – decided to put an end to its existence. Following the usual pattern, DCPM was converted from a public limited company to a private limited company on April 10, 1952, and on February 18, 1953, taken into voluntary liquidation. Its assets were transferred to another sister company, Delhi Glass Works Ltd, taking recourse under sections 153 and 153-A of the Indian Companies Act, 1913. Thereafter, its books and records were destroyed to avoid and obviate possible investigations and civil and/or criminal proceedings. In many cases, the COI was unable to determine how the accounts were finally squared up, as the books of accounts of DCPM were not available. The reluctance of witnesses to come forward and Ramkrishna Dalmia seeking refuge from self-incrimination (see below) forced the COI to reach conclusions and affix responsibility based on available evidence, direct or circumstantial.

Control over DCPM was exercised by appointing relations and or employees as directors of the company. They were subservient to the group/Ramkrishna, with no personal stake in the company. Several of them admitted to the COI that they were unable to exercise independent control. Ramkrishna Dalmia controlled and directed the overall policy of DCPM including matters relating to investments, borrowings, loans, etc., although he was never a director or an office bearer of DCPM.

Shanti Prasad Jain was the managing director from December 20, 1941 to November 01, 1947; and Jaidayal Dalmia, the deputy managing director from August 26, 1944, to November 03, 1947. They thus shared the control with Ramkrishna Dalmia during those periods.

The increasing concentration of ownership of this company in the hands of a few, in tandem with its journey of withdrawing public wealth from companies, is also interesting.

In 1943, the shares of DCPM were registered in the names of 428 entities, which increased to 728 in 1950. In November 1951, the number of registered shareholders had dropped to 23. By February 1952, the number had dropped to 20 and on April 14, 1952, (a few days after DCPM went private), all shares were held by 6 persons, including Ramkrishna Dalmia and Govan Brothers (which we have seen was 100 per cent owned by Ramkrishna Dalmia). Both SN Dudani, Secretary DCPM, and Ramkrishna Dalmia himself in their respective affidavits and statements on September 30, 1952 and October 10, 1952 respectively, averred that nearly all shares belonged to Ramkrishna Dalmia. Thus, between 1951-53, Ramkrishna through his large shareholding effectively controlled DCPM, although he wasn't a director.

In its role as "Financial Agency" described above, DCPM's balance sheets for the years ending February 28 in the following table reveal the pattern of borrowing and lending:

YEAR END	AMOUNT BORROWED (RS)	AMOUNT LENT (RS)
1947	3,58,92,289	-
1948	5,09,05,289	2,65,59,383
1949	6,75,57,073	6,34,52,603
1950	6,67,96,357	4,19,52,831
1951	7,53,25,790	7,35,49,077

The borrowings (with or without security) were mostly from Bharat Bank Ltd, Punjab National Bank Ltd, LES, DJ Airways, SSB, MDM and Bharat Insurance Co Ltd, in which the investing public had their hard-earned money. Loans and advances by DCPM (mostly unsecured) were made to Ramkrishna Dalmia, Jaidayal Dalmia, Rashtriya Financial Corporation Ltd, Bennett Coleman & Co Ltd, Ashoka Marketing Co Ltd, Ashoka Agencies Ltd, Vyapari Ltd, Dalmia Investment Co Ltd, Allenberry and Co Ltd, and Rashtriya Investors Ltd.

Funds borrowed by DCPM were either not repaid fully or were shown extinguished by transferring assets of sister companies of doubtful value, making adjustments towards selling and managing agency compensation received either by DCPM itself or for and on behalf of sister companies, or then by gifting itself extended years of repayment.

As with other entities, both Shanti Prasad and Jaidayal in their evidence dissociated themselves from all affairs of DCPM post May 31, 1948, the date of the alleged split. According to them, all loans granted by DCPM prior to May 31, 1948, were sound and recoverable, and were duly repaid to DCPM. They further dissociated themselves from all DCPM's exposures to Ramkrishna Dalmia or companies controlled by him.

The group argued that the funds borrowed by DCPM were for purposes of nation building. The COI disagreed. While Bharat Bank Ltd was indeed a large lender of funds, particularly during the later years of the war period and immediately subsequent thereto, it was a DJ group entity from whom DCPM obtained cash credit accommodation. Punjab National Bank too was under the control of the DJ group in the relevant period, in the era before the nationalization of banks. In 1948, the group directly held 15.7 per cent shares and another 36.5 per cent indirectly through the National Investment Trust. The group argued that banks would have done the due diligence before they lent monies to DCPM. This too was suspect.

As on February 28, 1949, the total amount borrowed by DCPM from Bharat Bank and Punjab National Bank totalled Rs 151 lakhs, whereas the value of DCPM's assets provided as security (stock-in-trade and investment) was only Rs 123 lakhs. A large value of the hypothecated stock included unexcavated pipes etc., security not readily available for disposal/sales. Somewhere around January 1947, Bharat Bank determined that the shares held as security were mostly unapproved and insufficient and sought these to be augmented by approved shares. This was overruled by the managing director of the bank presumably because during that period, Ramkrishna Dalmia was the chairman of the bank and Shanti Prasad Jain, VH Dalmia and Shriyans Prasad Jain were directors.

The COI also found that the assets/securities hypothecated/pledged were registered with the registrar of joint stock companies *after* more than three years from the date of advance!

DCPM's borrowings from Bharat Bank appeared to have declined steadily from Rs 107 lakhs as on February 28, 1948 to Rs 70.79 lakhs as on February 28, 1951, though the COI could not ascertain whether this was a part of the window dressing or not. The security for the above advances included shares valued at Rs 82.69 lakhs (main contributors were shares of MDM and SSB with a market value of about Rs 74.70 lakhs). It was surprising that any bank would allow such a high level of concentration risk[43] on its security.

Borrowings similarly from Punjab National Bank were significant; outstanding between the financial years ending February 28, 1948 and February 28, 1950 were between Rs 39.40 lakhs to Rs 49.84 lakhs.

There were substantial borrowings from group companies as well.

a. Borrowings by DCPM from LES increased from Rs 100.27 lakhs in March 1947 to Rs 113.53 lakhs in March 1949. During LES's financial year ending March 1950, DCPM transferred many shares of sister companies of the value of Rs 77.45 lakhs to reduce its indebtedness to LES to about Rs 38 lakhs. This, however, climbed up to nearly Rs 116 lakhs by December 1952. DCPM 'repaid' the same to the extent of nearly Rs 115 lakhs by the transfer of shares of Bennett and Coleman, DJ Aviation and Jaipur Udyog, amongst others. Government securities held by LES worth about Rs 66 lakhs as on March

---

43 The potential for financial risk/loss due to overexposure on one/few stocks, sector, counterparty, country etc.

31, 1946 were gradually sold, and the sale proceeds were used by the group and later Ramkrishna Dalmia through DCPM.

b. DCPM's maximum unsecured borrowings touched a high of about Rs 241 lakhs from SSB and Rs 125 lakhs from MDM.

c. Borrowings from Bharat Insurance Co Ltd of Rs 80.50 lakhs (maximum amount) between February 1948 to February 1951 were unsecured. Shriyans Prasad Jain, an employee of DCPM up to November 30, 1949, was also a director and vice chairman of Bharat Insurance. DCPM transferred shares and other assets of the DJ group to Bharat Insurance by way of repayment of the debt. These included SSB, MDM, DJ Aviation shares, and Nahur land.

d. There were large borrowings from Jaipur Traders Ltd, a Ramkrishna Dalmia company. Outstanding dues stood between Rs 67.63 lakhs to Rs 86.22 lakhs between 1950-51. Since Jaipur traders had only Rs 25,000 as the paid-up capital, its source of funds to lend such large sums were unknown. The COI could only infer that these were either the secret money of the DJ group or of Ramkrishna Dalmia. Since Jaipur Traders went into liquidation and was finally dissolved on May 10, 1954, and its books of accounts were destroyed, the COI failed to ascertain if and how DCPM had repaid Jaipur Traders.

From the foregoing, DCPM's borrowings from sister concerns were large, unsecured, and repaid not in cash but by way of shares/asset transfer or adjustment entries and often awarded generous discounts.

A study of some of DCPM's loans and advances reflected the following:

a. Between February 1948 and February 1951, DCPM's unsecured/partially secured interest bearing (6 per cent) advances to Ramkrishna Dalmia increased from Rs 17.30 lakhs to Rs 152.14 lakhs. On April 20, 1953, Ramkrishna Dalmia gave a certificate that nothing was due to/by him from/to DCPM, i.e. the Rs 152.14 lakhs stood discharged. There was however no evidence of how this amount was repaid. The COI inferred that the credit balance of the profit-and-loss account of DCPM as on February 28, 1951, for Rs 57.52 lakhs and the discount of Rs 98.78 lakhs is it received from DJ Aviation for DCPM's dues to it on or about February 13, 1953, was adjusted against the amount due from Ramkrishna Dalmia as he was the sole beneficiary of DCPM at that time. When the COI tried to investigate the exact mechanism of repayment/settlement of such a large sum by Ramkrishna Dalmia, instead of furnishing the required information, he claimed protection under Article 20 (3)[44] of the Constitution.

b. Jaidayal Dalmia too had borrowings from DCPM, which stood at Rs 30.94 lakhs by the year-end February 1948. In his books, Jaidayal transferred these dues to Vyapari Ltd, a company incorporated in July 1948. By September 04, 1950, Jaidayal extinguished his dues to Vyapari by transferring many investments and other receivables. Vyapari also had borrowings from DCPM, which stood at Rs 103.32 lakhs as at year-end February 1950. In the absence of the books of DCPM, the manner of settlement of Vyapari's dues remained unknown to the COI.

c. Rashtriya Financial Corporation (RFC), a private limited company, incorporated in September 1948, with a capital of

---

44 Article 20 (3) of the Constitution of India states that the defendant has the right against self-incrimination. However, witnesses are not offered the same protection.

Rs 2,000 subscribed by Ramkrishna Dalmia concerns, was later doubled in January 1952, to Rs 4,000.

Between February and March 1949, DCPM sold shares of SSB, MDM, and LES worth nearly Rs 132 lakhs and shares of Govan Brothers valued at Rs 16 lakhs to RFC. This indebtedness of RFC to DCPM for about Rs 148 lakhs was extinguished within two months in the books of RFC by it transferring the following investments:

i. Transferred to DCPM: Rs 106 lakhs.

ii. Transferred to LES through DCPM: Rs 38 lakhs.

iii. Transferred to Ashoka Marketing: Rs 4 lakhs.

These transactions followed close one upon the other without an event or consideration supporting them and without balking in even using a poorly capitalised company like RFC to do so. These were not just pointers to book adjustments and accommodations to confound the audit trail but the brazenness with which they were done.

There was a certificate dated April 20, 1953, signed by SK Sanghi, the liquidator of RFC (taken into liquidation in March 1953) stating that the account of DCPM stood fully adjusted in its books. Since RFC's last available dues to DCPM stood at Rs 288.43 lakhs, it was never known how such a large debt by RFC was repaid.

d. Between March 31 and May 31, 1949, DCPM transferred 11,250 Preference shares of Bennett Coleman & Co Ltd, for a total value of Rs 63.03 lakhs to Gwalior Bank Ltd (Rs 50.42 lakhs) and Bharat Journals Ltd (Rs 12.61 lakhs). On May 31, 1949, RFC transferred to LES 11,250 shares of Bennett Coleman for only Rs 22.5 lakhs. LES in its turn transferred these shares to DCPM on December 29, 1950, for the same price. Thus, DCPM got back the 11,250 shares of Bennett Coleman & Co Ltd, for Rs 22.50 lakhs as against their previous "sale" price of Rs 63.03 lakhs. Since Bennett was a private concern, there was no ready market value for the shares. If the value of the shares of Bennett were indeed higher than Rs 22.5 lakhs, RFC would have suffered a huge loss. How this was accommodated by its paltry paid-up capital of only Rs 2,000 is unclear. In the absence of the books of DCPM and the other three companies, it wasn't possible to probe further and ascertain which of the three companies suffered the loss on the resale of preference shares of Bennett Coleman to DCPM.

e. In April 1946, the control of Bennett Coleman and Co Ltd was acquired by the DJ group. Effective control passed from the group to Ramkrishna Dalmia, and towards the latter part of 1955, it went under the control of Shanti Prasad Jain. Between 1949 and 1951, large sums of monies were advanced by DCPM to Bennett Coleman (end-of-year outstandings grew from Rs 41.34 lakhs to Rs 94.42 lakhs, with intra-year exposures during these years peaking at Rs 160.77 lakhs). These advances were unsecured and carried an average interest at 4 per cent. As in the other cases, the outstanding amount of Rs 94.42 lakhs along with interest payable wasn't repaid, but adjusted by Bennett transferring to DCPM, shares valued at Rs 100 lakhs. These comprised SSB (Rs 62 lakhs), MDM (Rs 20 lakhs) and DJ aviation (Rs 18 lakhs). The COI determined that the real value of the combined SSB and the MDM shares were lower at Rs 54 lakhs and hence the transfer at Rs 82 lakhs to DCPM had benefitted Bennett to the extent of Rs 28 lakhs in liquidation of its debt to DCPM. The reason for such accommodation was unclear.

f. There were transactions and book adjustment/transfer of shares between DCPM and other companies in the DJ Group. The main ones in terms of exposure are as under, excluding Allenberry, which has been discussed earlier. The figure in brackets is the maximum indebtedness by these companies to DCPM:

i. Ashoka Marketing Co Ltd (Rs 87.70 lakhs)

ii. Ashoka Agencies Ltd (Rs 200 lakhs)

iii. Vyapari Ltd (Rs 103.32 lakhs)

iv. Dalmia Investment Co Ltd (Rs 105.86 lakhs)

v. Rashtriya Investors Ltd (Rs 56.95 lakhs)

THE DCPM CESSPOOL: POOR INVESTMENTS AND THE ABUSE OF CONTROL

DCPM also bought and sold shares of joint stock companies mostly under the control of the DJ group and later of Ramkrishna Dalmia. The primary objects of these investments were:

a. To acquire the control of companies outside the DJ group such as Bennett Coleman, SSB and MDM.
   i. Once control was taken, the shares of the acquired companies were transferred to the public limited companies, banks, and insurance companies towards repayment of the funds borrowed.
   ii. Additionally, Dalmia and his concerns derived benefits as selling and managing agency commissions from such companies taken over.
b. To control the overall taxation liability of the group by wrongful diversion of taxable profits from other companies to DCPM.
c. To adjust the indebtedness of DCPM to other companies and vice versa by making purchases and sales at rates manipulated to suit the convenience of the DJ group/Ramkrishna Dalmia.
d. To retain the control by the DJ group/Ramkrishna Dalmia, through the agency of DCPM via the large investment in shares of the companies.

e. To window-dress the balance sheets of sister companies.

DCPM was very highly leveraged on its investment portfolio (high level of borrowings as compared to own funds), with total investments as a percentage of its paid-up capital averaging 320.7 per cent between 1947-51. The figure crossed 400 per cent in three of the five years.

The profit-and-loss position on these investments reveal the following:

YEAR ENDED 28 FEBRUARY	PROFIT ON SALE OF INVESTMENTS (RS)	LOSS ON SALE OF INVESTMENTS (RS)	SPECULATION LOSS (RS)	TOTAL LOSS (RS)
1946	01,80,670		Not Available	
1947	05,31,173		Not Available	
1948		12,99,601	Not Available	12,99,601*
1949		13,85,027	04,75,392	18,60,419
1950		02,82,082	02,04,751	04,86,833
1951		24,14,080	19,48,485	43,62,565
Total	07,11,813	53,80,790	26,28,628	80,09,418

*Includes the loss of Rs 12,00,000 on transfer of 500 shares of Darbhanga Trading Co Ltd to Shanti Prasad Jain.

Most of these shares were not quoted in any stock exchange and belonged to group companies. In most of the cases, no cash payments were made either for the purchase or for the sale; it was done by book adjustment. Also, the company did not get the shares registered in its own name but retained these with blank transfer forms. The rates at which shares were traded were manipulated to suit the convenience of the group and often the same (type of) shares were exchanged at varying rates at short intervals.

As earlier mentioned, the same block of shares included as assets in the balance sheet of one company would appear within a few months thereafter as assets of another company. The has already been dealt with in the transactions we saw between DCPM (year ending February) and DJ Airways (year ending June) regarding the transfers of the 21,800 shares of SSB and the 7,200 MDM shares, and how these shares were further transferred by DCPM to RFC. The same shares again came to DCPM, and it received dividends in 1952 by way of return of capital from the liquidators of SSB and MDM. Similar transactions have been essayed earlier with the 11,250 Bennett shares.

The fact that DCPM booked cumulative losses of over Rs 80 lakhs (see table above) and earned a poor dividend income of a little over Rs 5 lakhs made it clear to the COI that DCPM's investments were not prudent. The way the shares were traded also indicated that these transactions were for the benefit of the DJ Group and later Ramkrishna Dalmia.

BENNETT COLEMAN & CO LTD

British-owned Bennett Coleman was a private limited company with a paid-up capital of Rs 38.79 lakhs (comprising 38,053 Preference Shares of Rs 100 each and 7,370 Ordinary Shares of Rs 10 each) and it owned a first-class press publishing, inter alia *The Times of India*. Its financial position was sound, with accumulated profits of about Rs 30 lakhs and additional reserves of Rs 53 lakhs as on December 31, 1945. It had an investment book in readily marketable government securities of over Rs 30 lakhs and its cash and bank balances of Rs 14 lakh plus indicated good liquidity.

On April 02, 1946, DCPM paid Rs 99.92 lakhs by cheque to Bennett Coleman towards the cost of its shares. DCPM's overdraft with Bharat Bank then stood at Rs 79.43 lakhs, indicating that this was a leveraged buy.[45] On April 25, 1946, Bharat Bank purchased

[45] An acquisition with significant amount of borrowed funds.

15,000 preference shares of Bennett Coleman from DCPM for Rs 87 lakhs (at Rs 580 per share) and six months later, on September 30, 1946, sold them to the Gwalior Bank Ltd (another DJ group concern at Rs 560 per share). The resultant loss of Rs 3 lakhs to Bharat Bank was compensated by the dividend received by Bharat Bank of Rs 3 lakhs on these shares. On March 01, 1947, Bharat Bank repurchased this very lot of 15,000 shares from the Gwalior Bank and on the same day sold it to SSB for Rs 84 lakhs. The sum of Rs 84 lakhs due from SSB was set off against the amount payable to the Gwalior Bank. Interestingly, the 15,000 shares do not appear in the balance sheet of SSB as on March 31, 1947. The COI inferred that SSB between March 01 and 31, 1947, had transferred these to some other concern of the DJ group, probably to DCPM as these 15,000 shares appear in DCPM's financials as on February 28, 1948, at a cost of Rs 84.04 lakhs. Thus, the block of 15,000 shares purchased by Bharat Bank and transferred to the Gwalior Bank and thereafter to SSB, ultimately came into the possession of DCPM. Another example of the rampant game of inter-company asset transfers indulged by the group, because DCPM now had almost the entire ownership of Bennett (Rs 99.92 lakhs paid initially, plus the 15,000 preference shares at Rs 84 lakhs).

The Gwalior Bank went into voluntary liquidation, the liquidator being SK Sanghi, an employee of Bennett Coleman. By a resolution passed at the Directors' meeting held on July 02, 1953, its books of accounts and records were destroyed.

The COI estimated that the total amount invested by the DJ group in April 1946 for acquiring the control of Bennett Coleman was Rs 186.92 lakhs, comprising investment by DCPM of Rs 99.92 lakhs and the investment via Bharat Bank of Rs 87 lakhs. Looking at certain other transactions involving DJ Charity Trust, RFC, LES, Bharat Journal Ltd, etc, the COI concluded that Ramkrishna

Dalmia had invested Rs 203.71 lakhs in the acquisition of Bennett Coleman.

This figure approximates the figure quoted by Neelima Dalmia Adhar in her book as well. She has an interesting anecdote to recount on the acquisition of Bennett Coleman:

"When Ramkrishna Dalmia wanted to acquire *The Times of India* from its imperialistic owners, he had deputed the chief editor of *The Statesman* to negotiate the purchase, who in turn took six months in London to persuade the managing director of *The Times* to come to meet Ramkrishna Dalmia in Bombay.

"The managing director said, 'You want to snatch away my baby, whom I have nursed for forty years?'

"He was undaunted, 'Now the baby needs two nurses instead of one, sir!' he said.

"Those words became legendary and in the most startling chain of events, *The Times* along with its allied publications came into the hands of its first Indian owner.

"The deal was clinched within twenty-four hours in total secrecy after Ramkrishna Dalmia placed a signed blank cheque on the table. It cost him an astounding sum of twenty million rupees. The takeover made Ramkrishna Dalmia the undisputed leader of the Indian industry of the century."[46]

The hefty premium paid by Dalmia for acquiring Bennett, underscored his fascination for the media.

To liquidate its overdraft with Bharat Bank, DCPM thereafter transferred the shares of Bennett Coleman it had acquired for Rs 99.92 lakhs to other companies as under:

a. On April 30, 1946: 4,500 shares were transferred to Bharat Insurance Co Ltd, for a sum of Rs 26.10 lakhs. These shares

---

[46] Dalmia Adhar, Neelima. *Father Dearest: the life, and times of R.K. Dalmia*. New Delhi: Westland Ltd, 2017.

were resold by Bharat Insurance before the end of the year to DCPM for a sum of Rs 25.42 lakhs resulting in a loss of Rs 67,500 to Bharat Insurance.

b. On or about April 26, 1946: 5,000 shares were transferred to Bharat Fire & General Insurance Co Ltd, for a sum of Rs 29 lakhs. These shares continued with Bharat Fire & General Insurance till December 27, 1946, when they were retransferred to DCPM at a loss of Rs 1.5 lakhs to Bharat Fire & General Insurance.

c. The shares so re-acquired by DCPM from Bharat Insurance, and Bharat Fire & General Insurance along with other shares it held were transferred to SSB (9,500 preference shares) and MDM (6,850 preference shares). As we will see later in the chapter dealing with SSB and MDM, they too lost heavily in this investment in Bennett Coleman shares.

The DJ group and later Ramkrishna Dalmia had effective control of the following companies at all relevant times – Bharat Bank, Bharat Insurance, Bharat Fire & General Insurance, SSB, MDM, RFC, Gwalior Bank, and LESCO It was, therefore, possible for the group and Dalmia to use the funds of these companies for their own benefit, and to manipulate the rates at which shares were to be purchased and sold.

After it was acquired, Bennett Coleman declared dividends only for two years, i.e. for the years ending December 31, 1946, and 1947; No dividends were declared for the years 1948 to 1954. In December 1955, however, arrears of dividends on preference shares were declared and the sum of Rs 26.64 lakhs were paid to BUA, a company under the effective control of Ramkrishna Dalmia.

THE USE AND ABUSE OF GOVERNMENT SECURITIES

As agents, DCPM purchased and sold shares and securities for and on behalf of companies under the control of DJ group, some of them being Bharat Insurance, Bharat Bank and Dalmia Provident Fund. The COI concluded that DCPM fraudulently retained and used the sale proceeds of government securities (or monies advance for their purchase) as under:

a. Rs 6.93 lakhs of Bharat Insurance, from March 1948 to September 1948.

b. At least Rs 63.60 lakhs of Bharat Bank Ltd from August 1948 to January 1949.

c. Rs 109.04 lakhs of Bharat Bank Ltd, from December 1946 to February 1947.

d. About Rs 2.97 lakhs of Dalmia Provident Fund, Dalmianagar, from March, 1948 to September, 1948. The employees of the DJ group concerns as subscribers to the provident fund were the beneficiaries of the Dalmia Provident Fund, Dalmianagar. Shanti Prasad Jain was a Trustee of this fund in September 1948.

It was further observed that in (a), (b) and (d) above, DCPM fraudulently misrepresented to the said insurance company, bank, and the trustees of the Provident Fund that it had purchased government securities on their behalf, even though it had not done so. DCPM deployed the said money without furnishing securities and thus saved considerably by way of interest expense if it had to borrow funds from elsewhere. In the case of (a) and (d) above, the delay in purchase was a period of six months.

In the case of (c) above, the facts were as under:

In October 1946, the DJ group acquired control of two textile mills – SSB and MDM – from Provident Investment Co Ltd for Rs

368.5 lakhs. As with the other acquisitions, this was a leveraged buy with DCPM availing of an overdraft from Bharat Bank. As on October 18, 1946, the amount of the overdraft was Rs 161.63 lakhs.

Immediately after the acquisitions, SSB and MDM borrowed Rs 52 lakhs and Rs 28 lakhs respectively from Bharat Bank on or about October 22, 1946, against the security of finished goods and stores of the mills. This borrowing was unnecessary, given their healthy liquidity position. On the very same day, the total borrowed sums of Rs 80 lakhs were diverted as advances to DCPM, which DCPM deposited in its account with Bharat Bank. On December 31, 1946, DCPM sold government securities of Bharat Bank for Rs 109.04 lakhs (face value Rs 105 lakhs). The sale proceeds were also deposited in DCPM's account with the Bharat Bank and then used to repay the loans totalling Rs 80 lakhs from SSB and MDM.

SSB and MDM repaid this money back to Bharat Bank and cleared their overdraft. The overall effect of this transaction was that the loan of Rs 80 lakhs by SSB and MDM from Bharat Bank was repaid out of the sale proceeds of government securities belonging to Bharat Bank! The sale proceeds of the government securities that were credited to the account of DCPM with Bharat Bank on December 31, 1946, was reflected as a loan from Bharat Bank in DCPM's books with effect from January 10, 1947. In effect, DCPM had unauthorized use of the sales proceeds of Rs 109 lakhs from December 31, 1946, to January 10, 1947.

DCPM couldn't have obtained funds from Bharat Insurance for purposes other than what was permissible under Section 27A of Insurance Act, 1938. Monies from the provident fund could not be utilised for granting loans and a bank wouldn't have advanced funds without adequate security. DCPM was thus guilty of having used these funds (listed on the previous page) fraudulently. In the absence of the books of accounts of DCPM, the COI again had to use circumstantial and indirect evidence to pin responsibility, such as dates of directorship and evidence of control via direct or indirect ownership.

The COI found an account called "Government Securities Business Account," where the sale proceeds on behalf of Bharat Insurance, Bharat Bank, etc., would be credited and purchases of government securities debited.

As Shanti Prasad Jain ceased to be a director of DCPM from November 1947 and Jaidayal Dalmia from December 1947, both contended that they were not directly connected with any of the transactions. Both argued that the account was not only for the companies of the group for whom DCPM acted as an agent, but also reflected DCPM's own trades. They also stated that a purchase order from a client in the market may not have been affected by DCPM immediately, but could have been supplied from their own holdings to be covered later. DCPM would take the risk of fluctuation in the market and the customer would make payment to the dealer (DCPM) either against delivery of government securities or in advance and in the latter case, would become entitled to interest from the date of payment. The COI found this explanation weak as it was very rare for banks and insurance companies to advance monies in the first instance for purchase of government securities, and then allow the broker to buy them later, allowing the broker to use the funds in the interim.

NAHUR LAND

DCPM's dues to Bharat Insurance in December 1950 stood at Rs 29 lakhs. In repayment, 4.55 (of the total of 5.02) lakh square yards of undeveloped land at Nahur village Thane district near Bombay, purchased a few years back by DCPM at a total cost of Rs 11.40 lakhs, was transferred to Bharat Insurance. The sale consideration at the rate of Rs 8 per square yard, translated to Rs 36.43 lakhs, about three and a half times the purchase price.

At a meeting of Bharat Insurance on December 16, 1950, chaired by Ramkrishna Dalmia, KL Agarwal, and RL Chordia (brother-in-law of Ramkrishna Dalmia) as directors of the company, this purchase was approved and ratified by an agreement dated December 30, 1950. Under this agreement, Bharat Insurance was given the option of purchasing the balance land measuring 0.47 lakh square yards at the same rate, provided the option was exercised on or before February 07, 1951.

The agreement stated that the land was one single continuous piece suitable for a compact colony to be developed by DCPM at its own cost for a residential colony. Alternatively, Bharat Insurance would have the option to develop the land themselves and to recover the cost. DCPM also undertook, if so desired by Bharat Insurance, to arrange for the lease of the land at a rent yielding not less than 4 per cent per annum of the amount invested.

Next, DCPM arranged for the said lease by Bennett Coleman (under the effective control of R Dalmia at that time) at Rs 24,000 per month up to December 1951 and at Rs 16,000 per month thereafter, well above the floor rate of 4 per cent per annum. On January 31, 1951, Bharat Insurance Company was made to exercise the option of buying the remaining land for an additional sum of Rs 3.77 lakhs, bringing their total cost of the purchase to Rs 40.2 lakhs. A sum of Rs 11.2 lakhs (Rs 40.2 lakhs less than the outstanding debt of Rs 29 lakhs), was paid by Bharat Insurance in March, 1951 to DCPM, with the latter making a profit of Rs 28.80 (Rs 40.2 lakhs sale price less Rs 11.40 lakhs cost), adequate to extinguish the debt to Bharat Insurance in its books.

After the execution of the conveyance deed, Bharat Insurance discovered that land measuring about 30 square yards could not be used for non-agricultural purposes; that the time limit allowed for the purpose of putting up a colony was only up to January 31, 1952; and that the measured land fell short by 7305.5 square yards and effectively stood at 4.95 lakh square yards. Bharat Insurance claimed compensation for these deficiencies.

The deficiencies also prompted Bharat Insurance to conduct a valuation exercise for the land, by Messrs KR Irani & Co who assessed the same at Rs 24.52 lakhs. The insurance company realized that they had been duped and overpaid Rs 15.68 lakhs for this fairyland, a sum belonging to the policy owners.

To compensate Bharat Insurance, DCPM transferred land in Mahalakshmi Bombay, valued by Messrs KR Irani & Co at Rs 16.60 lakhs, which belonged to SSB and another open land and six houses at Ghaziabad.

SSB Mills was persuaded to transfer the Hains property to DCPM for Rs 7.60 lakhs. This amount of Rs 7.60 lakhs wasn't paid in cash by DCPM, rather the usual ploy of debiting DCPM's account in the books of SSB was used. The COI determined that the choice of the Hains property as compensation to Bharat Insurance was not by chance. Rather it was done for the following reasons:

a. To dispose of the valuable properties of SSB, before it was taken into liquidation.
b. To divert the capital profit on sale of the land which if realized by the company and finally distributed on liquidation to its principal shareholders would have been liable to income tax in their hands and;
c. To ultimately benefit Ramkrishna Dalmia through DCPM.

The Hains road property sale yielded a profit of Rs 9 lakhs to DCPM (Rs 16.60 lakhs less Rs 7.60 lakhs), hence in its profit-and-loss account, DCPM recorded a profit of Rs 21.20 lakhs on the entire transaction (earlier profit of 28.8 lakhs less Rs 16.6 lakhs plus

9 lakhs). This amount, in the final analysis, was what was lost by the investing public policy holders of Bharat Insurance to the gain by Ramkrishna and the DJ group.

Though the COI apportioned the guilt for the collusion and fraud to the directors of DCPM – VD Agarwala, MK Roy, HD Bishnoi and others – and also the directors of Bharat Insurance, namely Ramkrishna Dalmia, KL Agarwal, RL Chordia, and MK Roy, the one person who was really responsible for this fraud was Ramkrishna Dalmia as he had a control over both, Bharat Insurance and DCPM.

RU(I)N OF THE MILL(S)

SSB and MDM were two flourishing textile mills with large reserves and liquid resources. SSB was incorporated as a public limited company during the WWI and MDM even earlier, in the nineties of the previous century.

As on March 31, 1946, their position was as under:

IN RS (LAKHS)	SSB	MDM
Paid up Capital	85.84	30.08
Reserves	87.16	32.82
Investments, cash, and bank	87.42	43.62

As mentioned earlier, the DJ group acquired their control from the Provident Investment Company in September 1946, with a majority stake, for a consideration of Rs 368.5 lakhs (SSB 226.84 lakhs, and MDM 141.66 lakhs). The artful methods used by the DJ group for milking these two mills was a combination of managing and selling agents. The device used was exploiting the supposed breaches in agreement, as compensation paid thereon wasn't subject to taxes. After this was done, the plan was to take the two companies into voluntary liquidation and destroy their books and records. On July 01, 1950, Bharat Union Agencies (BUA) was appointed as the managing agent of SSB, and Vastra Vyavasaya (VV), the managing agent for MDM. Shanti Prasad Jain and Jaidayal Dalmia were the first directors of the two companies.

The acquisition of the two mills was initially funded by DCPM along with borrowings from Bharat Bank for Rs 161.63 lakhs (as seen earlier).

Interestingly, within a few months of the acquisition, DCPM transferred a large number of shares to the following public limited companies as under:

PUBLIC COMPANIES TO WHOM SHARES TRANSFERRED/SOLD	SHARES OF SSB RS (LAKHS)	SHARES OF MDM RS (LAKHS)
Bharat Insurance	63.31	23.00
Bharat Fire and General Insurance	10.20	7.50
LES	54.44	25.48
Total	127.95	55.98

The monies of the depositors, and investing and premium paying public in companies under the control of the DJ group funded the expensive purchases of SSB and MDM. The total of the above share sales and the borrowing from Bharat Bank stood at Rs 345.56 lakhs, close to the acquisition price of Rs 368.50 lakhs.

12,000 shares of SSB and 6,000 shares of MDM were registered in the name of Ramkrishna Dalmia and were pledged by Dalmia with the Central Bank of India for a sum of Rs 25 lakhs, which was used by DCPM to reduce the borrowing from Bharat Bank.

Earlier we have seen how SSB and MDM availed of overdrafts totalling Rs 80 lakhs to enable DCPM reduce the outstanding with Bharat Bank.

The mills were also made to advance to DCPM large sums from time to time. Between the balance sheet dates of February 1948-52, average dues from DCPM were Rs 160.8 lakhs to SSB and Rs 77.65 lakhs to MDM.

Additionally, MDM and SSB also invested in preference shares of Bennett Coleman and Company Ltd, and LES. The exposures of the two mills as on February 28, 1951, to the DJ group companies stood at an astounding Rs 425.22 lakhs much more than what was invested in acquiring them! 76 per cent of the exposure was to

DCPM (Rs 325.52 lakhs), and the balance to Bennett Coleman (Rs 90.6 lakhs) and LES (Rs 9.1 lakhs).

The investment in Bennett and Coleman is worth expanding upon. Two months after its acquisition by the DJ group, in December 1946, SSB bought 9,500 preference shares of Bennett Coleman at Rs 557 per share for Rs 52.92 lakhs from DCPM. Similarly, MDM also bought 6,850 preference shares at Rs 550 per share for Rs 37.68 lakhs. The balance sheet of the two mill companies, as on March 31, 1946, shows that neither had enough surplus funds to enable them to make these two investments. On the contrary, the result of these investments was that they were obliged to borrow large sums of money to enable them to carry on their own business. Neither was it their business to invest in shares, more so in a private company whose shares were not traded in the market.

The total dividends received by SSB from Bennett between March 31, 1947 to April 16, 1951, was only Rs 5.46 lakhs, while for MDM it was only Rs 3.94 lakhs. This was because after Bennett's acquisition by the DJ group, it declared dividends for only two years. Hence the returns for the period 1947-51 translated to an annual return of about 2.6 per cent for the two mills. Had these mills invested their funds in a safe investment such as a bank, they could have earned at the rate of 4 to 5 per cent. These shares remained on the books of the two mills till about May 1950.

The COI found from the books of DJ Aviation that it had bought 16,350 preference shares (9,500 shares from SSB and 6,850 shares from MDM) at Rs 200 a share through Jaipur Traders Ltd In the absence of the books of the two mills and of Jaipur Traders Ltd and in the absence of any objections to the contrary, the COI inferred that these were the same block of shares. The two mills thus sustained a combined loss on the Bennett Coleman and Co

Ltd investment of Rs 57.91 lakhs. The COI had no way or evidence to show that the market for these shares had fallen in the interval because Bennett Coleman was a private limited company whose shares were not quoted on the Stock Exchange. The two mills and Jaipur Traders Ltd were all Ramkrishna Dalmia concerns. All three were taken into liquidation and their books were destroyed.

In an earlier chapter 'How Control was Abused,' we have mentioned the exploitation of breaches of agency and selling agency agreements.

DCPM was appointed in October 1948, the sole selling agent of MDM and SSB Limited for a period of 10 years. Thereafter on account of purported breaches of the selling agency agreement DCPM was paid by way of compensation Rs 17.8 lakhs by MDM and Rs 29.1 lakhs by SSB.

The manner of the breach was curious as well. DCPM's appointment as a selling agent (for a 10-year period with a commission at 2.5 per cent of the net sales proceeds) came two years after the acquisitions, in October 1948. One of the conditions of the selling agency agreement was that if (and when) the two mills transferred their business, they would seek that DCPM be appointed as a distributor for the transferee company. SSB and MDM entered into agreements with Ram Sahay Mull More Limited on October 27, 1950, for the sale of their undertakings, without advising/ensuring this precondition. In February 1951, DCPM claimed compensation for a breach. On behalf of the mills, BL Chokhani accepted DCPM's claim and negotiated for a lower amount, while PS Patke represented DCPM for their claim settlement. Conveniently, Patke was private secretary to Ramkrishna Dalmia and Chokhani was a relative. On the date of the compensation settlement (February 28, 1951), DCPM owed SSB Rs 211.58 lakhs and MDM Rs 113.56 lakhs. And both mills were taken into liquidation before the year was out (December 1951).

Similarly, BUA and VV, private limited companies under the control of Ramkrishna Dalmia were fraudulently and collusively appointed as managing agents of SSB and MDM, respectively. Ramkrishna Dalmia was the sole beneficiary of both these managing agency companies.

By March 1950, accumulated reserves for the two mills had grown to Rs 157.25 lakhs from the Rs 120 lakhs at the time of acquisition. About this time, all the conversion shares[47] of SSB and MDM were held by Ramkrishna Dalmia and companies under his control. He also held over 60 per cent of the deferred shares in SSB and 37 per cent in the case of MDM. Per extant laws, the shareholders could have drawn out the accumulated profits only after payment of super tax.[48] Also, in the case of liquidation, these profits could be subjected to super tax in the hands of the shareholders, and in some cases, subject to both income tax as well as super tax. The COI surmised that the appointment of DCPM as a selling agent for both SSB and MDM, the appointment of BUA and VV as managing agents as well as the liquidation of the two mills was to thwart these provisions of law.

BUA and VV were appointed as managing agents for SSB and MDM, respectively, for a period of twenty years from July 1950 on attractive terms including a commission of 10 per cent of profits, and office allowance and all expenses paid. The contracts had similar compensation clauses if the mills were sold or wound up before 20 years from the date of the appointment of the managing agents.

47 Shares of common stock that are issued or can be issued upon the conversion of another kind of security such as preference shares (preferred stock) or bonds.

48 A tax imposed over and above the income tax payable as per provisions of Chapter XI of the Income Tax Act 1922.

While the resolution to appoint BUA and VV as managing agents w.e.f. July 01, 1950, was taken on July 05, 1950, the contractual managing agency agreements were executed on October 26, 1950, between SSB and BUA and on August 30, 1950, between MDM and VV. However, both these managing agency agreements had been inked on dates *later* than the authority to sell the undertakings, which had already been obtained on August 16, 1950. The sales constituted a breach of the terms of the managing agency agreements according to BUA and VV and they claimed compensation for the unexpired period of 19 years and 8 months though the companies had acted as managing agents for a period of only 4 months. On February 28, 1951, astronomical amounts of compensation of Rs 46.80 lakhs in the case of MDM and Rs 73.10 lakhs in the case of SSB were mutually settled amounting to 76.24 per cent of the combined free reserves and profits of SSB (Rs 82.05 lakhs) and MDM (Rs 75.20 lakhs).

Had these funds not been siphoned off under the garb of contractual breach, the shareholders on liquidation would have been liable to tax as they would receive these sums as dividends.

Also, a large sum of Rs 166.80 lakhs had been drained from the accumulated reserves of the two mill companies. These amounts, classified as business expenses, were tax deductible and resulted in a lower tax liability.

The COI estimated the loss of tax collections by the government not less than Rs 12.3 lakhs for the selling agency breach compensation and Rs 30.58 lakhs for the management agency breach compensation. As the income tax records of the companies concerned were not available with the COI, a more accurate determination wasn't possible.

The amounts of selling and managing agency compensation were the first instance adjusted to reduce the indebtedness of

DCPM to SSB and MDM. DCPM received a credit of Rs 46.9 lakhs for compensation on breach of the selling agreement and Rs 54 lakhs as part payment for the compensation payable to BUA and VV for managing agency breaches and hence was able to "pay back" over Rs 100 lakhs to the two mills. Thereafter, SSB and MDM were taken into voluntary liquidation on December 31, 1951.

The assets and liabilities of the two mills were then transferred by the liquidators to South Asia Industries Ltd, (formerly known as Lahore Electric Supply Co Ltd or LES) in May 1953, pursuant to a Scheme of Arrangement under Section 208 C of the Indian Companies' Act, 1913. South Asia Industries Ltd (which was then under the full control of Ramkrishna Dalmia), authorized destruction of such books and records of these two companies as were not required for settling the claims of the shareholders. Under the terms of the Scheme, the books were accordingly destroyed after a board resolution of May 25, 1953. The two mill companies, SSB and MDM, were finally dissolved three months after the presentation of the final liquidation accounts on February 01, 1954.

NO ASSURANCE IN INSURANCE AND FINAL WORDS

Bharat Insurance Company was incorporated in 1896 and was taken over by the DJ group in 1936. Ramkrishna Dalmia became a director and chairman of the company, a position he held till 1942, when he was succeeded by his brother, Jaidayal. However, Ramkrishna Dalmia was re-appointed as the chairman and principal officer of the company with effect from August 20, 1954. As the period when the crimes were committed spanned August 1954 to September 1955, Dalmia was held responsible.

During this relevant period, Bharat Insurance had its current account no. 1120, in the Chartered Bank of India, Australia, and China Ltd (hereinafter called the Chartered Bank) at Bombay, and an account for the safe custody of its securities. Another current account was maintained with the Punjab National Bank (PNB), Bombay. At its Delhi head office, the company also had an account for the safe custody of securities with the Imperial Bank of India, New Delhi.

GL Chokhani was an employee of the insurance company in Bombay. Chokhani and Chordia (Ramkrishna's brother-in-law) were authorized to operate the Chartered Bank account, though Chokhani alone operated on that account between the years 1951-53. On October 01, 1953, the Board of Directors changed the authorized signatories on the account to be operated jointly by Chokhani and Raghunath Rai. Rai had joined the company in

1921 as a clerk and had worked his way up to become the secretary-cum-chief accountant by August 1954. He was stationed at the head office in Delhi. The prosecution's case against Dalmia and others rested principally on Rai's evidence.

Despite the change in mandate, Chokhani continued to operate the bank account alone. He would get several blank cheques signed by Rai and countersign these cheques upon issue. Thus, Rai wasn't aware when and to whom and for what amount the cheques had been issued. To ensure availability of signed cheques when needed, two chequebooks were used. When the signed cheques in one were close to depletion, Chokhani would send the other chequebook to Rai for his signatures. This system resulted in the misuse of the company's funds for unauthorized purposes.

The by-laws of the insurance company empowered the chairman to grant loans to persons with or without security. The chairman was also empowered to negotiate, transfer, buy, and sell government securities and to pledge, endorse, withdraw, or otherwise deal with them. Chokhani was not empowered by any resolution of the board to purchase and sell securities. He did so under the instructions of Ramkrishna Dalmia, who by his own volition had permitted Chokhani.

Chokhani would purchase and sell securities on behalf of the company in Bombay. Most of the securities were sent to Delhi and kept with the Imperial Bank of India there. The other securities remained at Bombay and were to be kept with the Chartered Bank.

During the investigations, it was revealed that most of the securities were purportedly held in the Bombay office of the insurance company and not deposited with banks. This was simply because they didn't exist. The plea of the accused that this was done to avoid bank charges was specious.

The transactions were conducted through recognized brokers to window-dress them as normal transactions. For security purchases, Chokhani would instruct the broker to transact with a company named Bhagwati Trading Company. Bhagwati was a proprietary concern owned by Vishnu Prasad, Chokhani's nineteen-year-old nephew.

Chokhani would advise the brokers that he would take the purchased securities directly from Bhagwati. However, this didn't happen. Chokhani would issue cheques to Bhagwati, who wouldn't deliver the securities against monies received. The sale transactions consisted in the sale of the securities held (or supposed to be held). The monies received from the sale would then be diverted in purchasing further securities. These securities were however not received by the head office in Delhi.

In a few cases, securities purchased and not received were received later when fresh *genuine* purchases of similar securities took place from the funds of Bharat Union Agencies or Bhagwati Trading Company. These securities were endorsed in favour of the insurance company.

The reason why genuine transactions were conducted were two – first, these were interest-bearing securities with scheduled interest payment dates. It was therefore necessary to procure these securities or to enter a paper transaction of their sale prior to the scheduled interest payment dates to obtain the necessary income tax deduction certificate from the Reserve Bank of India. The second reason was when audit called upon physical evidence of securities to record the security certificate numbers, these needed to be furnished.

The funds of the insurance company, ostensibly spent on the purchase of securities or from the sale proceeds of securities held by Bharat Insurance, were diverted to another company, the Bharat Union Agencies (BAU). Chokhani was a full-time servant of the

BAU as well. BAU, practically owned by Ramkrishna Dalmia, inter alia speculated in shares.

BAU suffered heavy losses in its forward transactions[49] between August 1954 to September 1955. To fund these losses, monies were diverted from Bharat Insurance to BAU

Between August 09, 1954 and August 08, 1955, funds totalling Rs 237.48 lakhs were diverted from the coffers of Bharat Insurance to those of BAU and between August 09, 1955 and September 30, 1955, a further sum of Rs 55.43 lakhs was similarly misappropriated. All transactions were routed through the intermediary Bhagwati's bank accounts.

In addition to fictitious purchase of securities, securities were also withdrawn from the safe custody accounts of Bharat Insurance with Imperial Bank Delhi and Chartered Bank Bombay, sold in Mumbai and funds similarly routed. Such withdrawals of securities were authorised by Ramkrishna Dalmia.

Excluding the funds so diverted but used for genuine transactions, the total estimated misappropriation of the monies of the insurance company amounted to nearly Rs 258 lakhs.

The real nature of the sale and purchase transactions of the securities did not come to the notice of the head office of Bharat Insurance at Delhi as Chokhani communicated to the head office the contracts of sale and purchase with the brokers' statements of accounts, with a covering letter stating the purchase of securities from the brokers, without mentioning that the securities had not been actually delivered/received and that the cheques in payment were issued to Bhagwati and not to the brokers.

---

49 Forward transactions as the name suggests are speculating on the future price of securities. The buyer in a forward transaction speculates on a rise in the value of the underlying assets. The seller, on the contrary, speculates on a drop in the price of the underlying assets.

Whenever Rai in Delhi would inquire from Dalmia about the transaction, he would be told that Chokhani had purchased them under Dalmia's instructions. Thereafter, the usual procedure of making the entries with respect to the purchase of securities was followed in the head office and then the transaction(s) confirmed (with an office note, which recorded that the purchase was under the instructions of the Chairman) at the meeting of the Board of Directors.

Dalmia, however, denied that Rai had ever approached him for the confirmation or approval of the purchase transaction or that he told him such transaction had been under his approval. He also maintained that he had authorised Chokhani in 1953, to purchase and sell securities and that thereafter Chokhani had acted on his own and Dalmia had no knowledge of Chokhani's modus operandi. Though Dalmia admitted being aware of BAU's losses, he maintained that Chokhani advised him that funds would be arranged, but no details had been shared.

RP Gurha was a director of BAU and looked after the work of its office in Delhi. At Delhi, there was a ledger with respect to the account of the transactions by the Bombay office of BAU. Under the directions of Chokhani, a cash statement and a journal of the Bombay office transactions were sent to Gurha personally at BAU Delhi. These cash statements correctly reflected the entries of the amounts received from Bhagwati by BAU as well as the payments by BAU to Bhagwati. Gurha allegedly substituted the actual cash statements with fictitious ones with no mention of Bhagwati. Receipts/payments from Bhagwati would be reflected as receipts/payments from/to the Delhi Office of BAU through Chokhani.

Later, during the investigations and trial, Chokhani admitted that he carried out the transactions in the form alleged to meet the losses of BAU. He stated that he did so as he expected that the BAU would, in due course, make up the losses and the money would be returned to Bharat Insurance.

Chokhani simplified the entire fraud defending that what he did, amounted to giving of a loan by Bharat Insurance to BAU and that there was nothing wrong with it. He asserted emphatically that had he known what he was doing, was wrong, he would've raised money through other means.

The firm of Khanna and Annadhanam, Chartered Accountants, was appointed by Bharat Insurance as its auditors for the year 1954. Shri Khanna carried out the audit and dissatisfied with certain matters requested for the counterfoils of the cheques and to produce securities. He sought an explanation of why the securities were not with the company's bank at Delhi.

The matter, however, came to a head not on account of the auditors' report, but because of Shri Kaul, Deputy Secretary, Ministry of Finance, Government of India. Kaul had heard murmurs in Bombay that Dalmia had incurred heavy losses amounting to over two crore rupees through his speculative activities and had been drawing upon the funds of the insurance company in which he was the chairman, to cover his losses. Kaul asked Dalmia on September 14, 1955, to see him on the next day in connection with the securities of the insurance company. When Dalmia met him on September 15, in the presence of Mr Barve, joint secretary, Kaul asked whether he had brought with him an account of the securities of the Bharat Insurance Company. Dalmia expressed his inability to do so for want of sufficient time and promised to bring the account the next day, on September 16. However, Dalmia did not go to Kaul's office; instead, Shanti Prasad Jain and others met Kaul and made certain statements. Kaul submitted a note to the finance minister on September 18, 1955, and recommended an investigation.

Matters moved swiftly. The Government of India appointed Shri Annadhanam under the Insurance Act 1938 to investigate into the affairs of the company. This was done on September 19, 1955. Dalmia signed a confessional statement to Annadhanam on September 20, 1955:

"I have misappropriated securities of the order of Rs 2,20,00,000 of the Bharat Insurance Company Ltd I have lost this money in speculation. At any cost, I want to pay full amount by requesting my relatives or myself in the interest of the policy holders."

The reason why Dalmia signed this confession is curious. Dalmia contented that he had signed the confession upon the promise that if he quietly made good the amount, he would not be prosecuted. He was apparently made to believe that the government did not want adverse publicity in the matter, as it would cause policyholders to lose faith in insurance companies, and hence had offered him a way out. This was denied by Annadhanam and Khanna (partners in the firm) who were present when Dalmia confessed in writing. Also, it could not be established that there had been any threat or duress on Dalmia. The court contented that his confession was voluntary, even though it might have been made for the purpose of screening the scheme of the conspiracy.

Dalmia's counsel, the famous British barrister Sir Dingle Foot QC, was unable to exclude Dalmia's confession as admissible evidence. Nor could the confession seek protection of Article 20(3) of the Constitution, i.e., protection against self-incrimination, since it was not made by Dalmia at a time when he was accused of an offence.

As Dalmia did not have the funds to put back to Bharat Insurance and had no one to bail him out, he was forced to sell a piece of his heart, *The Times of India,* and the Jaipur Udyog Industries to Shanti Prasad Jain for Rs 250 lakhs. Even after he had made good the monies to Bharat Insurance, the matter was handed over to the Police, and a case was registered under the Indian Penal Code (IPC).

While the Bharat Insurance scandal triggered the process of nationalization of the insurance business in India, Dalmia's trial was bitter. Despite his expensive and spirited defence over seven long years, moving from the Sessions to the High Court, he was sentenced to two years in prison and incarcerated in the Tihar Jail.

Eight others, including Chokhani, Gurha, and Vishnu Prasad, were sentenced. All their appeals too were turned down by the Supreme Court on April 05, 1962. The dismissals of their appeals came slightly ahead of the COI findings report of June 18, 1962, which found Dalmia guilty of multiple misdemeanours.

In the words of his daughter Neelima, "...he had been sentenced even before the trial began. In a single stroke, he lost everything – his honour, his money, his reputation, and his freedom."

Dalmia emerged from prison after two years, decimated in every sense of the term, a man broken and disillusioned, with a broken business and a fractious family...

FINAL WORDS - WHAT WAS THE SCAM SIZE?

It is difficult to quantify the value of the scam involving Ramkrishna Dalmia and the DJ group for the following reasons:

- The investigation was conducted by the COI for only ten of the group's companies. That was only a fraction of the total portfolio of the DJ group.
- Even in the ten companies, the trail ran cold on account of the unavailability or destruction of the books of account.
- The system of complex intercompany transactions made the audit discovery extremely difficult. Additionally, every trick in the book was used, from interest subsidy to falsification/

fabrication of accounts to siphoning off through managing and selling agents to liquidations and amalgamations.

Notwithstanding, the COI tried to arrive at the losses the investing public suffered and placed this figure at Rs 260.50 lakhs. This loss excluded the losses inter-se the companies in the DJ group or companies where Ramkrishna Dalmia was wholly or near-wholly interested, since the COI treated these losses "out of one pocket into another."

The details were as under: *(Note: Annas converted to decimals for calculation purposes where necessary)*

	DETAILS	IN LAKHS (RS)	IN LAKHS (RS)
1	**DJ AIRWAYS**		
a	On acquisition of 4,29,935 shares from the public by DCPM at an average rate of Rs 3 plus per share. Loss of Rs 7 per share (Face Value Rs 10).	30.10	
b	On acquisition of 12,27,905 shares by BUA from the public at an average rate of Rs 3.8 per share. Loss of Rs 6.2 per share. (*Although BUA acquired 15,32,340 shares, the COI excluded 3,04,534 shares that were acquired from the DJ group*)	76.13	
c	On 15,37,725 shares with the public at the time the scheme of liquidation entered into, the shareholders were to receive about 50 per cent of the face value, hence a loss of Rs 5 per share. (*As DCPM & BUA owned 19,62,275 shares as in (a) & (b) above, the investing public owned 15,37,725, as the total number of shares were 35 lakhs*)	76.89	183.12

	DETAILS	IN LAKHS (RS)	IN LAKHS (RS)
2	**DJ AVIATION**		
	On 6,600 preference shares subscribed by the Bharat Insurance in which the policy holder's interest (the public) was paramount.		1.98
3	**SSB AND MDM.**	**SSB**	**MDM**
a	Loss of interest after deducting dividends on investment in Bennett Coleman Shares.	5.56	3.91
b	Loss on sale of Bennett Coleman Shares.	1.77	1.28
c	Loss of profits on sale of Haines Road Property.	0.47	
d	Payment of Selling Agency Compensation.	0.52	0.65
e	Payment of Managing Agency Compensation.	1.29	1.70
	Total	9.61	7.54
	(Note: Item (a) is the total loss to the Company. However, the rest of the items represent losses to the investing public according to the percentage held by them at the times the losses were incurred.)		17.15
4	**DALMIA DADRI CEMENT**		
a	In acquisition of the ordinary & deferred shares from the public at rates well below the intrinsic value of the shares by Coys, such as DCPM, Asia Udyog & BUA in which Ramkrishna Dalmia was wholly beneficial shareholder,	10.94	
b	Arrears of dividends on preference shares which were denied to the shareholders but subsequently paid to DCPM, Asia Udyog & BUA,	0.82	11.76
	(The shareholders sold their shares well below the intrinsic value because of the purposeful policy of not declaring dividends which unduly depressed the value of the shares.)		

	DETAILS	IN LAKHS (RS)	IN LAKHS (RS)
5	**DCPM**		
a	Gain on sale of SSB & MDM shares to Bharat Insurance at Inflated rates due to which Bharat Insurance made a loss. (i) On 15,900 shares of SSB at Rs 10 per share Rs 1.59 lakhs (ii) On 5,200 shares of MDM at Rs 10 per share Rs 0.52 lakhs.	2.11	
b	Profit on sale of Nahur Land to Bharat Insurance.	21.20	23.31
6	**LES**		
a	Loss up to March 31, 1955, on sale of SSB and MDM shares Rs 32.34 lakhs.		
b	Loss up to March 31, 1955, on interest Rs 81.95 lakhs.		
	Proportionate loss to the public according to its holdings on the respective dates on (a) and (b) above.	23.18	23.18
	TOTAL		**260.50**

In addition to the amount lost by the investing public, if we add the funds diverted from Bharat Insurance to BUA (approximately Rs 258 lakhs, though the amounts were recovered/paid back by Dalmia), the figure doubles to Rs 518.50 lakhs. It is assumed here that the inflation of closing stock, selling expenses and other unauthorized business expenses are all captured in the assessment of concealed income by the Income Tax Investigation Commission of Rs 419 lakhs. The figure of the scam rises to Rs 937.5 lakhs.

To this, we need to add the interest subsidy enjoyed by DCPM from all its borrowings from Bharat Bank, Punjab National Bank, Gwalior Bank, and other public companies. We have seen that between 1947-51, DCPM's average borrowings were Rs 592 lakhs. Even if we were to conservatively estimate the interest subsidy at 2 per cent over commercial rates, this works to a figure of about Rs 12 lakhs annually or Rs 60 lakhs over the five-year period. To this we need to add the loss of the present value of rescheduled loans as excused to DCPM by many companies. In the case of DJ Airways alone, we have seen this figure at Rs 128 lakhs.

If one were to total this all up, the "scam value" for the DJ group would be well over Rs 11 crores, and we are unaware of the misdemeanours in the other twenty odd companies. The figure as a rough guesstimate in the very least would be at least Rs 12 crore or about Rs 1100 crore in current-day terms (using our multiplier of 92).

MACHIAVELLIAN MUNDHRA

FROM OBSCURITY TO NOTORIETY

Little is known about Mundhra's beginnings. He was born into a trading family with two younger brothers – Tulsidas and Manmohandas. He was married to Yashoda Devi, whose brother Rameshwar Daga (mentioned later) was a stockbroker and worked closely with Haridas. Mundhra started his career as a light-bulb salesperson. Though initially thought to be "self-made", Mundhra's graduation as an adventurer into the world of business, perhaps was due to the considerable support from the Marwari business circles and from tea export traders.

His initiation began with the funding of 50 lakh rupees each, provided by the firm of Bansilal Abhirchand of Nagpur and Vallabhswami, a Vaishnavite guru from Rajasthan.[50]

He started with tea exports before WWII, and apparently retained in pound sterling, his sale proceeds, as well as his profits in Britain. Using this capital as collateral, he managed to raise further capital in India, which he used to buy his way into British Indian companies. A question often asked is the reason for Mundhra's success for this funding leverage. Finance minister CD Deshmukh's note to the prime minister provides a clue: "the main appeal which he has as a potential purchaser in the British market is preparedness to refrain from general interference with the internal workings of

---

50 Tyabji, Nasir. *Forging Capitalism in Nehru's India: Neocolonialism and the State, c 1940-1970* – New Delhi: Oxford University Press, 2015.

the companies he buys… at least one big insurance company in the United Kingdom is prepared to support him… it is difficult to see how he has been able to do all that he has without the knowledge of the UK exchange control authorities. The support which the UK exchange banks[51] give him would necessarily mean at some stage or other a guarantee with the head offices of the exchange banks for Mundhra's loans in India and for that purpose some kind of approval or acquiescence by UK exchange control would be necessary."[52]

Whatever the modus operandi used by Mundhra to curry favour and support to obtain their guarantee and comfort to banks in India, he used the bank loans to purchase shares and ownership/directorship of companies in India. For every company so purchased, he would pledge its shares with banks to obtain additional finance, often rigging the prices of pledged securities[53] to manipulate margin requirements[54].

---

51 Banks with foreign ownership, operating in India and regulated by the RBI. These banks provided services such as foreign currency exchange, remittances, and financing of import-export transactions.

52 (Letter no.084/PSF/55 dated 21 September 1955 from the finance minister to Jawaharlal Nehru, JN papers, File no.385. pp.116-17) Tyabji, Nasir. *Forging Capitalism in Nehru's India: Neocolonialism and the State, c 1940-1970* – New Delhi: Oxford University Press, 2015.

53 By rumour mongering and using circular trading, which is a fraudulent practice where a group of traders buy and sell shares among themselves to create artificial demand and liquidity for the shares, thereby inflating their prices.

54 The amount, based on the market price of securities, which needs to be provided by the borrower from his own funds. For example, if the market price of 'n' shares is Rs 100 and the margin is Rs 30, the borrower can borrow a maximum amount of Rs 70. If the price of the securities goes up to say Rs 110, the borrower can borrow Rs 77 (70 per cent of Rs 110). Similarly, If the security price falls to say Rs 95, the borrower can borrow

According to a secret report sent to the Central government by the deputy governor of the RBI Ram Nath in February 1956, Mundhra bought his controlling interest in the British India Corporation by paying its former owners Rs 10-12 per share. Subsequently, he drove the price of these shares up to nearly Rs 14 per share. He then obtained finance from banks of up to Rs 11 per share, thereby managing to finance the takeover almost entirely with borrowed funds. The borrowed funds would be used to drain the resources of the acquired company for his next acquisition. When funds fell short, he even pledged fictitious, forged shares of his companies to raise monies. AD Shroff, an eminent industrialist, banker and economist, and an author of the Bombay Plan (discussed in Appendix 2) called as an expert witness by the Chagla Commission reportedly deposed, "It was fairly common knowledge in Bombay that against the 6 lakh shares of Richardson and Cruddas, there were nearly half as many duplicate shares floating in the market and this was the best of the Mundhra companies."[55] Mundhra was even indicted by the Bombay Stock Exchange in 1956 for selling forged shares.

By the mid-1950s, his personal wealth had built to about 1.5 crore rupees. Interestingly, apart from the Vaishnavite guru, Mundhra was also rumoured to have access to the resources commanded by the Punjab National Bank and its chairperson, Shanti Prasad Jain, a prominent player in our earlier chronicle.

There were several companies across industries that Mundhra acquired. To dovetail the narrative, we will focus on some of the

---

Rs 66.50. If the borrower's current outstandings are over Rs 66.50 (based on his earlier limit of Rs 70), he must correct the position by funding his account or providing additional securities.

55 Dalal, Sucheta. *AD Shroff: Titan of Finance and Free Enterprise.* Gurugram, Haryana: Penguin Random House India, 2001.

six companies into which LIC had made the infamous investments and add a couple, to encompass the breadth of Mundhra's misdemeanours. The six companies were Richardson and Cruddas Ltd, British India Corporation, Smith and Stanistreet, Jessop and Co Ltd, F & C Osler (India) Ltd, and Angelo Brothers. Though there are mixed reports on his sequence of takeovers, an RBI report[56] indicates that he began with F & C Osler (India) Ltd.

Following the indictment of the Chagla Commission, Mundhra was arrested from his luxury hotel suite at *The Claridges* in New Delhi, tried and finally imprisoned from January 17, 1961, to June 01, 1963.

His surprising acquittal in a little over two years in a prison sentence, which was for twenty-two, clearly underscored his ability to wheel-deal in high places, a refrain that will persist in our entire narrative about this man. In the prison too, there's ample evidence to show that he (and Dalmia) led comfortable lives, in exchange for money and gifts. "Haridas Mundhra, a businessman who was convicted of fraud, was another rich man who spent some time in Tihar. Not only did he have all the facilities, but he could also go out of the jail whenever he liked; at times, he would be out for several days and travel even up to Calcutta. All this, of course, cost a lot of money. An even richer prisoner was Ramkrishna Dalmia; he spent most of his jail term in hospital. He was known for his generosity to jail authorities, and one doctor received a car as a gift..."[57]

Unlike Ramkrishna Dalmia – who was a broken man after his prison sentence – Haridas Mundhra tried to return with gusto

---

56 The Bank and the Mundhra Affair - Reserve Bank of India, 25 Jun 2022.

57 Rakesh Kaushik v. B.L Vig, Superintendent, Central Jail, New Delhi And Another, Supreme Court Of India (Apr 30, 1980) CASE NO. Writ Petitions Nos. 393 and 549 of 1980, decided on April 30, 1980: reference Kuldip Nayar's book: "In Jail"

to play the marauder. The developments in the Turner Morrison Limited case (see in chapter 'And the (corporate) bodies keep piling...') exemplify this. Mundhra was adjudicated insolvent in 1974.

The main wrongdoings company-wise are as under.

F & C OSLER (INDIA) LTD

On March 13, 1946, this Indian subsidiary of a well-known British concern, F & C Osler – whose products included tablewares and lighting devices – passed to Indian management. The subscribed capital of the company was 1 crore rupees. J Osler, PA Osler, MC Bagri, Gwaldas Mundhra (Haridas Mundhra's father), Haridas Mundhra (as an alternate shareholder[58]), D Kothari, FT Griffinchif, GD Binani, CC Pyne and LR Josse, were the first directors. SB Industrial Development Co Ltd (SBIDC) was the managing agent of the said company. The Mundhras were the directors of SBIDC, having 99 per cent controlling shares, with Haridas Mundhra as the chairman. There were rapid changes in the board of directors of the company with Haridas Mundhra and his men taking control. In 1949-50, the board comprised Gwaldas Mundhra, Manickchand Bagri, Rameshwar Daga (Haridas's brother-in-law who ran a

---

[58] An alternate shareholder, also known as a substitute shareholder, is an individual or entity that is designated to exercise the voting rights of a shareholder who is unable or unwilling to do so. This can occur for a variety of reasons, such as the shareholder being out of town, incapacitated, or having a conflict of interest.

Alternate shareholders are typically appointed by the shareholder in writing, and their authority to vote on behalf of the shareholder is limited to the specific meeting or matter for which they are appointed. They do not have the same rights and privileges as the actual shareholder, such as the right to receive dividends or inspect the company's books and records.

stock broking firm in Calcutta), GD Binani, LR Josse and Haridas Mundhra, who in 1953 became the chairman as well. By March 1958, the directors were Rameshwar Daga, Haridas Mundhra, his brother Tulsidas Mundhra, Gwaldas Mundhra, and SB Mohta. Osler was wound up by an order on November 26, 1958, a mere twelve years after being set up.

During this period, the directors in a breach of trust and misuse of authority, misappropriated funds amounting to about Rs 71.19 lakhs, which resulted in Osler becoming insolvent. More than Rs 20 lakhs were advanced recklessly to various parties and soon became bad debts. In 1955, Rs 4.9 lakhs were invested in Osler Properties Ltd, a public company incorporated on February 17, 1955, which was controlled by Haridas Mundhra, SB Mohta, and one GK Maheswari. This company filed only one balance sheet on March 31, 1956, and soon became defunct. The shares of Osler Properties were never delivered to the official liquidator (for Osler), nor any explanation was provided about the whereabouts of these shares.

Osler also invested Rs 10 lakhs in one F & C Osler (Pakistan) Ltd, despite the knowledge that the amount could never be received back or recovered. No dividend was received on this investment. Further, as evidenced from the financials of Osler as on March 31, 1954, an unsecured loan of Rs 9.69 lakhs too was outstanding, which met a similar fate, without recovery of the principal or payment of interest.

Based on an alleged board resolution on May 23, 1951, 5,900 fully paid-up shares of Brahmapootra Tea Company Ltd of the face value of £5 per share were purchased at £24 per share, for a rupee equivalent of Rs 18.91 lakhs. This amount was first transferred to the account of SBIDC, and then to the personal account of Haridas Mundhra. Neither were the shares ever traced, nor any rationale provided why a company engaged as electrical engineers would acquire 19 per cent of the shares of a tea company at a premium of five times.

DN Guha Roy, the chartered accountant who was appointed by the court to investigate Osler in liquidation concluded in his report on September 12, 1967 that the total loss suffered by Osler for the collusive negligence of the directors was over Rs 375 lakhs, far higher than the call by the official liquidator for its case of misfeasance for Rs 71.19 lakhs. In his report, he argued that Osler not only allowed the loot of the share capital but also that of funds borrowed by the company.

Haridas Mundhra, Gwaldas Mundhra and Manickchand Bagree, were the directors of Osler as well as SBIDC, along with Tulsidas Mundhra. Haridas Mundhra was also a director of Brahmapootra Tea Co (India) Ltd. These same names figure in the list of debtor companies that had suspect businesses and had been used to siphon off the funds.

Indian Cable Company Limited supplied cables and other electrical goods on credit to Osler (Rs 11 lakhs) and SB Trading Co (P) Ltd (Rs 15 lakhs) between March 1955 and February 1956. These were secured by personal guarantees of Haridas Mundhra. By September 1957, these debts increased to Rs 11.37 lakhs and Rs 15.34 lakhs respectively, due to non-payment and interest charges. Haridas Mundhra guaranteed these liabilities as well, on the assurance of which, Indian cable had deferred filing suit for recovery of their dues. Later, Mundhra denied any liability in court.

Though we will not be discussing Mundhra's acquisition of tea companies, which met with mixed results for him, it would be important to underscore serious charges of violations under the Foreign Exchange Regulation Act (FERA), 1947 levied upon him. Brahmapootra Tea Co Ltd (BTC) with pound sterling capital was registered in England. Mundhra was a director of both BTC and Brahmapootra Tea Co India Ltd (BTCI). The managing agents of BTC were SB Industrial Development Company (UK) Ltd (SBIDC-UK). BTC had two accounts with Eastern Bank London, one where Haridas Mundhra and Gwaldas Mundhra were the authorized signatories and other established by SBIDC-UK. Some cheques drawn by Haridas Mundhra on these London accounts were dishonoured for want of sufficient funds. Between December 1955 and January 1956, Mundhra remitted three cheques for £9000, £2500, and £1500 to fund the BTC accounts. Mundhra denied that he had sent out the cheques for £9000 and £1500. The cheque for £2500, he explained, was proceeds of a loan arranged by SBIDC-UK for BTC from a foreign national in India, and he was simply the post office. Mundhra's defence did not stick. The 'foreign national' in India was one Mr Drissen, who though a UK citizen, was then employed by the India Cable Ltd at Calcutta. Per extant rules, such a remittance by Mr Drissen could only be made to a family member for purposes of maintenance. A cogent reason for such a remittance to BTC couldn't be presented nor its relationship with Mr Drissen established. It was thus concluded that the cheque had been sent to cover the overdraft in BTC's UK account by Mundhra and Mr Drissen must have been compensated in the Indian currency, in Calcutta. This amounted to a FERA violation, punishable by imprisonment for which Mundhra was held guilty.

RICHARDSON AND CRUDDAS LTD

Richardson and Cruddas Ltd, (Richardson) carried on business, inter alia, as structural and mechanical engineers. Haridas Mundhra was the chairman of the board of directors of Richardson, and the managing director of its managing agents SB Industrial Pvt Ltd (SBIPL).

Allegedly, Mundhra misused his position to effect payments by Richardson against two forged bills for Rs 4.12 lakhs and Rs 6.49 lakhs to a fictitious company – Indian Machine Tools Company Ltd Additionally, the accounts of Richardson were falsified to reflect receipt of machines supplied by Indian Machine tools and inflated with these assets, which existed only on paper.

Life Insurance Corporation of India (LIC), a shareholder of Richardson, moved the High Court on December 09, 1957 (following the alarming developments of spurious shares months after the infamous LIC investment - discussed later). The court then appointed DN Mitra as the Special Officer. Mitra engaged Messrs Fergusson & Co, to audit the accounts of the company. They reported that the case of Indian Machine tools was only one of the many offences. Failure and neglect to maintain proper vouchers and accounts and for wrongful withdrawal of monies and/or alleged loans and advances taken from the company amounted to nearly Rs 78.40 lakhs. A police complaint was lodged, and investigations followed.

While the chargesheets of this case added to the many against Mundhra for which he was eventually indicted, the board of directors who were the representatives of the shareholders, were removed on grounds of mismanagement. DN Mitra, the special officer already appointed was authorized to enter into an arrangement with the State Bank of India (SBI) and to consolidate all accounts of Richardson into a single account and operate the same and also to execute all bank documents necessary for the cash credit and the security creation and with SBI. The Government of India stepped in to guarantee the indebtedness of Richardson to SBI to the extent of Rs 95 lakhs. A board of advisors was appointed to assist the special officer in managing the business of the Company, comprising Richardson's two largest customers – Messers. Hindusthan Steel

(Private) Ltd, and a member of the Railway Board as well as a representative of the Ministry of Commerce and Industry and a representative of SBI. No representation of the shareholders was included for fear that it would encourage back door entry for the ousted directors. Hindusthan Steel also advanced Rs 10 lakhs to enable Richardson to execute its orders. By an act of the parliament, Richardson was eventually nationalised in 1972.

JESSOP AND COMPANY LTD

Haridas Mundhra was a director of Jessop and Company Ltd, (Jessop), a reputed engineering concern under European management in Calcutta.

In November 1955, Jessop purchased 3 lakh ordinary shares of British India Corporation Ltd (BIC) from Rameshwar Daga and another 25,000 shares early in October 1956, through a firm named Ramanarayan Kayan and Brothers. These purchases were made at a total cost of Rs 38.81 lakhs.

Subsequently, at the end of October 1956 the 3.25 lakh shares were sold to a firm of share brokers, Messrs Sohanlal and Company at the same purchase price. However, Messrs Sohanlal and Co paid only Rs 8.57 lakhs from its own funds while Haridas Mundhra and Tulsidas Mundhra paid the majority share with Rameshwar Daga funding the balance. One of Haridas Mundhra's cheques bounced and thus Jessop received, in November 1956, only about Rs 31 lakhs, leaving a shortfall (loss) in the transaction of Rs 7.81 lakhs.

By a letter dated May 27, 1957, Messrs Sohanlal and Co confirmed this balance to be due; however, soon repudiating the same, alleging that the letter had been forged.

Jessop instituted a suit in November 1959 for recovery of the shortfall, a police complaint was filed and a chargesheet was submitted in April 1960, alleging that Haridas Mundhra, along with

Rameshwar Daga had conspired with the secretary of the company GM Robins (who was absconding by then), to use Jessop's funds to invest in the shares of BIC where Mundhra was a director too. Further, Mundhra had also caused the sale to Messrs Sohanlal, a firm acting as a front for Haridas Mundhra. It also appeared that Jessop's resources were used to the extent of Rs 60 lakhs to buy shares of Richardson and Cruddas.[59]

Incidentally, when Jessop, in another matter, had appealed to set off the loss on their sale of shares against profits for an amount of Rs 2.45 lakhs for the year 1955-56, this was disallowed by the commissioner of income tax. The income tax officer opined that Jessop was speculating in shares and that the shares were never purchased or sold from real shareholders. The transactions were done through brokers on blank transfers, never registered in Jessop's name and sold within a month of their purchases. It was clear that Mundhra and his people were misusing their authority to speculate with company funds, against the memorandum and articles for which Jessop was set up.

Except for the purchase of the shares of the Indian Cable Co, all the other purchases and sales had been made either from or to Haridas Mundhra. It appeared that the only purpose of these transactions was to enable Mundhra, either to acquire control of other companies or to amalgamate them, or to help him to dispose off his own shares. In the case of BIC as well, the shares were never delivered to or held by Jessop.

In May 1958, the Government of India took over the management of Jessop and Co Ltd Jessop was eventually nationalised in 1973.

---

59 Dalal, Sucheta. *AD Shroff: Titan of Finance and Free Enterprise.* Gurugram, Haryana: Penguin Random House India, 2001.

NETTING THE BIG FISH, AND THE WHIFF OF A QUID PRO QUO

BRITISH INDIA CORPORATION LTD

British India Corporation (BIC) was the product of a collaboration between five British merchants in Cawnpore (now Kanpur), who, between 1876 and 1894, started woollen mills, cotton mills, and leather factories in the city. The South African War provided a fillip for army supplies. Of every 1,00,000 pairs of military boots, 60,000 were made in Kanpur. By early 1920s, Sir Alexander McRobert, a self-made millionaire, acquired these mills in Kanpur and established BIC as a public limited company. Spurred by the demand for sugar during the world war, BIC soon started sugar production and became an attractive proposition for buyout after India's independence.

The Dalmia-Jain group made an abortive bid for control of BIC in 1954. Mundhra had some BIC shares as well. In 1955, he persuaded the trustees of the McRobert Trust in England (which owned the controlling block), to sell their holdings to him. The Singhania group too was interested and already held a substantial number of shares. They were prepared to buy Mundhra's block if he failed to persuade the McRobert Trust. With this, the Singhanias would have gained control. "However, Deshmukh wrote, that very day's edition of the *Statesman* newspaper had reported that

Mundhra had succeeded in his effort, on the condition that he did not sell off. Mundhra's own managing agency, (SBIDC introduced earlier), managed many of his acquisitions in name, but his main appeal as a potential buyer in the British market lay in his preparedness to refrain from detailed interference in his managed companies." [60] Mundhra's ability to finance the entire acquisition of BIC through bank borrowings has already been chronicled earlier.

Sometime in September 1955, Haridas Mundhra acquired 48 per cent shareholding in BIC. At that time, Sir Robert Menzies and WHJ Christie were chairman and deputy managing director (DMD) of BIC. When Sir Robert Menzies retired in April 1956, Haridas Mundhra was elected a director and chairman in his place and soon, in July, his brother, Tulsidas Mundhra, was also elected a director. That was the starting point of BIC's woes.

BIC, a profit-making entity till 1953, had a subscribed share capital of Rs 406 lakhs, with substantial reserves, which stood at Rs 127.73 lakhs in 1957, despite suffering losses in 1954, 1955 and 1957 totalling Rs 48.26 lakhs. Its fixed assets rose from Rs 41.04 lakhs in 1950 to Rs 108.38 lakhs in 1957. Between September 1955 to April 1958, it owned and operated the Cawnpore Woollen Mills, Kanpur (popularly known as Lal-Imli), the Cawnpore Cotton Mills (known as Kakomi), North-West Tannery, Kanpur (popularly known as Flex), Cooper Allen, Kanpur and The New Egerton Woollen Mills, Dhariwal, in Punjab (popularly known as the Dhariwal).

BIC's 100 per cent subsidiary and its managing agent Messrs Begg Sutherland and Company Pvt Ltd (Sutherland), had a share capital of Rs 30 lakhs and reserves of Rs 2 lakhs in 1957. For most

---

[60] Private Industry and the Second Five-Year Plan: The Mundhra Episode as Exemplar of Capitalist Myopia – Nasir Tyabji, Institute for Studies in Industrial Development, Working Paper 2010/04, May 2010.

practical purposes, Sutherland was a branch or a department of BIC, with BIC, taking all decisions on its behalf.

Through Sutherland, BIC controlled several companies engaged in sugar, engineering, and textiles till 1957 - such as Cawnpore Sugar Works Ltd, Champaran Sugar Co Ltd, Purtabpore Co Ltd, Saran Engineering Co Ltd, Brush ware Ltd, Elgin Mills Co Ltd, Cawnpore Textiles Ltd, Samastipur Central Sugar Co Ltd (Samastipur) and Balrampur Sugar Co Ltd (Balrampur).

BIC thus commanded control over the aggregate subscribed capital of Rs 6.5 crore of its own and those of its pyramided subsidiaries. It was a mammoth combine, controlling vast share capital, fixed assets, reserves and diverse businesses.

Till 1955, BIC (16.8 per cent) and Sutherland (8.4 per cent) together owned a little over 25 per cent of Samastipur's 1,19,000 issued shares. Of Balrampur's issued shares numbering 2,80,000, BIC held 13.8 per cent. Mundhra later, averred in court that in October 1955, chairman Menzies, and the DMD Christie, had sought his assistance in securing a controlling interest in Samastipur and Balrampur. However, BIC and Sutherland had no spare liquid funds to make the proposed acquisitions. Mundhra promised to arrange the necessary finances and deposited Rs 20 lakhs in an account opened in his name with Sutherland. Between October and December 1955, Mundhra purchased 54,825 Samastipur shares and sent Sutherland a bill for the same. These included 51,000 shares at the rate of Rs 36 per share and the rest closer to the then market price of Rs 15.75 per share. Allegedly, this netted Mundhra a profit of Rs 10.33 lakhs. Mundhra argued that the purchase had been expensive, at substantial premiums over market rates, but necessary to secure Sutherland and BIC a 50 per cent, voting power in Samastipur. No one questioned why he couldn't have purchased only 30,000 shares, which would have been adequate for the purpose.

In the same period, Sutherland purchased through Haridas Mundhra and upon his insistence 1,03,418 shares of Balrampur at an average price of Rs 14.40 per share when the market price of the share was about Rs 11.50 per share, netting Mundhra a profit of Rs 3 lakhs plus to Sutherland's detriment/cost. Here again, a lesser number of shares would have sufficed. Mundhra failed to prove the exact price paid for the shares and refused cross-examination in court. He denied having given any promise to finance Sutherland but stated that he did advance a loan of Rs 80 lakhs for making share-purchases.

This was, however, not the truth that emerged from the minutes of the various board meetings in November and December 1955. In a meeting of BIC's board on January 07, 1956, which Mundhra attended on invitation, he convinced the board that the only way to restore the trading and financial glory of BIC was to increase production and to modernise the plant and machinery. The outlay would cost Rs 1.25 crores. The board of directors resolved to accept his proposals and his offer of a loan of Rs 80 lakhs at 4 per cent per annum interest for the purpose, on his assurance that he would not demand repayment until BIC had ample liquid resources. Yet funds had been used not for modernization, but expensive share acquisitions.

It was also strange that the shares had been purchased by Mundhra when he was only a shareholder of BIC, without any board sanction from either BIC or Sutherland. Rather, it was only a post facto ratification, with no director questioning the advisability or the cost of the acquisitions.

Records show that Mundhra's advances to Sutherland (deposit balances in his account opened with Sutherland) reached a maximum of Rs 70.48 lakhs as on October 31, 1956, of which over Rs 68 lakhs was withdrawn within a year. Sutherland's dues to Mundhra were paid with borrowings from its parent, BIC. BIC was already heavily borrowing in August 1955 (its debit balance with the State Bank of India, Kanpur stood at Rs 387.94 lakhs), this increased its indebtedness further to accommodate Sutherland. Its borrowings from SBI stood at Rs 436.74 by March 1957. It began to delay creditor payments.

To alleviate the pressure on BIC, on February 09, 1957, BIC's board resolved to sell shares of Samastipur and Balrampur, authorizing Mundhra and the management to negotiate the sale. By the end of the month, Mundhra had a deal on the table, which was authorized by the board. Sutherland's 64,825 Samastipur shares were proposed to be sold at Rs 30 per share along with the purchaser also repaying Sutherland's short loan to Samastipur of Rs 10 lakhs. Additionally, BIC agreed to relinquish the managing agency of Samastipur to the purchaser *without* compensation. Sutherland also authorized the sale of 1,03,418 Balrampur shares at Rs 12.32. On March 02, Mundhra brought a new deal. A group of buyers was ready and willing to purchase 70,000 Samastipur shares and 1,43,000 Balrampur shares at Rs 26 and Rs 15 per share, respectively. He disclosed that the group of buyers consisted of Jumnadas Kayan of Ram Narain Kayan & Co, Matadin Khetan of Hind Sugar Co, Sheo Chand Dabriwala of Hind Sugar Co, *and himself*. He said that he had a 50 per cent interest in the group.

DMD Christie informed the board that another prospective buyer, Jhunjhunwala was willing to buy 1,53,000 Balrampur shares at Rs 15 per share but unwilling to purchase Samastipur shares. The board resolved that Balrampur and Samastipur shares should be sold together in view of the urgent need for cash. Jhunjhunwala made an alternative offer in the same meeting of purchasing 1,43,000 Balrampur shares at Rs 20 each or of purchasing 1,43,000 Balrampur shares at Rs 18 each and 60,000 Samastipur shares at Rs 35 each, the aggregate price being payable in three years. This offer too was rejected on grounds of the need for immediate cash infusion.

The purchase by the consortium (where Mundhra had 50 per cent interest) was preferred and voted at Mundhra's behest in the same meeting, along with the following conditions: (a) Payment in cash against transfer of shares to be completed by the first week of March 1957. (b) Purchaser to also repay short loans advanced by Sutherland to Balrampur and Samastipur for Rs 6 lakhs and Rs 8 lakhs respectively. (c) The consortium to buy an additional 14,873 Samastipur shares at Rs 15 each, upon Sutherland relinquishing the managing agency to the purchaser. On March 04, Mundhra authorized Sutherland to debit in his account for a sum of Rs 23 lakhs in part-payment of the deal.

However, Mundhra and his group backed out of the transaction. They did not pay the price and take delivery of the shares, and yet the BIC board did not enforce the contract or claim damages for its breach. Surprisingly, despite his authorization, neither was Mundhra's letter placed before the boards of BIC or Sutherland, nor was his account debited by Sutherland for Rs 23 lakhs, which would have locked him and the group to the deal. Between March and May 1957, Mundhra kept assuring the board that he was pushing the group to honour their contract. The board of BIC was getting increasingly desperate to realize cash for those investments not only to meet immediate business needs but also to pay about Rs 19 lakhs as dividends, which were likely to be declared in the annual general meeting of the Corporation's shareholders on June 22, 1957! The search for a new buyer began.

Haridas Mundhra, as a member of the group, was jointly and severally liable for breach of contract. Outside the board, he was collectively destroying the contract; inside the board, he was putting up a pretense of enforcing the contract. He could not serve both himself and BIC.

Eventually, Sutherland's board (under the chairmanship of Christie) approved the sale of 24,000 Samastipur shares and 2,000 Balrampur shares it owned at Rs 9 and Rs 5 per share respectively to Mundhra with a buyback clause at the same prices anytime within two years. Mundhra was to be compensated for interest at 5 per cent per annum, for the purchase price paid by him. On July 31, 1957, purchase amounts were further reduced. An eo nominee sale[61] to Ram Narain Kayan & Co for 18,000 Samastipur shares at Rs 9 per share and 1,500 Balrampur shares at Rs 5 per share was concluded.

Ram Narain Kayan & Co eventually purchased an additional 20,048 Samastipur shares from BIC and Sutherland's holdings of 39,952 at Rs 19 per share. They also purchased an additional 6,873 shares from Sutherland at Rs 11 per share, along with taking over Sutherland's managing agency without compensation.

Similarly, Sohanlal Pachisia & Co purchased holdings of Balrampur shares (BIC's 38,604 shares and Sutherland's 1,01,918 shares) at Rs 16.25 per share along with taking over the managing agency of Balrampur.

When compared to the book value (acquisition price) of the shares of these two sugar mills, BIC and Sutherland suffered a loss of Rs 5.57 lakhs, and even the courts pegged the loss which Mundhra was directed to compensate Rs 6.65 lakhs (for they evaluated the Samastipur transaction alone). However, the actual loss for the combined entity for both sugar mills factoring (a) Proposed repayment of the Rs 14 lakh of loans provided by Sutherland which was to be paid by the Kayan-Mundhra consortium and (b)The contracted prices against the actual transaction done, the real loss

---

61 An eo nominee sale is a legal term that refers to a sale transaction where the buyer purchases the property in the name of another person, who is not the actual owner of the property. The eo nominee is a person who acts as a trustee for the actual owner of the property.

on the sell side was Rs 19.17 lakhs. This taken together with the loss on the buy side suffered of Rs 13.33 lakhs pegged the total cost to the BIC-Sutherland entities at Rs 29.50 lakhs. This does not account for the substantial hidden costs of surrendering the managing agency remunerations of Sutherland from Samastipur and Balrampur, nor the cost of borrowings by BIC (a primary driver of its losses) on account of Mundhra withdrawing the promised support and the delay on the share sales due to Mundhra's skulduggery.

The case of Cawanpore (Kanpur) Cotton Mills (CCM), a mill operated by BIC, becomes important for it took centre stage as one of the explanations on why the Congress government had allowed the LIC investment into Mundhra's companies. In addition to Mundhra's purported donation of Rs 2.5 lakhs to the Congress party (Rs. 1.5 lakhs to the UP Congress and Rs 1 lakh to the Central Congress Party), the government had apparently requested him not to close CCM, with the concomitant loss of thousands of livelihoods, as it would reflect badly upon them in an election year.[62] Govind Ballabh Pant, then chief minister of Uttar Pradesh, had apparently appealed to the government that the parlous state of BIC and other Mundhra concerns in Kanpur had caused large-scale layoffs from his companies, that this unemployment was causing great discontent in Kanpur and the only way to get the BIC going again was to buy Mundhra shares so that Mundhra could put the proceeds of the sale into reviving his undertakings.[63]

Between 1952-57, CCM suffered a loss of Rs 1 crore on account of surplus labour, old machinery, and want of rationalization. There was accumulation of huge unsold stocks of manufactured goods and the mill was a dead weight on BIC. Sometime in 1957, BIC's

---

62 Second General elections were held in February-March 1957

63 Nehru, B.K., *Nice Guys Finish Second: Memoirs*. Gurugram, Haryana: Penguin Random House, 2012.

MD and director Christie and Powell negotiated for its sale for about Rs 52 lakhs to Roop Narain Ram Chandra Pvt Ltd (RNRC).

Mundhra, however, prevailed against this decision on grounds that the prospective buyer's financials were not sound and as selling agents for CCM, Kanpur Textiles Ltd and Elgin Mills Co Ltd, RNRC were indebted to BIC to the tune of Rs 30 lakhs. A certain buyer was lost, and BIC suffered great loss in operating the mill as no better offer could be secured.

Initially though, Mundhra was in consonance with the decision to close the mills. At a board meeting on April 27, 1957, it was decided that due notice to the employees would be given for closure with effect from May 12, 1957. However, on May 07, at another board meeting of BIC it was reported that labour and the government were both opposed to the closure and there was apprehension that if the mills were closed, the government might appoint an authorized controller over BIC. A new resolution to find a buyer and extend the closure date to June 16 was taken. Significantly, at this meeting Mundhra stated that he met Mr TT Krishnamachari along with Mr Bhattacharya, the Chairman of the State Bank, and discussed with him "the whole matter."[64] This meeting was a little over a month before the actual investments were made by LIC into the Mundhra companies and *thus provided the fuel for the rumour that LIC's investments in Mundhra's companies was in exchange for his agreement to keep CCM operational.*

On June 05, closure was ruled out, with the only choices being to sell or operate, though the latter wouldn't be possible without financial assistance. Accordingly, application for a loan from the National Industrial Development Corporation (NIDC) was recommended.

---

[64] 'Rajya Sabha discussion on the Government's resolution on the Life Insurance Corporation Inquiry: September 11, 1959' - Observations by Lavji Lakhamshi, MP representing Gujarat in the Rajya Sabha.

By July 12, negotiations with RNRC had yielded better terms. RNRC would purchase the fixed assets of the mills for Rs 35 lakhs, with Rs 10 lakhs payable immediately as earnest money, and the balance Rs 25 lakhs in equal instalments over three years along with interest at 6 per cent per annum. RNRC would also pay Rs 11.76 lakhs for the new machinery already purchased and paid for by BIC within two months of the date of the sale deed, plus Rs 5.42 lakhs for new machinery purchased and not paid for by BIC within one month of the sale agreement. Outstandings by RNRC as selling agents of the three mills would be reduced immediately from Rs 29 lakhs to Rs 7.50 lakhs, before the execution of the sale deed. RNRC also agreed to pay 75 per cent of the current assets – the value of the stocks of cloth, yarn, and cotton held by the mill and the balance of 25 per cent within two months.

Mundhra opposed this offer as well, assuring to "make arrangements for another similar or even better offer from another party almost immediately." He also mentioned that in his high-level discussions with the Government of India, he had indicated that BIC would be able to continue to operate the mills if financial assistance were received.

MD Christie had serious misgivings. Although RNRC's offer was not perfect, it would allow the immediate and much-needed cash infusion of Rs 75 lakhs. The mills had suffered losses for six years and further operations would require cotton purchases at unremunerative prices. Such continuance projected the loss for 1957 at about Rs 21.25 lakhs. Christie opined that even after the installation of new machinery, CCM wouldn't be able to turn profitable. As the board was split on the decision, BIC deferred the final decision to July 20.

At that meeting, where Mundhra was absent, MD Christie informed the board that Mundhra had given an undertaking to

Sri Morarji Desai, minister for commerce and industries, that BIC would operate the mills if it were promised financial assistance by the NIDC. He had also undertaken to arrange for sale of unsold stocks of cloth and yarn to the extent of Rs 50 lakhs by the end of August. It was recorded that Mr Hill, a director of BIC had discussed with the Loan Advisory Committee of the NIDC in Bombay and it "was his impression" that if BIC decided to continue the mill operations, NIDC would be willing to consider a loan of Rs 65 to Rs 75 lakhs. The board then resolved to drop negotiations for the sale of the mill with RNRC.

The elected directors of BIC were eventually evicted for mismanagement; Haridas Mundhra was directed to pay certain compensation to BIC and an interim committee of management appointed from four years to January 31, 1963.

In 1962, Bhagwati Prasad Bajoria and others (hereinafter Bajorias) applied for dismissal of the interim committee. They sought immediate election of directors by the shareholders and for entrusting management of the affairs of BIC based on their having wrested 26.5 lakh shares of BIC. Along with the LIC and the President of India they now owned about 75 per cent shareholding. Their petition was supported by the LIC and Government of India.

There was some opposition based on allegations that the Bajorias were a front for Mundhra and if Mundhra succeeded in the ongoing litigation in the Calcutta High Court with the banks from whom the LIC and the President of India had purchased shares once held by Mundhra, the combined shareholding of these persons would be considerably reduced form the 75 per cent claimed by the consortium. These were dismissed and the new directors took control of BIC in November 1962. BIC, however, failed to recover its position of eminence and was nationalised in 1981.

...AND THE (CORPORATE) BODIES KEEP PILING...

TURNER MORRISON AND CO PVT LTD

The Turner brothers, John Geoffrey, and Nigel Fredric held the entire controlling interest in Hungerford Investment Trust Ltd (HIT), which in turn controlled the entire share capital of Turner Morrison & Co Pvt Ltd (TML), a Calcutta managing agency. Subsidiary and controlled companies under TML were Shalimar Tar, Angelo Brothers, Lodna Colliery, Smith Stanistreet & Co Ltd, Shalimar Works Ltd, and two other companies. Most of these companies were treated by TML as its departments. TML would provide finances, loans, and guarantees for loans advanced by the banks in respect of these companies.

The way Mundhra commandeered control over TML by paying for less than half its shares, underscores his deviousness.

TML's shareholding comprised 4,500 shares of Rs 1,000 each. Haridas Mundhra with BIC as his nominee, entered an agreement at the end of October 1956 with the Turner brothers to purchase 49 per cent in TML with the further option to purchase the balance 51 per cent for a sum of Rs 86.60 lakhs, within 5 years from the date of acceptance of the offer by HIT. Mundhra paid for and obtained a transfer of 49 per cent (2,205 shares) while HIT retained 2,295 (51 per cent) shares of TML. The 2,205 shares were held by BIC (2,187 shares) Mundhra (3 shares) and 3 shares each in the names of five officials of BIC. On September 07, 1957, Mundhra became entitled to exercise the option and to purchase 51 per cent of the remaining shares.

In December 1960, Mundhra exercised his option to buy the remaining 51 per cent. Since the shares were not transferred to him, Mundhra filed a suit on April 19, 1961 (Suit No 600 of 1961: Haridas Mundhra v Mrs Mary Theresa Turner). There was a hiatus thereafter, possibly on account of Mundhra's imprisonment.

On February 25, 1964, a court decree directed HIT to deliver to Mundhra 51 per cent ordinary shares of TML against payment of the consideration fixed at Rs 86.60 lakhs. An injunction was also issued restraining sale of the shares to anyone but Mundhra as well as prohibiting HIT (and other defendants in the suit) exercising their voting rights, except in accordance with the instruction of Mundhra.

In another development, on February 28, 1964, the certificate officer, 24 Parganas attached the decree in Suit No 600 of 1961, (essentially the sum of Rs 86.60 lakhs) for failure on the part of Mundhra to satisfy six certificates (claims) then pending against him. Besides the attachment by the certificate officer, attachments were levied in three other execution proceedings. [Decrees obtained by Champaran Sugar Co Ltd and British India Corporation Ltd, (Kanpur Sugar Works Ltd), and Life Insurance Corporation of India].

Thus, Mundhra was prohibited and restrained from alienating, transferring, or charging his right title and interest in the decree in Suit No 600 of 1961 (for the option of 51 per cent in TML). It was alleged by HIT's counsel that these attachments were at Mundhra's behest to thwart his payment of Rs 86.60 lakhs.

In another development, on February 03, 1965, Bank Hoffman AG obtained a decree in London, against Romanigo Holdings SAH and HIT. This decree was transmitted for execution to the court of the district judge, Delhi for attachment of the 2,295 shares of

TML held by HIT, subject to any option rights of Haridas Mundhra on the same shares per Suit No 600 of 1961. In addition to Bank Hoffman, the Indian income tax authorities had an interest in the shares as well for their claims against Mundhra. An order was also issued, directing the deputy commissioner of police Calcutta, to produce 707 shares of the company, being withheld by TML on grounds that they were Mundhra's property.

HIT appealed on August 30, 1965, seeking Mundhra's payment of Rs 86.60 lakhs and the simultaneous release of the 51 per cent of shares *within a time to be fixed by the court,* failing which the contract should stand rescinded. This application was dismissed by the court in view of the complex litigations, claimants, and the various attachments on the proposed payout by Mundhra and the shares held by HIT.

In a sudden and strange turn of events, on November 15, 1965, TML instituted a suit against HIT (Suit No 2005 of 1965) claiming Rs 127.67 lakhs on account of payment made by it on behalf of the HIT to the income-tax authorities. To secure this claim of nearly Rs 128 lakhs, TML requested for the appointment of receiver and the possession and sale of 2,295 shares (51 per cent shares of TML) from HIT in exercise of its lien under Article 22 of the Articles of Association of TML. This suit was dismissed in 1968. Mundhra appealed against that decision to the Supreme Court, which too was dismissed in March 09, 1972.

It must be stated that though TML was a party to Mundhra's Suit No 600, Mundhra had refused to proceed against TML; hence, all claims and charges against TML had been dropped. Suit No 2005 was believed to be a diabolical move by Mundhra, not to pay Rs 86.60 lakhs, since the injunction against HIT to either vote or sell to another party meant that he could control 100 per cent the company having paid for only 49 per cent of it! Also, Mundhra was trying his best to thwart other claimants such as Bank Hoffman.

There is a devil in the detail on the income tax payment made by TML. The offer made by Mundhra to purchase 49 per cent shares of TML had a Clause 9, which allowed TML to pay Indian super tax payable under the Indian Income Tax Act to the extent of Rs 46 lakhs. In other words, TML was to pay out of its assets, the said sum to the income tax authorities on behalf of the shareholders of HIT. Although Mundhra acquired virtual control of the affairs of the company by reason of the course of events, he denied that he was under any obligation to cause the company to pay income tax up to Rs 46 lakhs. Hence, he instituted the suit by TML against HIT.

On March 21, 1967, HIT renewed its appeal that Mundhra pay the necessary sum to the receiver against the delivery of the said 2,295 shares of TML, else the agreement dated October 30, 1956, be rescinded and the injunction in favour of Mundhra stand vacated.

On July 14, 1969, the court ruled that Haridas Mundhra committed breach of the contract, which was directed to be specifically performed by the decree and that he created a situation that showed that he was never anxious to perform his part of the contract and pay the Rs 86.60 lakhs during the last five-and-a-half years.

All Mundhra's attempts, either through TML or otherwise, failed. Eventually, the Supreme Court rescinded the decree in Suit No 600 of 1961 in early March, 1972. Consequently, the injunction order, the voting rights of 51 per cent shares to Haridas Mundhra, was vacated and the majority shareholders became entitled to voting rights in respect of 51 per cent shares. On an application by the majority shareholders, the central government called an annual general meeting in July 1972 and new directors were elected in the said meeting. Mundhra's further legal challenges in the matter were dismissed in September 1972 and the entire management of TML replaced.

SHALIMAR TAR, ANGELO BROTHERS AND LODNA COLLIERY

These three companies were profitable and had large reserves prior to Haridas Mundhra and his nominee directors working at his behest taking over their control. Their control became complete after the February 25, 1964 ruling, discussed earlier.

TML owned:

a. 64 per cent (27,950 ordinary shares) of Shalimar Tar's (Shalimar's) 43,644 shares of Rs 100 each.

b. 32 per cent (1,43,625 shares) of Angelo Brothers' (Angelo's) 4,50,000 ordinary shares of Rs 10 each

c. 53.44 per cent (4,64,940 shares) of Lodna Colliery's (Lodna's), 8,70,000 ordinary shares of Rs 10 each.

All these were duly recorded as TML's holdings in the books of these subsidiary companies till March 1972.

After the dismissal of the TML (Mundhra-led) board following the Supreme Court judgement in March 1972, an application was successfully filed for the removal of the board of directors of Shalimar, Angelo, and Lodna.

When Mundhra realized that the courts were against him and that his control over TML would be lost, he began to undermine the financial condition of TML. TML's entire holding of shares of Shalimar and Angelo were sold at rates much below the market to one Ganapat Rai & Sons (1946) Ltd (Ganapat Rai). Similarly, 4,07,225 shares in Lodna were sold to one Metal Craft (India) Ltd (Metal Craft). Such sales were allegedly made by Mundhra through the directors of TML under his influence. The buyers didn't have the wherewithal and the money used was Mundhra's. HIT, the majority shareholder, learnt of these transactions on April 14, 1972.

Mundhra's clique, including his son VK Mundhra, held multiple positions across TML and the three companies. A board resolution was drafted for the purported sale of shares of TML's holding in the companies on February 15, 1972, and sales concluded by March 15, 1972. Reasons mentioned in the minutes were pressure by TML's bankers for loan repayments by February end, failing which the assets secured against the loans would be sold by banks. Letters from National & Grindlays Bank Ltd and Central Bank of India about sale of securities pledged were mentioned, but no evidence of such letters was submitted in support. Outstanding loans by TML to the three companies totalling Rs 50 lakhs with easy repayment terms was also put forward as the reason for TML's cash crunch. There was, however, no evidence of delays in statutory payments like tax or provident fund to have warranted the sudden need by TML for cash. Neither was any liquidity problem mentioned in the board meeting of TML a month before the sales, nor was there any due diligence for the proper publication of the sales or a tendering process. Shalimar's (not a listed company) shares had been sold at Rs 15 each, Angelo at Rs 5, and Lodna at Rs 2.50. The minutes referred to the stock exchange quotation in respect of shares of Angelo brothers for February 14 and 15, though no such quotation was made available. The valuation of Lodna shares too was apparently assessed by one of the directors BP Moody at Rs 2 per share, though the basis of such valuation was never sighted. Nor was the purported offer for purchase by Ganapati Rai and Metal Craft available.

Records revealed that a sum of Rs 51 lakhs was due from Shalimar towards loan, interest, rent, services, and other charges to TML. It was suspect and unreasonable for TML to have sold its shares of Shalimar for Rs 4.19 lakhs (27,950 shares at Rs 15 each), at a discount of 85 per cent of its face value, when a sum of over 12 times this amount was due.

The balance sheet of TML for the year ended December 31, 1968, showed secured loans to the extent of Rs 25.27 lakhs from Grindlays Bank and Rs 6.05 lakhs from Central Bank, in addition to other liabilities. There was indeed a call from the banks for reduction in outstandings and liquidation of collateral in failure, but TML's position had improved after August 1971, and there was no cause for distress sale of the company's assets. Total liabilities for TML for March 1972, stood at Rs 27.10 lakhs, a much-improved position.

Shalimar earned a profit of Rs 18.28 lakhs in 1971-72 and Rs 22.88 lakhs in 1972. Hence, its sale at Rs 15 per share when similar transactions had concluded in the market at Rs 100, was indefensible.

Angelo's financials for the year that ended on August 31, 1972, reflected sales of Rs 262.34 lakhs, advance tax payments of Rs 5.54 lakhs and cash and bank balance of Rs 1.52 lakhs. Yet the books of the share transfer register of Angelo showed that 1,43,625 shares were sold at 50 per cent discount to the face value.

Lodna was sold at Rs 2.50 apiece, at a discount of 75 per cent to the face value, when transactions in the market revealed that no transaction had ever been done below Rs 5 per share.

While Shalimar was profitable, Angelo had been profitable till 1969 and Lodna till 1968. The fortunes of Lodna had suffered after taking over of Coking Coal Mine for which it needed to pay a heavy compensation, but it still had robust revenues and a distress sale at 75 per cent of the face value was unwarranted.

Both Ganapat Rai and Metal Craft were loss making and their state of finances was deplorable in March 1972. Though Metal Craft argued that they had borrowed large sums for the transaction and pledged the Lodna shares as collateral, this appeared specious, as their balance sheet simply wouldn't support a large debt. Some directors of the purchasing companies were also directors earlier in TML and Angelo.

The court held the sales as fraudulent, illegal, and void.

There is legal evidence from another case where the DIG (CID, Government of West Bengal) appointed as a Special Officer averred that Mundhra had fraudulently rented out Angelo's multi-crore property and later denuded it of all asset and valuables.[65]

Thereafter an FIR was registered against six accused persons, including Haridas Mundhra, who were found to be absconding.

---

[65] February 28, 2014: Angelo Brothers (in liquidation) Vs Nawdeep Singh, CA 401 of 2013.

THE MUNDHRA MURMURS, THE ECONOMIC AND POLITICAL TRIGGERS...

The Indian polity had become aware of Mundhra as early as mid-1955, possibly after his large acquisitions of Jessop and BIC. On August 23, 1955, Tiruvellore Thattai Krishnamachari (TTK), the industry and commerce minister, wrote to CD Deshmukh, the finance minister, "It seems very strange that despite so many stringent measures in the Companies Act, right at our very nose HD Mundhra can do what he likes. I do think that we must have some reserve powers for Government at least to secure information and to prevent mischief when a large block of shares of any company whose capital and assets are more than Rs 20 lakhs are to change hands." It is strange indeed that TTK then got embroiled in the controversy as the finance minister less than two years later!

As an aside, it must be mentioned that while the developments chronicled hereafter do paint a less than satisfactory picture of TTK, the Mundhra episode was a blemish in an otherwise brilliant political career. His contributions to shaping the Indian constitution and astute handling of the portfolio of commerce and finance remain undisputed. His profound impact on the growth of Indian industrialization, especially the setting up of the developmental financial institutions, too, have been well documented. Most importantly, no investigating body, the Chagla Commission, the Bose Board or the UPSC found any evidence of corruption or personal loot by any of the persons held accountable in LIC's investing in Mundhra shares, be it TTK or HM Patel, or the RBI governor, or LIC's chairman or managing director, et al.

Mundhra's exploits captured international attention too. Mystified by an article about this unknown name, in the '*Time*' magazine, United States, Prime Minister Nehru had even sought details from Deshmukh. In September 1957, just before the entire issue of LIC's investment in Mundhra blew up, Nehru, acting as the finance minister in TTK's absence (who was away on a USA visit) had remarked about Mundhra, "So far as I know the reputation of this gentleman is not good. Certain prosecutions have been launched against him for breaches of the provisions of the Companies Act."[66]

From the mid-1950s, murmurings about Mundhra from various quarters had reached the RBI. In December 1955, RBI decided to investigate Mundhra's use of his sizeable bank borrowings. They learnt that nine banks had substantial exposure to Mundhra or his companies. These included the SBI, whose advances were fully secured against Jessop's and BIC's inventories. Three exchange banks and a commercial had lent Rs 3.3 crores to Mundhra, secured principally against the pledge of his companies' shares. RBI's inspection of the accounts of the exchange banks in March 1956 revealed many irregularities. It appeared that the managers in Calcutta, in two of these banks, had financed Mundhra's acquisition spree, far exceeding their sanctioning authority and had even concealed this from their head offices in London. The ploy used was to get Mundhra to temporarily regularize his overdrawing

---

66 Setalvad Motilal, C. *My Life: Law, and other things*. New Delhi: Law & Justice Publishing Co, 2022.

every month end for a couple of days, when the relevant reports for their head office would be prepared.

When Mundhra failed to fund his account in time, at the end of November 1955, the head office was advised that necessary cash and shares had been deposited by Mundhra at the manager's residence rather than the bank! The excuse provided was that Mundhra couldn't reach the bank offices before closing hours due to traffic congestion caused by the Calcutta visit of Nikolai Bulganin, the Soviet Union Premier and his ally, Nikita Khrushchev.

RBI also found the three exchange banks guilty of overvaluing Mundhra's shares, held as collateral, in lending to him. RBI's inspection reports led to the resignation of the Calcutta managers of these banks.

The RBI had kept the government abreast of developments. On February 17, 1956, RBI's Governor B Rama Rau wrote a letter to the Principal Finance Secretary, HM Patel. Rau pointed out that Mundhra had met him the previous month with various documents explaining how to secure funds to acquire a controlling interest in large firms. Mundhra had also informed Rau that he (Mundhra) had explained the position personally to the finance and commerce ministers. Rau annexed to his letter a note prepared by the deputy governor of the RBI, explaining the operations of Mundhra. The letter warned that Mundhra was building up an industrial empire of considerable magnitude but did not appear to possess the experience or the background for successfully managing it. He had also quoted a remark of Justice Tendulkar of the Bombay High Court "that a thoroughly dishonest attitude had been adopted by Mundhra." The deputy governor warned that the entire edifice built up by Mundhra was liable to collapse and that action should be taken to restrain the activities of Mundhra not only in the interests of the shareholders and the banks which were involved, but also to safeguard the soundness of the industrial structure of the country.[67] On March 08, 1956, the deputy governor wrote to Patel enclosing a preliminary report of RBI's inspection officer indicating the manipulations in the accounts of some of Mundhra's concerns.

It appears that the governor's February letter was shown to TTK as well on May 07, 1956, by Mr Mazumdar, Secretary of Company Law Administration.

Mundhra had earlier attempted to have an audience with the then finance minister, Deshmukh as well, on several occasions. Finally, when he managed to do so, Deshmukh asked him to leave within a couple of minutes. The Bose Board Report (discussed later) finds Deshmukh categorical against support for Mundhra. On April 23, 1956, Deshmukh had stated that "we should never go in for any investments in Mundhra concerns."

From 1956, RBI tightened the screws, conducting half-yearly reviews of banks lending to Mundhra and his concerns. These reviews showed that the exposure of the four banks to Mundhra had increased from Rs 3.3 crores at the start of 1956 to Rs 14.5 crores by the end of the year and to Rs 15.6 crores in May 1957.

In December 1956, RBI was alerted by the government that Mundhra was using finance from banks to corner shares of some Calcutta-based companies. Inquiries by the central bank revealed that six banks (including one exchange bank) had sanctioned advances to share-brokers against the shares of Mundhra's companies. Following this, RBI issued instructions to all banks in April 1957 to refrain from financing takeovers and speculation in shares. This stymied Mundhra's methods, and he was driven to a corner and became desperate to stay afloat.

There were economic and political contributions at play as well. By the start of the second Five-Year Plan in 1956 (also see Appendix

---

67 Ibid.

2), the private sector was feeling fairly stifled by the government's control. The Nehruvian model of socialism, the 'License Raaj,' the nationalization of the Imperial Bank under SBI in 1955 and that of the insurance industry, under the LIC in early 1956, added to their concern.

The government sought to exercise greater control over the financial sector too. To some degree, this was prompted by the history of bank failures that the previous decade had seen.[68] The apprehension that public funds (as in insurance) were being mishandled under private ownership was another reason. Under the amendment of the Banking Companies Act, December 1956, the RBI acquired powers to direct banks on matters of policy administration and was also empowered to appoint observers on the boards of directors of banks. This hampered the banks in their wayward lending practices, which had been milked by the likes of Mundhra.

The large-scale imports of capital machinery and goods to enable India's industrialization along with the insidious practice of 'gold plating' (also discussed in Appendix 2), had put an enormous pressure on India's foreign exchange reserves. The proposed benign lending rates offered by the DFI's subsidized by the government added to the fiscal deficit. This was already precarious in India's efforts to meet the second Five-Year Plan planned public sector investment outlay of Rs 4,800 crores. The harvest shortfalls during the plan period also added to the misery.

At the end of August 1956, TTK, till then the minister for commerce and industry, took over the reins as finance minister from CD Deshmukh, as the latter resigned.

---

[68] As against 566 commercial banks operating in 1951, only 89 survived by 1969, the rest went into liquidation or amalgamation during 1951–69 (Indian Financial Sector: Structure, Trends and Turns - Rakesh Mohan and Partha Ray, IMF Working Paper, January, 2017)

TTK found that the calculations in the 1955-56 budgets had gone awry and there was an urgent need to shore up government finances. As part of these measures, in November 1956, he raised the stamp duty on usance bills.[69] Since the lending rate under the Bill Market Scheme (BMS)[70] had been raised in the same month (from 3.25 per cent in March 1956) to 3.5 per cent, this took the effective lending rate beyond 4 per cent and defeated the very purpose of the BMS which was a window for banks to borrow from the RBI at concessional rates (below or around the bank rate, which was then 3.5 per cent).

RBI governor, Rama Rau put up RBI's board note on December 12, 1956. "The board requests the government to consult RBI in advance on all matters which significantly affect the monetary structure and policy." When TTK rejected Rau's protest, the case went up to the prime minister who put it up to the cabinet.

Nehru threw his weight behind TTK, and wrote to Rau that it would be "completely absurd" if the central bank had policies contrary to those of the government. Rather, RBI's monetary policy must be subservient to the government's industrial policy. Rau resigned before the end of the year, just short of the expiry of his second term in January 1957. He had served as the RBI governor for over seven years. The "Rama Rau affair," many believed, resulted

---

[69] A bill of exchange (bill) is a negotiable instrument used in a trade transaction, drawn by a seller on a debtor (buyer or a bank) with instructions to pay immediately or in the future (signifying that the seller is extending a credit period to the buyer, the period being called the usance).

[70] A scheme provided by the RBI where banks could take refinance against eligible trade bills financed by them. On the due date on receiving the payment from the buyer, banks would return the advances taken from the RBI.

in the RBI losing its autonomy at that time. It became another subordinate government office, headed by Rau's replacement, HVR Iyengar, under the diktat of the Ministry of Finance. Perhaps a stronger and autonomous central bank would have been able to put up a greater resistance to the LIC investment in Mundhra shares. Rau was first RBI governor to have resigned before the expiry of his term. In independent India, the only other instance was Dr Urjit Patel's resignation in 2018.

The final straw that broke the camel's back were TTK's tax proposals. On November 30, 1956, alarmed at the state of government's finances, TTK underlined the need for fresh taxes and resources for the government, even before the next budget presentation, wherein he introduced a tax on capital gains and provision for compulsory deposits.[71]

Then again, when he rose to make the budget speech for 1957-58 on May 15, 1957, he went ahead to introduce wealth and expenditure tax, without any reduction in the rates of income taxes, despite being dissuaded by his senior finance officials at a meeting before his speech. His Principal Secretary HM Patel, AK Roy, chairman of the central board of revenue, MV Rangachari, expenditure secretary, HVR Iyengar, governor of the RBI, PC Bhattacharya, chairman of the State Bank, and BK Nehru, secretary to the government of India in the department of economic affairs – all had warned him that these proposals would adversely affect investor confidence, collapse the stock market and the economy would begin to flounder.

---

[71] Compulsory Deposit Scheme to mobilize resources for economic development. The scheme required individuals above a certain income or some criteria such as land holdings etc., to deposit a certain portion of their income for a specified period of 5 years. The deposits earned interest, and after the maturity period, depositors could withdraw the principal along with the accrued interest, in installments.

Perhaps TTK was hopeful that the high activity of Indian business houses buying out tea, textile, and engineering industries, in the vacuum created by the repatriation of British interests would continue to keep the stock markets buoyant, notwithstanding their state of stasis since August 1956. Or then perhaps it was just TTK's rigidity in his beliefs.

While the government justified these onerous tax measures for the size and scope of the Second Five-Year Plan, there was opposition in the parliament itself and from the public. "The index number of industrial securities declined from 121.6 in 1955-56 to 117.4 in December 1956 and to 111.1 in March 1957. The Calcutta index, which was 113.5 in 1955-56, gradually declined to 100.2 in February 1957 and registered of sharp fall to a record low level of 90.1 by June 1957."[72]

It must however be noted that it were not just the budget proposals that had teetered the stock market in Calcutta. For a few months preceding, they remained in an extremely depressed state on account of the continuing losses reported by most jute companies, investment in whose shares was normally regarded the mainstay of the Calcutta market.

Though dismissed by some (and negated eventually by the findings of the Chagla Commission), it was also believed that the drag on the Calcutta market was also on account of Mundhra's shares. "Disturbing reports of his position and manipulations continued to circulate acting as a major depressing factor... It was widely known at that time that Mundhra was frantically trying to lighten his commitments by liquidating some of his holdings and or disposing some of the companies in the group."[73]

---

72 Patel, HM. *The First Flush of Freedom: Recollections and Reflections.* New Delhi: Rupa Publications India Pvt Ltd, 2010.

73 Writings of Parekh, HT. *India In Transition Through the Eyes of a*

However, it is also true that the Calcutta Stock Exchange had been heading downwards since August 1956 and that Mundhra's shares had been a drag on the market for close to two years. The timing and the panic to invest in Mundhra's shares in June 1957 was thus questionable. Hence, the "drag theory of Mundhra's shares" as one of the reasons ascribed for the LIC investment into Mundhra's companies failed to stand up to scrutiny.

Visionary, 1940-1990s: Volumes I & II: A Tribute by HDFC and ICICI. Mumbai: HDFC and ICICI, 1995.

THE LIC FIASCO

After the flounder of the stock markets, soon after his budget speech, TTK adopted a two-pronged approach to restore confidence and maintain the balance of the financial system.

The first was to support the stock markets by purchasing sound equities using LIC funds in the private sector. LIC came forward in the middle of May 1957 and purchased substantial shares of Tata Iron and Steel Co (TISCO), Indian Iron and Steel Co (IISCO) and Associated Cement Company (ACC). Incidentally, like the investment in the Mundhra's companies' scrips, these investments too were made at the behest of the government, without taking the prior approval of LIC's investment committee (see below). However, these were profit-making blue-chip companies, leaders in their field, and sound investments. Using this as a precedent to invest in Mundhra scrips was incorrect.

More fundamentally, the task of stabilizing markets was not incumbent upon LIC or a part of its charter. "Nowhere is it laid down that LIC should buy or sell shares to regulate prices or yields. Nor has LIC the resources of technical competence to undertake such a task... Equity prices by their very nature are subjected to wide variations and no corporation is expected to take up an impossible adventure."[74]

Around the same time, RBI began to fear that Mundhra's financial difficulties would prevent banks from realizing their

---

[74] Ibid.

debts without unloading his shares on the market. This might have triggered a crash in their prices, eroding the realizable value of the banks' securities. RBI examined the possibility of Mundhra's creditors forming a consortium to coordinate the recovery of their advances to him. The banks, however, refused to participate as their legal counsel warned that they could be liable to civil suits by Mundhra, should he suffer any loss or adversity because of their action.

By June 1957, Mundhra was in serious trouble. He had approached GD Birla for help in liquidating a part of his holdings, but Birla felt that with the tight conditions in the money market, no one would be prepared to buy the shares. Birla suggested that Mundhra should meet TTK and ask for his advice. By this time, the Punjab National Bank, which had been accommodating Mundhra, was pressing him to repay, and Birla felt that Mundhra risked losing control of Turner Morrison.[75]

The LIC Act, 1956 had provided for the setting up of an investment committee, as an advisory body, for prudent investment of the corporation's funds. It began functioning in September 1956, comprising seven members: four official and three non-official. The official members included the chairman, the managing director of the LIC and two government representatives, one representing the Ministry of Commerce and Industry and the other, the company law department. The three non-officials included the presidents of the BSE and the Calcutta Stock Exchange (CSE), and HT Parekh, then the deputy general manager of Industrial Credit & Investment Corporation of India, (now ICICI Bank).

The committee met fortnightly and decided on investments

---

75. Private Industry and the Second Five-Year Plan: The Mundhra Episode as Exemplar of Capitalist Myopia – Nasir Tyabji, Institute for Studies in Industrial Development, Working Paper 2010/04, May 2010.

based on (a) a proper examination of prospects of each industry and of each company, (b) comparative rates of return from different investments, (c) the extent of LIC's present investments in each company, to ensure that there was no concentration of risk or anything that could indicate partiality/preference, (d) the standard of management in the companies where public funds were being invested, and (e) the contribution which LIC might make to promote industrial development by doing that investment.

LIC's investments in the steel and cement companies mentioned above were ratified post facto at the next meeting of the investment committee. The committee didn't express an opinion in the way the purchases had bypassed the committee and thus accorded their tacit approval.

TTK's second measure was to allay the apprehensions of industrialists and other businessmen. Towards this, he held several meetings in Calcutta and Bombay along with his advisory team on economic affairs, comprising HVR Iyengar, PC Bhattacharya; and HM Patel.

A meeting was held on June 18, 1957, with the businessmen in Calcutta. While happy that LIC had stepped in to stabilize the market, some of them voiced their concern on the unstable stock markets on account of Mundhra's shares. TTK and his team were aware that not just banks, but brokers and individuals holding Mundhra shares by way of pledge were in difficulties. Mundhra could neither redeem the shares held, nor pay the margins. They appeared to have little option but to sell the shares and cut their losses.

After the meeting of June 18, SC Chaturvedi, president, CSE reportedly told Iyengar and Patel that the biggest single cause of the trouble in the market was that a large quantity of Mundhra shares was likely to be thrown on the market at distress prices. Though moot, hopefully Chaturvedi's concerns were made and received as those stemming from a worried President of the CSE rather than as a member of LIC's investment committee. However, there is evidence that Mundhra was a close friend of Chaturvedi, hence the story may have been fabricated and propounded by Mundhra himself to throw the scare of brokers' selling and to prompt LIC to invest.

TTK and his team decided to reconvene on June 22 in Bombay, to discuss the issue further. On June 21 morning, Bhattacharya asked Patel if he could give Mundhra an audience (Mundhra had travelled from Calcutta to Bombay for the meeting as had Patel and TTK). At that meeting, Mundhra spoke about his difficulties in a general way and made certain proposals. Patel asked him to send his proposals in writing, which Mundhra did on June 22, sending copies of his letters to Iyengar and Bhattacharya as well. Mundhra's proposal was that LIC should buy shares worth Rs 80 lakhs from him and pick up another Rs 30 to 40 lakhs from the market to stabilize it. Additionally, he wanted a loan of Rs 1 crore from LIC. He also suggested that LIC should buy fresh issues of preference shares of BIC and Jessops to the extent of Rs 1.25 crores, and offered as a sweetener, fire insurance business worth Rs 15 lakhs. Attached to Mundhra's letter was a list of his total liabilities amounting to about Rs 5.25 crores of which Rs 3.93 crores were owed to banks and the rest to brokers. His unencumbered assets amounted to Rs 1.55 crores. On the morning of June 22, at a meeting along with Iyengar and Bhattacharya, Patel showed Mundhra's letter to TTK. They agreed that of the various proposals, the purchase of shares was the only feasible way. TTK approved Patel's discussing the matter with the LIC.[76]

---

[76] Patel, HM. *The First Flush of Freedom: Recollections and Reflections*. New Delhi: Rupa Publications India Pvt Ltd, 2010. There is great debate

The same afternoon, Patel met LIC Chairman GR Kamat, along with Bhattacharya to discuss the proposal. On June 23, which happened to be a Sunday, Patel, Kamat, and Bhattacharya met Mundhra. At this meeting, Mundhra was invited to come up with definite proposals. Patel, Bhattacharya and Kamat agreed to purchase shares mainly of BIC, Jessop, and Richardson Cruddas for about Rs 1 crore.

Thereafter Patel and Bhattacharya met TTK along with state finance ministers. TTK was satisfied at LIC's willingness to purchase the shares but warned about the need for caution on account of news circulating about Mundhra's spurious scrips.

The following day, Mundhra's proposals were tabled in a meeting. In addition to the others at the Sunday meeting, LS Vaidyanathan, Managing Director LIC; RG Vaidya, General Manager Oriental Insurance, and Mundhra's representative ML Sodhani were present. Proposals such as the formation of a holding company alone on immovable property or the purchase of shares in the open market, etc., were rejected. Then came the decision of the amount necessary for the investment. Mundhra gave details about his most pressing liabilities. It emerged that it would be necessary for him to have about one and a quarter crore rupees, if the pressure on the Calcutta market was to be effectively reduced. The total number of shares of each individual company to be purchased was discussed next. Mundhra's request for purchase of shares at prices higher than the current (depressed) rates was denied; he was also asked to provide a written assurance that he would replace any scrip if found to be spurious or unsatisfactory.

On June 25, 1957, LIC wrote to Mundhra, communicating its willingness to buy from him an agreed list of shares of six of

---

whether express approval was given or not by TTK as he had denied the same. Discussed later.

his public companies at prices prevailing at close of trading the previous day, Monday June 24.

The deal finalized by LIC on June 25 was however, not the first investment by the corporation in shares of Mundhra's companies. In March-April 1957, LIC had bought 50,000 shares of Jessop without the advice of the investment committee, directly from Mundhra at prices higher than the market. Shares of two other companies had been purchased, with only one of the two deals being concluded through brokers. These investments occurred apparently at the behest of HM Patel who was then the chairman of the Corporation. This was surprising since the then finance minister, Deshmukh had clearly proscribed involvement in Mundhra companies.

In September 1957, LIC entered four more purchase transactions through a firm of brokers, which included shares of Jessop and Richardson & Cruddas. But the deal of June 25, 1957, was the biggest by far of any single investment the LIC had undertaken until then. It appears that LIC's total investment in Mundhra firms for all purchases was about Rs 156 lakhs.

While both the Chagla Commission and the Bose Board (discussed later) found that the statements of those involved were conflicting and that the entire truth hadn't been revealed, from the speed and sequence of events it becomes clear that LIC (at the government's initiation) was indeed bending over backward for Mundhra.

Interestingly, the Bose Board Report reveals that Mundhra and Sodhani were in touch with TTK directly as well.[77] They saw him on September 23, 1956. On April 27 and May 07, 1957, they met with him and Bhattacharya when a discussion about LIC also occurred. Mundhra met TTK on June 18 at Calcutta as well

77 Discussion on the Government Resolution on the Life Insurance Corporation Inquiry, Rajya Sabha Papers, September 11, 1959.

before his meeting on June 23 at the RBI. Sodhani appears to have met TTK on or about June 13 and sent a telegram to Mundhra in Bombay, "Life Insurance Corporation prepared to purchase Jessops and BIC Ordinaries at negotiated prices. Necessary instructions being issued from this end. Please phone."

There is a fair bit of intrigue about the meeting of Sodhani with TTK between June 12 and June 13. The Bose Board Report mentions that between June 06 to June 17, 1957, the gate registers at the North Block of the Central Secretariat in New Delhi were missing and hence there wasn't a record of Sodhani's visit and whether Patel too was present at the meeting. It was also alleged that at the June 18 meeting in Kolkata, TTK and Iyengar had met with Mundhra and Chaturvedi as well. There is reference to an entry in the diary of the governor (Iyengar) which too couldn't be found.

Feroze Gandhi's assertions in the parliament (see next chapter) make it clear that the deal sealed between LIC and Mundhra on June 25 were at inflated prices, (as brokers had rigged up prices leading up to June 24 when markets closed) to the detriment of the policy holders. This is entirely possible as we have seen that the LIC deal was being discussed for quite some time before June 25 and may have been leaked. LIC ended up paying over Rs 10 lakhs more for the purchases. However, from Mundhra's position, on the overall portfolio, he suffered a loss as discussed below.

On June 25, 1957, LIC invested a sum of Rs 124.44 lakhs in six public sector concerns of Mundhra – BIC, Jessop, Richardson, Angelo, Smith Stanistreet, and Osler.

At its meeting held on July 09, LIC's investment committee was informed of the purchases. As the deal was concluded without prior reference to the committee, they could only make a note of the transaction. The committee believed that the chairman and the managing director of LIC could not have entered this large single deal on their own responsibility and they presumed that it was done in consultation with and under instructions of the government.

While the investment committee only took note of purchases, its uneasiness on the deal is recorded in a note submitted by HT Parekh on August 20, 1957, which stated, "… It would have been preferable had the investment committee been consulted in advance particularly when Rs 50 lakh of the investment would yield practically no return… the case also had the effect of indirectly supporting wanton acts of persons who might have taken over control of companies without having the resources by means of financial manipulations without intent to run industrial concerns in a serious fashion… it lays down a precedent not capable of serving the best interests of policyholders unless suitable safeguards are taken."

So here was an autonomous body dealing with public funds, clearly without the interests of the policyholders in mind, as 40 per cent of the investments were unproductive, and in enterprises of someone whose antecedents made for dismal reading. Even stranger when TTK had earlier clearly stated as one of the investment objectives of LIC being a minimal return of 5 per cent on investments, unless the same had been made in government securities.

Delving deeper, it became clear that the objective of the transaction was to release the pressure of brokers and bankers from whom Mundhra had to receive delivery of shares purchased or to whom he had to pay for the losses they had incurred. The transaction could not have saved Mundhra permanently, but only provided a temporary respite because it did not provide him with adequate funds to square the losses in his portfolio. For instance, one major LIC purchase, BIC, was at Rs 6 per share, whereas the shares had been purchased by Mundhra at about Rs 11 apiece, which meant that he had incurred a loss in this transaction.

Of the total amount of Rs 124.44 lakhs invested in shares of the six companies, preference shares of four companies accounted for about Rs 30 lakhs, the balance being invested in ordinary shares of all six. Richardson's 5.5 per cent tax-free preference shares bought at Rs 80 each yielded a net return of 6.875 per cent (5.5/80) and comprised the lion's share of the preference investments. Jessop's 5 per cent tax-free preference shares at the prices bought yielded a lower return of 5.556 per cent. Both these companies were good and profitable. Smith Stanistreet yielded 6.14 per cent tax-free. The smallest preference investment of Rs 4.5 lakhs was in Osler. The yield on the face value of Rs 100, on paper here was 4.5 per cent tax-free; and at Rs 75 per share paid by LIC, promised a 6 per cent yield. The only problem was the workings about the company were not known and it had no dividend record.

For equity (ordinary) shares, BIC won the largest amount of LIC's purse. Shares with a face value of Rs 5 had a poor dividend record of late and yielded only 1.67 per cent at the purchase price of Rs 6 per share. Shares were purchased at the lowest market price in the previous ten years. Despite the low yield, this investment could perhaps be excused on account of BIC's intrinsic value, its diversified business and assets and future potential, if the management (by Mundhra and his men) could be changed.

The second largest investments were in Richardson's and Jessop's shares. Both these companies were reputed and important engineering concerns with large order book positions, and their last dividend payouts had been attractive. However, future yields couldn't be extrapolated on these numbers on account of their increase in capital and the fact that recent financials of Richardson had not been published. In the hands of good management, these companies could do well. Both Angelo and Smith Stanistreet showed a high yield, a regular dividend record, and a satisfactory financial position. The investment in Osler ordinary shares was unsatisfactory, as there had been no dividend for a long time, and little was known of its financial position.

In addition to the poor return on the overall investment, unlike the blue-chip investments of TISCO, IISCO, and ACC, Mundhra's scripts were not active and the poor confidence and trust in Mundhra's managerial ability had already been factored in their subdued prices. In addition, these were private transactions and not market interventions by LIC. Hence, it was highly unlikely that LIC's support would galvanize the market, the primary excuse for the investment! In short, these were akin to short-term accommodation finance for Mundhra, providing him transient relief.

Thus, the entire rationale of these investments became suspect and theories of the investment being quid pro quo for Mundhra's donation to the Congress of Rs 2.5 lakhs or for his agreement to defer the closing of the Cawnpore Cotton Mills gained currency. What is however certain was his reach and access to those holding high public offices, despite his poor reputation. The Mundhra episode is perhaps one among the very few, where the disrepute of the embroiled person preceded the event rather than be born because of it.

The temporary breather for Mundhra's misadventures soon ran out of steam and his misdeeds grew as Mundhra struggled to stay afloat. By about September-October 1957, rumours swirled that the shares in circulation exceeded Richardson and Cruddas's share capital, indicating the presence of duplicate/forged share certificates in the market. These were confirmed when two banks reported to the RBI that they were holding duplicate shares of BIC and Richardson. In a blatant lapse of due diligence, one of these banks held two sets of shares pledged by Mundhra with the same serial numbers, with two of its branches, and both sets were forged!

RBI then conducted a study on the Mundhra shares pledged to various banks and discovered that between Mundhra and three of his concerns, shares totalling 3.5 per cent to 92 per cent of the capital had been put up as collateral with banks. In five cases, the shares pledged exceeded half of the respective firm's paid-up capital, and in three cases, 75 per cent. Investigations also revealed large-scale duplication, triplication, and in one case, even quadruplication of his companies' shares. Notwithstanding, as seen earlier, even in September 1957, LIC had invested in four of Mundhra's concerns, albeit through brokers.

Alarmed at the volume of fictitious shares in circulation and the possible systemic risk they posed to the financial system, Iyengar wrote to the finance minister in November 1957, "the business of Haridas Mundhra is getting worse and worse." Inter alia, Iyengar advised that though both SBI and LIC were taking steps to ensure the security of their advances and investments in Mundhra's various firms, it was time "to stop Mundhra in his share certificate forging orgy."[78] Meanwhile, the Punjab National Bank offered for sale, a large block of shares pledged by Mundhra as he had been unable to pay his dues and his cheques had bounced. It was uncertain though how many of these shares were forged.

RBI initiated steps for legal proceedings against Mundhra. It was decided that the SBI and LIC should move courts under the Companies Act to change the management of Richardson and BIC. At Iyengar's instance, and in public interest, an investigation of all Mundhra concerns was ordered. Prodded by the RBI, one of the

---

[78] Private Industry and the Second Five-Year Plan: The Mundhra Episode as Exemplar of Capitalist Myopia – Nasir Tyabji, Institute for Studies in Industrial Development, Working Paper 2010/04, May 2010

banks holding bogus shares also agreed to lodge a complaint with the Delhi Police.

Mention must be made of the intrepid A Raman, research officer at RBI's Calcutta office who was the whistle blower, writing continuously to his superiors in Bombay about Mundhra's activities. Much of RBI's and government's intelligence on Mundhra was due to his dogged efforts.

His reports were quoted extensively in the report of the Chagla Commission, and detailed Mundhra's modus operandi, share price rigging, deployment of inflated bank loans, the drag his shares exercised on stock prices in Calcutta and even contained the rumours of LIC's intervention. His letters ominously had warned that Mundhra's troubles were chronic and that LIC's support would have a transient impact. The possible negative market impact of BIC's withholding dividend payments and Jessop's inability to provide audited financials were also highlighted in Raman's epistles.

As far back as September 1957, Raman's letter had urged for a governmental inquiry. This had been shared by RBI with the Finance Ministry. Reportedly, on the last of Raman's letters, TTK had noted with despondence that it did not 'make good reading'.

DL Mazumdar, secretary of the department of company law administration, too had written to Nehru in September 1957 when TTK was absent (he was travelling to the United States). He wrote a second note in December 1957. Mazumdar advised that LIC's share purchases didn't have any lasting results and the share prices of Mundhra's companies had continued to drop. He further counselled that there were two options that the government could choose from. The first was an investigation into the affairs of the Mundhra Group under provisions of the Companies Act; the second was action against the management of specific companies of the group for contravention of articles defining sound principles of corporate governance. Mazumdar wasn't in favour of a formal investigation process, which would be long-drawn-out and subject to judicial scrutiny and detrimental to investors and employees.

The feared scandal broke out soon, which burned not just Mundhra's industrial empire of cards, but also singed the reputation and careers of several in the public eye.

THE FIASCO BECOMES A SCANDAL...

On September 04, 1957, Dr Ram Subhag Singh, a Congress politician, and member of parliament, posed a question in the Lok Sabha to the finance minister referring to an insertion in *The Statesman* (Delhi edition) of August 03, 1957. Specifically, he sought a confirmation on the report, if indeed a sum of 1 crore rupees of LIC's funds had been invested in a private enterprise with its headquarters in Kanpur, the name of the enterprise and the reasons for such a deployment of public savings. Deputy Finance Minister Bali Ram Bhagat denied saying, "It is understood that the LIC has not invested, as stated in the report referred to, rupees 1 crore in any single private enterprise with headquarters in Kanpur." The answer was technically correct as LIC had invested more than rupees one crore across *several* Mundhra concerns, of which only one had its headquarters in Kanpur. The minister was intentionally vague in his response and was able to get away as it was an unstarred question, which is asked and answered only in writing without allowing supplementary questions.[79]

Armed with more information this time, a dogged Singh, on November 29, asked another question on the issue. In response to Singh's questions and the supplementary questions lobbied by Feroze Gandhi and others, Bali Ram Bhagat acknowledged that in

---

[79] LIC-Mundhra Scam: Independent India's First Mega Financial Scandal - Ashok K Singh, Peepul Tree, September 01, 2021.

June 1957, LIC had bought shares in firms that were connected to Haridas Mundhra. He said that LIC's decision was "dictated" by its investment committee, and that the "Government had no hand in the purchases." He added that LIC was guided by returns and safety and did not operate to favour an individual or business group. According to the Chagla Commission, the first to investigate the scam, Bhagat deliberately gave false information.

From an account of HC Heda (MP representing Nizamabad) on September 15, 1993,[80] who used to sit across Feroze Gandhi per the Lok Sabha seating arrangement, "When Ram Subhag Singh was asking his question, Feroze Gandhi saw that TTK's legs began to shake." They decided to take further interest in the matter at this show of anxiety and along with others asked questions.

According to Heda, Mundhra had visited him as well during the days of the turmoil in the parliament!

The deathblow was sounded by Feroze Gandhi (as he had done in the case of Dalmia) when he rose on December 16, 1957, to make his meticulously crafted and investigated report on the LIC investments.

Relevant extracts are as under:[81]

> Mr Speaker, sir, there is going to be some sharpshooting and hard-hitting in the House today, because when I hit, I hit hard and expect to be hit harder.
>
> ...There is nothing to be ashamed of if a public undertaking has made a mistake, if some people have made a mistake. We should confess it. Parliament must exercise vigilance and control over the biggest and most powerful financial institution it has created, the Life Insurance Corporation

---

[80] Falk, Bertil. *Feroze the forgotten Gandhi*. New Delhi: Roli Books, 2016.

[81] Ibid.

of India, whose misapplication of public funds we shall scrutinize today. Much as I have tried to, I have failed to understand how the Life Insurance Corporation became a willing party to this questionable transaction with the mystery man of India's business underworld.

.... It appears the Life Insurance Corporation has committed a breach of privilege of this House....

...On 29 November the finance minister stated in the House: 'The question is not one of favouring one particular individual or group but seeing that the corporation benefits and the policy holders, ultimately, benefit by the investment made.' I ask, was it in fulfilment of this policy that the corporation purchased by direct negotiation from an individual, Shri Mundhra, shares worth Rs 1,25,00,000 in his concern on 25 June 1957? In March, in April, in June, in July – July is the one, which the statement has left out – in August, in September, for six months in this year and on nineteen different occasions the corporation purchased shares of the Mundhra Group for a sum of Rs 1,56,00,000. If this is not favouring and financing one particular individual or group, then what else is it?

...the Life Insurance Corporation transacted business on a day when both the Calcutta and Bombay Stock Exchanges were closed.... To my own question: 'May I know whether it is a fact that a few months ago some shares were purchased at a higher price than the market price of those very shares on the particular day?' The finance minister gave an emphatic reply: 'I have been told that no such thing happened.' What does the statement reveal? According to the quotations on the Calcutta Stock Exchange given by the minister himself, on 24 June 1957 there is an overpayment of 77,000 rupees. According to the quotations on 25 June given by the hon'ble minister in the statement, there is an excess payment of about 3 lakh rupees.

...This is not an investment. This is a conspiracy to beguile the corporation of its funds. From the finance minister's statement, it would appear as if these investments were made through the open market. The truth is that this was a negotiated deal with Shri Mundhra himself.

...This was a device to help Shri Mundhra who happened to be in financial difficulties at that time, as I shall prove later. The sacred savings of the insured were misused for this purpose and, if I may say so, almost gambled away.

...Prevailing prices of these shares on the stock exchange must have been thoroughly scrutinized. Balance sheets must have been looked into. I am sorry, sir, I made a mistake. Some of these concerns have not published their balance sheets since 1955. I do not know what procedure the corporation adopted in the absence of balance sheets to arrive at a conclusion as to the value of the shares they were purchasing.

...The 25th was a Tuesday, 24th was a Monday, 22nd and 23rd were Saturday and Sunday when the stock exchange was closed. Let us see how much less the corporation would have paid had they concluded the transactions, say, on the 21st. The answer is, Rs 10,73,000... But let us move a little backward and see how much less they would have paid on the 20th. Again, according to the same source, the official report of the stock exchange it is Rs 9,42,000 less. On the 19th, Rs 11,52,000 less; on the 18th, Rs 13,47,000 less; on the 17th, that is Monday – Monday week Rs 13,62,000.

...The corporation could have purchased these very shares on the 10th for Rs 20,83,000 less than what was paid on the 25th of June. I have made no calculations of prices before the 10th. My nerves gave way.

...For purchases affected on the 25th, the prices were artificially created by crude market manipulations on the 24th, when, all of a sudden, all these shares reached their peak. On Monday, the peak was reached. On Tuesday, the purchases were made. What happened Tuesday? The peak had passed. The downward trend began and as on Friday, 13 December, the corporation's investment has depreciated by about Rs 37 lakhs against the total investment of Rs 1,24,44,000... (Feroze then proceeded to take the example of individual Mundhra companies and their share price movements to prove his point on how the market was manipulated).

...The corporation has an Investment Board. May I know why the chairman did not consult the Investment Board before the investment of 25 June was made? Rs 1,24,00,000 is not a small amount. I doubt very much if the chairman has got the sole right to go about investing these huge sums of money in any manner he likes on his own authority, without the consent of the Investment Committee.

...The point is this. Was the financial instability of these concerns known to the government and to the corporation? Was it known? Did they know that this money was going to be locked up in unstable financial concerns? It is here that I have an important clue contained in the report of the textile commissioner on the working of the British India Corporation and its subsidiaries and I shall read out the relevant portion from the report. I quote: The State Bank of

India has recently demanded the mills to mortgage the fixed assets of the British India Corporation also as a security for the hypothecation loan.[82]

...The State Bank of India and the Reserve Bank refused help in the month of March and in the month of March, the Life Insurance Corporation started investing money in these companies. 23rd March is very significant, because the financial condition of the Mundhra group was becoming worse and worse. The State Bank and the Reserve Bank refused help because of the unsoundness of the concern. But the Life Insurance Corporation was only too willing and rushed in. The textile commissioner's survey concluded on 10 June and the Life Insurance Corporation, a fortnight later, recklessly invested its funds in these very concerns.

...Mr Speaker, where are the scrips of these shares? Did the corporation receive the share scrips before payment was made on 25 June? That is a very important point. Or, did they make payment without having the share scrips in their possession? I would like to have that clarified. Have they even today in their possession all the shares? I would like that to be clarified too, and if they have, have they got the genuine scrips? There is nothing to laugh about – My information is that there are in the market originals, duplicates, and also forged scrips of these very shares. The House would like to know which variety the corporation has got. I hope I have established collusion between the Life Insurance Corporation of India and Shri Mundhra. I have, I hope, established a conspiracy in

---

82 Since the current assets were already hypothecated to the bank, additional security of the fixed assets meant that the bank wanted to enhance security.

> which public funds were wrongfully employed for financing the interests of an individual at the cost of the insured.
>
> ...I demand that the government institute an inquiry into this questionable transaction. There is already a precedent for such action. When charges less serious than this were levelled against the Industrial Finance Corporation, the then finance minister, Mr Deshmukh, appointed a committee and the chairman of the committee was a member of the opposition. Let us hope that our finance minister will follow the example of his predecessor.
>
> ...I would like the public to know, I would like the government to know, and I would like the members of Parliament to know that in the public sector, if such a thing happens, we are prepared to face an inquiry and get to the bottom of it. I hope that the finance minister will accept this suggestion of mine and appoint a committee in which this House shall be well-represented.

TTK replied immediately, saying that he knew little about the matter. This followed the line he and his team had taken in the previous session in answer to a question on the Mundhra purchases. The fact was that in the draft reply to that question proposed by Brahma Kaul, then joint secretary handling insurance, the full circumstances were stated and the justification for his action given in detail in the 'notes for pad'. TTK had crossed out the draft and replaced it with a denial of knowledge. There had been a furore and demand made for a judicial enquiry into the whole affair.[83]

Interestingly, this incriminating pad, which had gone missing, appears to have surfaced the very next day after Chagla had signed

---

83 Nehru, BK. *Nice Guys Finish Second: Memoirs*. Gurugram, Haryana: Penguin Random House, 2012.

and despatched his report. Chagla mentions, "Frank Moraes and Feroze Gandhi came to see me at Chief Justice House with news that they had discovered an important document which somehow could not be traced during the inquiry. As far as I remember, it was the pad, to use a parliamentary expression, which they said was given to the finance minister when he answered the original question in parliament with regard to this matter, and which, as I saw, contained information, which he did not then disclose. I told them that as far as I was concerned, I was functus officio. I had nothing more to do with the inquiry, or the report, or the results..."[84]

Nehru, a great supporter of TTK was greatly incensed by his son-in-law's temerity on the floor of the house and the humiliation that his favourite finance minister and the government had suffered on account of Feroze's onslaught. According to OP Mathai, private secretary to Nehru, "Nehru vehemently condemned him in (the) presence of Lal Bahadur and myself and said: 'This fellow Feroze is a bloody liar.'"[85]

Yet, the prime minister had little option but to proceed with an official inquiry, which proved soon enough that Nehru's "lying son-in-law" was in fact, right.

A one-man commission, which was appointed for the purpose with the Chief Justice of Bombay High Court, MC Chagla (Chagla), as chairperson, called upon Feroze as the first witness to appear.

---

84 Chagla, MC. *Roses In December: an autobiography*. Mumbai: Bharatiya Vidya Bhavan, 2019.

85 Falk, Bertil. *Feroze the forgotten Gandhi*. New Delhi: Roli Books, 2016.

THE FIRST INVESTIGATION – THE CHAGLA COMMISSION

Chagla and Motilal C Setalvad (Setalvad), the attorney general of India, were in Delhi towards the year-end in 1957, working together on the Law Commission. Chagla would stay with Setalvad whenever he visited Delhi.

At a dinner invitation by Home Minister, Pandit Govind Ballabh Pant, Chagla was requested by Pant to constitute a one-man tribunal to inquire into the affairs of the LIC, which had of late raised considerable controversy in the parliament. Pant mentioned that the prime minister had attached a great deal of importance to it. Chagla agreed. While they were in conversation, TTK walked into the dining room.

"I cannot say whether he was expected or not. When he sat down, Pant told him that he had just secured my acceptance of the proposal that I should constitute a one-man tribunal to inquire into the affairs of the LIC. I could see from TTK's expression that he did not welcome the idea at all – either he did not like the inquiry or did not like my being the person to conduct it."[86]

Chagla had two conditions. The first was that Setalvad should assist him in the inquiry. Setalvad and Chagla agreed that the former wasn't going to look after the interest of the government or any of its official, nor of any minister. Rather, since the government was as

[86] Chagla, MC. *Roses In December: an autobiography.* Mumbai: Bharatiya Vidya Bhavan, 2019.

much of an interested party in uncovering the truth, the attorney general would assist Chagla (the commissioner) in eliciting the same and in arriving at a proper decision. Chagla's second condition, and one sought after considerable thought and hesitation, was that the inquiry should be in public. Chagla explained in a statement that the public was entitled to know on what evidence any decision was based. Members of the public in possession of any relevant material would also be able to come forward at any time to throw more light on the facts disclosed by the evidence.

When the controversy on the appointment of the Commission arose, the joint secretary of the finance ministry shuttled back and forth, consulting Chagla and Setalvad on the one hand and the finance minister on the other in terms of reference of the Commission. Chagla was very keen that the question of the responsibility of the person or persons for this purchase of shares should be a subject matter for reference. The finance minister, though initially unwilling, finally relented.

The government notification appointing the Commission was issued on January 17, 1958, and the inquiry began on Monday, January 20, 1958, in a council hall in Bombay and continued till February 05. Chagla completed the proceedings, signed off, and submitted his report on February 10, 1958, the entire process completed in twenty-two days, a record of sorts. It was perhaps the first and the only time that any tribunal had completed its investigation and signed off on the report within a month of its being set up.

The public was extremely interested in the proceedings, and they thronged the room to capacity. Newspapers covered the inquiry at length, sometimes reporting every word of what a witness had said. Proceedings attracted the media, both at home and abroad.

One day the crowd became large and unruly, and the police

commissioner decided on his own volition to install a loudspeaker outside the office so that the people could hear all that was being said. Chagla, who was unaware of this development, summoned the police officer concerned, and sought the reason for installing the loudspeaker without permission. While the public had a right to know, Chagla didn't want that the proceedings in a court of inquiry to be treated as a theatrical performance. The police officer apologized, explaining the cause of his actions as the pressure of circumstances, and his perceived threat to public peace and order.

Surprisingly, soon after, Nehru, while addressing a public meeting in Chowpatty, commented on loudspeakers being installed during the LIC inquiry as though there was an intention to broadcast the proceedings. Chagla immediately wrote to Nehru, explaining the extenuating circumstances.

Nehru promptly replied, "I am glad that you wrote to me and cleared up the matter. I might mention that my remarks in Bombay were directed to the people."

However, the same day, whilst addressing a meeting at the Indian Merchants' Chamber, Nehru eulogised TTK. Chagla found this incorrect. "I cannot help remarking that it was hardly proper, when a judicial inquiry was being held involving the conduct of a Minister, for the Prime Minister to pay that very Minister a compliment in public."

On the first day, Chagla laid down the ambit and scope of the inquiry. This included determination if the share purchases were prudent, in accordance with the normal business principles, in consonance with LIC rules and to determine the person(s) ultimately responsible for the purchases. Chagla and Setalvad agreed that the former would examine the witnesses and the latter question (cross-examine) them and supplement the evidence in any manner thought proper. All those giving evidence would be taken under oath with attendant consequences for anyone giving false testimony.

Proposed witnesses included Feroze, Kamat, Vaidyanathan, TTK, Iyengar, Patel, Bhattacharya, Chaturvedi, KRP Shroff (Chairman, Bombay Stock Exchange), AD Shroff, M Hasham Premji (a renowned businessman), and HT Parekh.

There were some interesting developments behind the scenes.

Before the proceedings began, Kaul, the joint secretary in the Finance Ministry, and a director of LIC asked Setalvad whether a joint conference could be held with the counsel for LIC. Setalvad declined, opining that since the government was assisting the Commission, it should take an entirely independent attitude, rather than the LIC, which was under a cloud.

Setalvad was also approached by Munshi, seeking a meeting with Setalvad along with Patel and his attorney. Setalvad agreed if Patel was accompanied by his counsel and attorney. When they met at Setalvad's residence, Patel and his counsel made certain statements about the case. They advised that though these facts were known to the finance minister and other (high) officials, they were unlikely to disclose them in evidence. Setalvad advised that Patel seek his counsel and attorney's advice in the matter.

Another incident was the unannounced visit by Dr Baliga, a well-known surgeon of Bombay, to Setalvad's residence. He informed that Haridas Mundhra was waiting in the car below and wanted an audience with Setalvad. Setalvad refused to see Mundhra in the absence of the latter's lawyer. Baliga then related Mundhra's version of the affair, which appeared to Setalvad to be improbable, and one designed to implicate the finance minister. Setalvad told Baliga that Mundhra should give testimony under oath during his deposition before the commissioner (Chagla).

One morning, Setalvad read in the newspaper that Sachin Chaudhuri had met the home minister and the law minister in

Delhi and discussed matters regarding the pending inquiry. This was surprising as LIC was an independent statutory corporation, which had nothing to do with the government, except to the extent provided by Section 21 of the Act (which defined the government's role in guiding LIC in matters of policy involving public interest).

When Setalvad expressed his surprise at this development to Chaudhuri at the next sitting of the Commission, the latter was dismissive, and said that he was on his way to Calcutta via Delhi and had 'just happened' to see these ministers.

There was more. The finance minister was coming in for a fair bit of criticism during the inquiry and suddenly one day, Chaudhuri applied for permission to represent the finance minister at the hearing. Setalvad pointed out to the commissioner that Chaudhuri would be occupying two inconsistent positions, i.e. he could not represent both the LIC and a minister, both of whom were under investigation. Chaudhuri withdrew his application.

Chagla also turned down Sir Jamshedji Kanga's application to represent TTK at the inquiry and asked him, "Since when, Sir Jamshedji, are witnesses allowed to be represented by counsel at a hearing?"

From the evidence of the two key players, Patel and TTK, the following emerged from the evidence provided:[87]

Patel's stand was that he had given directions to LIC to enter the transactions hurriedly to avert the crisis on the CSE. Mundhra had made large purchases of shares in his own concerns and was unable to find funds to complete these purchases. Brokers were not ready to continue holding those shares for Mundhra, and unless this pressure or 'drag' in the market was relieved, a crisis was likely to overpower the CSE. Patel also forwarded this as a defence for

---

87 Setalvad Motilal, C. *My Life: Law, and other things.* New Delhi: Law & Justice Publishing Co, 2022.

the extreme urgency and speed with which events had transpired between June 18 and June 25 to precipitate the LIC investment. AD Shroff, while deposing before Chagla said, "If you allow me, sir, this is a cock-and-bull story. I would like to know who was interested in the Mundhra shares. The general public was not interested in that; of the 10 million shares held by Shri Mundhra, a majority were pledged to various banks while others were held by brokers. I can't see how these shares could be a drag on the market."

The "drag theory" was also negated by the evidence of Esplen, a prominent Calcutta broker, and KRP Shroff, in their evidence.

When Patel was asked why he had negotiated this transaction despite knowing Mundhra's dubious antecedents for over two years, and why had Mundhra approached him (when he had nothing to do with LIC) rather than Kamat, or why Patel had asked Mundhra to give him the proposal rather than to the LIC, Patel failed to provide cogent explanations.

Patel, however, mentioned that he had, at a meeting held at the RBI in Bombay on June 22, mentioned the transaction to the finance minister and that the minister had approved of it.

TTK later denied that he had given specific approval for the LIC investment, "So far as these transactions are concerned, I cannot specifically say on what day my principal secretary mentioned to me that there was some kind of offer made and there was some discussion. The companies mentioned to me were Jessop and Richardson and Cruddas. All I now recollect is that these are the companies into which there was some talk to look into the matter about which there were rumours."

When Chagla asked, "Do I take it you did not give any direction to Mr Patel with regard to those shares?"

TTK responded, "That would be correct."

Chagla persisted, "Do I take it that Patel was acting on his own responsibility and not under your orders or directions? What I want to know from you is whether he (Patel) was acting entirely on his own or whether he was acting under instructions or directions or advice from you as the head of the Finance Department?"

TTK replied, "That would not be correct. I think your Lordship, that the matter was mentioned to me. I cannot say when, but I did not go very much behind it. In fact, what happened subsequently at the RBI was that there was no order or desire that it should be done. I merely said that the matter may be looked into."

Chagla's attempt to get the truth continued, "There is bound to be some application of mind. What is puzzling me is this – that Mr Patel, who undoubtedly had full knowledge of the matter and was in possession of the whole record, should be in a great sense of urgency and put through the transaction in the manner it was done. He would not have done that, unless there was some driving force behind it?"

The finance minister, perhaps trying to protect himself, answered, "I did not supply that force."

Apart from TTK's evidence being vague and evasive, his demeanour as a witness was somewhat haughty and pontifical. Further, there was a rumour that after he had given evidence, the finance minister had seen Patel in the latter's residence and told him that he was sorry that he had let Patel down. Patel confirms this visit as well.[88]

The Commission found Patel's evidence to be much more definite when compared to TTK's vague statements. The commission also relied on the evidence of Iyengar and Bhattacharya as clearly corroborating what Patel had stated.

---

[88] Patel, HM. *The First Flush of Freedom: Recollections and Reflections*. New Delhi: Rupa Publications India Pvt Ltd, 2010.

There is further evidence of TTK's volte-face in the entire LIC drama. According to BK Nehru:

> "His own statement (for appearing before the Chagla Commission) had not been prepared and he asked me to draft it for him. This I did. It was a short statement stating the facts... TTK left the next morning for Bombay. Imagine my surprise when I read in the newspapers the morning after that the statement he had made was totally different from the one I had prepared. In effect, he denied all knowledge of what had happened, throwing the blame entirely on HM Patel...
> When TTK came back to Delhi, next morning, I barged into his room and asked him why on earth he said what he had. His answer was the most unsatisfactory. He said, 'I was advised that it would be best to say as little as I possibly could.'"

And what about the antagonist in the affairs, Haridas Mundhra?

According to Chagla, "I found him to be a colourful personality, extremely able and quick-witted, and prepared to dodge any inconvenient question, or give a plausible answer when dodging became difficult or impossible. His personal appeal was undoubted, and his capacity for evasion or sabotage so far as it related to the inquiry, infinite. Mundhra also stepped into the witness box, and gave his evidence in a nonchalant, cocksure manner, unaffected by the blaze of publicity that attended the inquiry, or the fact that he was the real cause of all the trouble. Far from being repentant, he seemed to enjoy the fact that he was instrumental in getting the attention of the whole country concentrated on what was happening in a small office and himself as the cynosure of all the eyes..."[89]

---

[89] Chagla, MC. *Roses In December: an autobiography*. Mumbai: Bharatiya Vidya Bhavan, 2019.

The Chagla Commission concluded the object of the LIC investment was to relieve Mundhra rather than satisfy any public interest and dismissed the "crisis in the market" theory. They found that Patel had abused his authority by causing Kamat to allow LIC to invest in Mundhra's shares and Kamat was negligent in dealing with the matter, particularly regarding the prices paid for the shares.

Kamat and Vaidyanathan were both "overborne" by Patel and failed to "exercise responsibility".

On the finance minister, the Commission said that "Clearly, there is acquiescence on the part of the Minister in the part played by Mr Patel… the lack of repudiation on the part of the Minister would go to support Mr Patel's story that the Minister had approved the transaction in Bombay on the 24th of June… It is clear that constitutionally, the Minister is responsible for the action taken by the Secretary with regard to the transaction."

Iyengar came under a cloud as well. Mundhra's letter to him on June 22 enclosing Mundhra's letter to Patel of June 21 had mentioned, "I shall request you to go through the same (the letter of June 21) and I would like to discuss with you further." This proved that there had already been an earlier discussion between Mundhra and Iyengar about the transaction. There was also a telltale note dated June 25, 1957, of Iyengar on this letter, which stated, "LIC is looking into this in consultation with the principal secretary." Setalvad observed, "The inference is irresistible that both these officers (Bhattacharya and Iyengar) were really in close touch with the transaction which was later on affected; but now that the things are taking a different shape, they don't want to come near it."

Indicting Mundhra, the Commission noted, "A man who has a flamboyant personality and is a financial adventurer whose only ambition is to build up an industrial empire by dubious methods. He is not very particular about the means employed so long as the end is achieved... He is not an industrialist in the real sense of the term. His interest does not lie in developing or enlarging the industrial output of the country. But his interest lies in being a financial wizard who can swallow up concern after concern..."

IN THE WAKE OF THE CHAGLA COMMISSION, AND TWO MORE...

Chagla concluded his report with the note that the inquiry would serve no purpose whatever if no general lessons could be derived from it, and added, "...the following principles seemed to be established as a result of a careful consideration of all the material that has been placed before me."

Six of the relevant seven lessons were:

1. Government should not interfere with the working of autonomous statutory corporations. Should they interfere, they should not shirk the responsibility of giving the directions in writing.
2. The chairman of the Corporation should be appointed from persons who have business and financial experience and who are familiar with the workings of the various stock exchanges.
3. If executive officers of the Corporation are to be appointed from the Civil Service, it should be impressed upon them that their duty and loyalty is for the Corporation. They should not be influenced by senior officials of the government or surrender their judgment to them. If they feel bound by the officials' orders, then they must insist on such orders being given in writing.

4. The funds of the LIC can only be used for the benefit of the policyholders and not for any extraneous purpose. Any such use for any extraneous purpose should only be in the larger interests of the country.
5. In a parliamentary form of government, the parliament should be taken into confidence by the minister at every stage, and all the relevant material must be placed before it. This would avoid difficulty and embarrassment at a later stage if and when the parliament were to get the necessary information from other sources.
6. A minister must take full responsibility for the acts of his subordinates. He cannot be permitted to say that his subordinates did not reflect his policy or acted contrary to his wishes or directions.

TTK, anticipating Chagla Commissions' verdict, submitted his resignation on February 05, 1958. Nehru received Chagla's report of February 10, and by his letter dated February 12, accepted the finance minister's resignation. Reportedly, Nehru's acceptance of TTK's resignation was at the behest of Maulana Azad who told Nehru that it would cause a national scandal if after the disclosures in the Commission's report; he continued to retain TTK in the cabinet.

While eulogizing TTK for his services, Nehru wrote to TTK, "So far as you are concerned, I am myself convinced that your part in this matter was of the smallest and that you did not even know much of what was done." Further, Nehru was critical of the Chagla Commission and noted that, "...this manner of approach to a complicated problem was hardly satisfactory.... It was neither judicial nor capable otherwise of eliciting all the facts.... In effect, there was rather a one-sided presentation of facts... I have still a feeling that all the relevant facts connected with this unhappy matter have not been brought out…"[90]

TTK suffered the ignominy of being the first minister in free India to have resigned due to his involvement in a scam. The prime minister reportedly went to the airport in person to bid him farewell, a gesture that was unique in the annals of India's parliamentarian history. TTK was provided with an Indian Air Force aircraft as well to travel, another first.

The Chagla Commission report was discussed in the Lok Sabha on February 19, 1958, and in the Rajya Sabha on February 21.

In the parliamentary debate on the report, some members pointed accusing fingers at Iyengar (and Bhattacharyya), while one member even charged Nehru with protecting Iyengar because he had earlier been Nehru's principal private secretary. Rejecting the allegation and defending Iyengar, Nehru pointed out that there was "nothing involving him at all" in the Commission's recommendations.

On February 20, 1958, after a cabinet meeting, the government passed a resolution recording the government's acceptance of the Chagla Commission's findings that the transaction resulting in the purchase of Mundhra shares was not entered into in accordance with business principles and was also improper on several grounds. The government was however undecided about adoption of the seven principles propounded, proposing, "to examine them carefully."

On the matter of personal culpability, the government decided to initiate "appropriate proceedings" against the officers responsible. Nehru said that they would be given an opportunity to defend themselves.

---

90 Setalvad Motilal, C. *My Life: Law, and other things*. New Delhi: Law & Justice Publishing Co, 2022.

The Chagla Commission's report thus was not the last word. In May 1958, the government appointed a three-member Board of Inquiry headed by Justice Vivian Bose, former Supreme Court judge (Bose Board) and included Sukumar Sen and WRS Sathianadhan to investigate the charges against Patel and Kamat under the 'All-India Service (Discipline and Appeal) rules 1955'. Since LIC also wanted an inquiry into Vaidyanathan, the inquiries against the three persons were consolidated into one. The Bose Board proceeded with the evidence provided before the Chagla Commission and twenty-five witnesses were also examined in camera. The evidence before the Bose Board was not on oath, nor were they made public. But from its report as well as the one submitted by Chagla earlier and the UPSC later, it was clear that all the obscurity surrounding the transactions in June 1957 had not been dispelled and that there was considerable variation in the appreciation of evidence by the three bodies.

In its report submitted in September 1958, the Bose Board upheld the findings of the Chagla Commission stating that the allegation against all three had been proved. It recommended Patel's removal from service and compulsorily retiring Kamat.

The Bose Board, after a long inquiry, found Patel guilty of the following two charges:

1. That in June 1957, Patel abused his authority by causing Kamat and Vaidyanadhan to enter a transaction, which was improper and resulted in investments, which the Corporation should not have made.
2. That in causing the above transaction, Patel was negligent to the extent that he failed to give a clear indication as to the prices to be paid for the various shares, thereby causing loss to the Corporation.

The Bose Board also found that TTK had given only vague approval of any deal with Mundhra along "with a cautionary rider that Patel's action was not covered by ministerial approval or authority."

Additionally, they also stated that not only was there no imminent danger in the Calcutta market in June 1957, and the "drag theory" propounded by Patel was an afterthought, and the transaction was entered into to help Mundhra. They also ascribed the motive for the investment of a crore and quarter of public money in the Mundhra concerns to be a quid pro quo for the donation of Rs 2.5 lakhs to the Congress party and perhaps for the loss being incurred by Mundhra by recalling certain closure notices relating to the Cawnpore mills. The Board never provided any clear and cogent evidence for this last conclusion/observation, though.

Not being accused persons, neither Iyengar nor Bhattacharyya appeared before the Board.

In addition to the quid pro quo angle, the Bose Board was also scathing in their observations how some of the highest officials of the land had behaved, when called forth to justify their behaviour under public scrutiny.

Incensed with the allegation of the "quid pro quo", Nehru made rather derogatory remarks about Justice Vivian Bose, questioning his intelligence. Later, Nehru had to express his regret in public after the Calcutta Bar Association passed a resolution condemning his actions.

As enjoined in the Constitution, in March 1959, the government then sought the Union Public Service Commission's (UPSC) advice on the show cause notices and the penalty proposed against Patel and Kamat by the Bose Board. The UPSC re-evaluated the evidence before the Bose Board in the light of the replies of Patel and Kamat, and in a surprising turn, advised the government (though one of their member J Sivashanmugham Pillai, dissented) that Patel should be exonerated of the charges and Kamat should only be censured.

The UPSC held that the charges that Patel had abused his authority were baseless, for he could not have "caused" Kamat and Vaidyanadhan to enter the transaction nor was the transaction improper as far as Patel was concerned. The UPSC also held that the second charge against Patel was also not proven. Regarding Kamat, the Commission held that the charge of impropriety and the unbusinesslike nature of the transaction was established only in the manner of price fixing and the resulting loss to the Corporation. It also held the other allegation against Kamat of failure to discharge his duties as chairman of the Corporation proved, since due care and caution were not exercised by him in fixing the prices.

The UPSC held Kamat responsible for entering the transaction, and *unanimously* recommended that he should only be censored. Further the UPSC held that "No ground for the inferences that either Shri Mundhra's donations amounting to Rs 2 ½ lakhs, or his agreement to defer the closure of the Kanpur Cotton Mills placed the Government under any obligation, express or implied, to enter into a transaction with him of the order of over a crore of rupees."

The government accepted the UPSC's recommendations on May 27, 1959 and dropped charges against Patel.

While Patel and Kamat both resigned and the latter retired into obscurity, Patel returned in 1977 as the finance minister under India's first non-Congress government (Janata Party) led by Prime Minister Morarji Desai.

After the 1962 elections, Nehru offered a re-elected TTK any cabinet post of his choice except finance (held by Morarji Desai after a brief interval following TTK's resignation in 1958). Strangely, TTK's appointment became possible on account of a confidential inquiry conducted by Intelligence Bureau chief BN Mallik, which gave him a clean chit. TTK wrote a bitter letter to Nehru, preferring to remain a minister without portfolio.

In this scathing letter, TTK claimed that it was Morarji Desai, who had played a major role in ensuring a situation in which his resignation in 1958 had become inevitable.[91]

"*... You will appreciate also that I cannot serve in any ministry charged with some economic mission with the present FM as economic director. There are two angles to it - one personal and the other a matter of principle. Mr Morarji Desai had a fair share in the launching of the campaign against me when I was Finance Minister. I know more of it after I left. His minions in the Lok Sabha & outside did the dirty work. You knew that he brought Moulana [Abul Kalam Azad] into it at one stage. He suborned the loyalty of officials whom I had trusted & even specially favoured by offers of preferment and made them give false testimony before the [first Vivian] Bose Commission. His agent, a journalist at the time, lobbied with the UPSC and got rewarded as news editor in All India Radio...*"

TTK then became the Minister for Economic and Defence Cooperation and finally the finance minister again in 1964.

A WRAP ON THE MUNDHRA AFFAIR

In the final analysis, it was indeed unfortunate that the sensationalism of the transaction put the media and public glare more on the individuals involved rather than the lessons learnt. Especially so, when it was well established that there was no evidence of graft or personal corruption of the individuals in government or institutions

---

[91] Handwritten letter, 24 March 1962, TTK Papers, correspondence with Jawaharlal Nehru, 1962, Pp. 11–14. Ref: 'Private industry and the Second Five-year plan: The Mundhra Episode as Exemplar of Capitalist Myopia'- Nasir Tyabji, Institute for Studies in Industrial Development, May 2010.

involved. And yet, in political graciousness, the men accepted their responsibility and resigned from public office/institution.

The seven recommendations by the Chagla Commission were never adopted formally. Sadly, those and the lessons that should have been learnt, elude us to this very day, regardless of the many scams and scandals in the interim.

First, the importance of allowing unfettered autonomy to public corporations free of governmental obstruction or direction and ministerial responsibility towards the same. We have seen governmental interference in the functioning of and policy matters of public bodies like the RBI, SEBI, and the LIC time and again.

Second, the dangers of the concentration of industrial power and wealth in a few hands and their resultant abuse. There have been examples abound in this practice as has been the unholy nexus between industry and politics and their symbiotic relationship, in the manner they feed off one another. The reach which Mundhra had in the highest echelons of power persists among many in the industry to this day.

Yet there are some positive lessons that the Mundhra episode brings out and perhaps will never ever be emulated.

First the importance of the government's conscience keeper; someone from their own rank and file, as was the role played by Feroze Gandhi. Without his initiative, it is unlikely that the justice meted, no matter how ephemeral or inadequate in measure, as witnessed in the Mundhra (or Dalmia) episodes, would have seen the light of day. Especially in a democracy with an effete opposition, a moral compass within the ruling party becomes indispensable. A voice that isn't stifled but welcomed and heard.

Second, the expeditious and fearless functioning of the judiciary, unfettered by executive interference. True, Nehru had some obtuse comments for the Chagla Commission and the Bose Board, but they were largely allowed a free hand in the investigations, including conditionality of the former to have evidence administered in public. One could of course argue that this came to naught with the UPSC overturning the findings of two eminent jurists and thus ensuring that the dispensation in some form or manner will find a way and continue to "protect" their ministers. Yet in Mundhra's case, due process was followed; the Bose Board was appointed under the 'All-India Service (Discipline and Appeal) rules 1955' as was the UPSC's appointment constitutionally valid. Whether the UPSC outcome was doctored or influenced is a moot point. We seldom would see a minister resign even before the conclusion of the due process as TTK did.

The conduct of the Chagla Commission and the Bose Board in a day and age unaided by the speed of technology was exemplary and would perhaps make the lawmakers and law keepers of today, red-faced.

An increasing ill is the blur between the independent functioning of the judiciary and the executive. India has witnessed increasing political involvement and interference in the fields of education, religion and even in the judiciary (for example, wanting a say in judicial appointments). In the same manner, the judiciary appears to be having an increasing overreach in deliberating issues on policy, religion and in matters clearly under the remit of the executive, with wide-ranging impact.

APPENDIX 1: MANAGING AGENCIES IN INDIA

Joint stock companies[92] in India owe their genesis to the British East India Company (the Company). By a royal charter, the Company was granted monopoly to trade in the Indian subcontinent and operated as a joint stock company on her shores. Its success and expansion prompted the British to regulate and facilitate the formation of joint stock companies in India in the mid-nineteenth century. These companies, predominantly owned and managed by British investors, were involved in various industries such as tea, jute, cotton, banking, railways, and mining. Over time, prominent Indian business families, such as the Tatas, Birlas, Dalmia-Jain groups and others established their own joint stock companies as entrepreneurs and investors.

The managing agency system, a peculiar form of corporate governance, evolved in the early nineteenth century, another British legacy. A "Managing Agent" or "Management Agency" was a person or a business enterprise (typically a partnership firm or a company) in charge of the management, in part or full of a joint stock company. The managing agent would derive his authority and power, either from an agreement with the "managed" (or target) company or by an enabling clause in its memorandum or articles

---

[92] A Joint-stock company is an incorporated association of two or more persons having a separate legal entity that is separate from its member. Its capital is divided into shares and is freely transferable (except in a private company). The shareholders are the owners of the company while the Board of directors who are elected by the shareholders manage the company.

of association.[93] Despite often holding limited shares in the target company, the managing agent would wield considerable control over the board of directors of the managed company. They would enjoy representation on the (target) company board and be able to solicit proxies from other shareholders.[94] Unlike a manager employed by the target company who would be directly supervised by the board, here the board was controlled by an external manager, the managing agent.

In addition to executing their managerial responsibilities, managing agents wore many hats. They would promote, finance, underwrite, and organize the joint stock company. Thus, the partners of the managing agency were able to control with minimum capital and risk, a vast number of large independent joint stock operating companies and enjoyed both autonomy and access to risk capital.[95]

---

93 The Memorandum of Association (MOA) sets out the company's constitution and purpose. The Articles of Association (AOA) comprises byelaws that govern the company's internal affairs, management, and conduct. Both MOA and AOA, are two fundamental charter documents of a company that require registration, with the appropriate authority, when the company goes for incorporation.

94 Soliciting proxies from shareholders is a process that allows shareholders to exercise their voting rights without being physically present at the shareholders' meeting. A proxy is a power of attorney allowing the company's management (or another designee) to vote the shares owned by a shareholder as directed by the shareholder or at the designee's discretion.

95 Risk capital typically refers to funds allocated to speculative activity and/or used for high-risk, high-reward investments. Any money or assets that are exposed to a possible loss in value is considered risk capital. Used here in the context that often the target company could be one not currently profitable but with a promise to be so. This allowed the managing agent to acquire the target company at low valuations.

The joint stock companies thus became the operating units of the central decision-making unit, the managing agency.

The managing agents could leverage investments in profitable or potentially profitable ventures with minimum investment of managerial resources. To acquire a new business, say jute, or textile, it would raise capital from friends or the partner or promoter of the managing agency and leverage the rest through bank borrowings. Thereafter, once the target company's fortunes had improved, the agent would offload majority of their shareholding, at a profit. The profits would be channelized to a new business opportunity (say a sugar mill) or to another profitable venture as decided by the managing agent. The managing agents, however, would continue to wield influence and managerial control over the earlier business, despite their status as minority shareholders, based on the long-term management agency contract. This process could be repeated many times based on the reputation and successful track record of the managing agent as well as his ability to raise the necessary funds.

The managing agent would decide for the operating enterprise, its products, markets, raw material sources, etc. In addition to to the funds raised from external sources, the agent also had access to the capital reserves of its managed companies. These were employed to finance new ventures or even subsidize dividends of its less successful ones so that the managing agent could extract his pound of flesh regardless of the performance or fortunes of the acquired companies. The risk-return equation clearly favoured the partners of the managing agency, as their agreement with the managed companies offered attractive commissions either as a percentage of sales or profits. Additionally, they earned other fees as well. In some sense and manner, the managing agents of yore functioned as the modern-day venture capitalist.[96]

The managing agent would leverage his entrepreneurial reputation to ensure significant control and disproportionate cash flow benefits, notwithstanding their relatively small ownership. Even when in 1913 the Companies Act was introduced which gave significant powers to the elected corporate boards and which resulted in an overlap with the extant powers and roles of the managing agents, the latter were able to wrest the initiative by inviting family and friends to take up directorial positions.

History has overwhelmingly berated the managing agency system for its high commissions, conflicts of interest leading to weak corporate governance, and its flawed structure where ownership and control were separated with the owners' (shareholders) interest subservient to that of the controlling managing agent. Incidences of the misdemeanours of the Dalmia-Jain group and Mundhra essayed in this book will support this argument on how the managing agency system was exploited to benefit a few at the cost of the shareholder. In fact, the twin episodes of both Mundhra and Dalmia-Jain contributed to accelerating the demise of the managing agency system in India. While Mundhra could be excused as his motive was speculative profits in the stock market, rather than managing the acquired companies, the involvement of one of the largest industrial houses (Dalmia-Jain) in a series of tax evasions and dubious inter-corporate transactions was unacceptable to the Indian government. Their practice of emaciating public companies of their reserves to the owners' private entities/managing agencies was inexcusable.

There, however, were positive examples too. Managing agents

---

[96] Venture Capital (VC) is a form of private equity and a type of financing that investors provide to startup companies and small businesses that are believed to have long-term growth potential.

did use their entrepreneurial expertise to act in the best interests of the managed companies. At a time when there was little possibility of public participation in share issues, industrial enterprises were floated with the business acumen of the managing agencies (whose track record and reputation were able to attract public participation), who nurtured these firms until their viability and profitability had been demonstrated. The managing agency system played a pivotal role in driving industrial growth in India, particularly in sectors like textiles, jute, tea, banking, cement, and more.

When the British took over the reins of the Indian colony from the East India Company after 1860, famous managing agencies took shape – such as Mackinnon, Mackenzie, Andrew Yule, Shaw Wallace, Martin Burn, and others.

With Indian entrepreneurs following suit, many like the Tatas, Birlas, and the Dalmias adopted the model of the management agency system. The low-risk managing agency structure was their avenue to either buy existing weak industrial enterprises or start new ones. The downside, however, was that they short-changed the learning curve of technological research and innovation, which had been the bedrock for the industrial revolution in the West. Using their financial muscle, they preferred to buy technology rather than create.

After the WWI, Indian entrepreneurs already had a formidable presence in the cotton textile industry. Now, through their managing agents, they forayed into the manufacture of jute, sugar, iron and steel, cement, chemicals, and engineering. British managing agents were caught napping. Indian businessmen acquired significant shareholdings in companies managed by British managing agents and began to assert themselves between the period 1936-70.

However, despite India's independence, British-controlled managing agents remained active till the '60s.

The managing agents, whether British or Indian, suffered from some common shortcomings. First, they held on to the control and failed to provide the managed companies the independence to think and grow on their own. Second, they denied their managed companies, the opportunities to develop and hone professional managers of their own.

The problems with the managing agency system increased with the upheavals caused by the Great Depression and events leading up to the WWII. With increase in competition and decline in profitability, dividends to shareholders dwindled. Managing agents, however, continued to protect their commissions and earnings, which often, were linked to sales and production figures, rather than profits. Shareholders grew restive and murmurs of abuse by the managing agents began to gather steam. The fundamental question of control versus ownership was raised and why companies couldn't replace managing agents with professional managers. Oversight and accountability would both improve.

Understandably, the British were not keen on rescinding the system, as this would adversely affect British interests in India. Only closer to independence, when the Indian influence on the legislative process gathered steam, were changes initiated. Bowing to the shareholders' protests, after almost a century of inaction, changes were affected via the Indian Companies (Amendment) Act 1936, which sought to clip the wings of the managing agents. Shareholders were empowered to remove managing agents guilty of offences, limit their compensation, curb their ability for inter-company fund transfers, and call for greater transparency in financial transactions between the company and its agent.

Additionally, managing agency contracts were limited to a maximum of twenty years, loans to managing agents by the company was forbidden as were the transactions of shares and debentures between two companies with a common management agent. Agency commissions were capped at a fixed percentage of annual net profits and contracts were prohibited between a company and its managing agency involving sales, purchases, supplies of goods and materials, unless approved by eighty per cent of the directors of the company.

Post 1947, the independent government of free India refused to annul the system, though further curbs were put in place. Indian businessmen tried to protect their turf and pushed for legislative bills designed to limit the sphere of operations of British managing agents on the grounds that they excluded Indian capital, management, and employees. Their proximity to and influence upon the ruling dispensation of the Congress, helped them and British managing agents began selling their interests to Indians.

The voices against abuse of the entire managing agency system grew louder with the shareholders coming together. "In 1949 the Bombay shareholders association in a memorandum listed questionable practices by managing agencies owned by Birla Brothers, Dalmia Jain, Karamchand Thapar, Jaipuria, Walchand, Surajmall Nagarmall, Sarupchand Hukumchand, Kamanis, and Bajorias among the more prominent business groups."[97] Additionally, changes were brewing in independent India's industrial policies with public sector reservations for certain categories of industries, and the influx of multinational corporations.

The other development responsible for the demise of the managing agency system was the access to bank-term finance

---

[97] The Politics of Industry in Nehru's India – Nasir Tyabji, Nehru Memorial Museum and Library, NMML Occasional Paper, History and Society, 2015.

for industrial growth. Hitherto, banks provided working capital finance, but were reluctant to offer long-term financing, necessary to set up industries with long gestation periods of generating returns. Hence, the dependence for term funding fell upon an investor willing to wait. This changed when government-sponsored Development Financial Institutions (DFIs) like Industrial Finance Corporation of India (IFCI) in 1948, the Industrial Credit and Investment Corporation of India (ICICI) in 1955 and the Industrial Development Bank of India (IDBI) in 1964, provided long-term loans at attractive interest rates. This offered attractive leverage, requiring the shareholder to put up lesser capital. Since the interest paid on such was tax deductible, it was attractive and reduced the cost of capital and the returns sought by the long-term shareholder. The pressure on promoters to access risk capital from the investor and entrepreneurial groups reduced, as did their dependence on complex structures and the use of the managing agency system.

With the insertion of Section 324A in the Companies Act 1956, the managing agency system was abolished on April 03, 1970. This was one of the series of radical measures taken by the then prime minister, Indira Gandhi, in addition to the nationalization of fourteen large banks in 1969 and the nationalization of coalmines. After a successful run of over a century and a half of dominating industrial capital in India, the managing agency system was laid to rest.

Though managing agencies legally demised in 1970, entrepreneurs and promoter groups continued to exercise control over corporate cash flows disproportionately greater than their shareholding. Most entrepreneurial groups/business houses in India have designed and sought to control their major listed entities through a complex labyrinth of cross holdings through private companies and later, offshore entities.

APPENDIX 2: INDUSTRIAL CLIMATE IN INDIAN POLITY - PRE AND POST INDEPENDENCE

Before independence, India's economy was primarily agrarian. The British implemented land revenue systems that put a significant burden on farmers and led to the concentration of land ownership. They also implemented exploitative economic policies that favoured their own interests over Indian businesses. Their focus was on extracting resources from India and promoting industries in Britain. Hence, only those industries in India serving this purpose, such as textile, jute, and mining, were allowed to flourish.

Thus Indian business enterprise (and capital generated thereof), remained limited largely to trading and money lending activities. However, by the mid-nineteenth century, green shoots of industrial capital were visible as cotton textile mills came up in western India to give competition to Lancashire. The Tatas set up the first steel plant in 1912 to challenge the steel imports from Britain and the Birlas started jute manufacturing after WWI. The end of the war also saw Indian engagement in other industries such as sugar, cement, chemicals, engineering, and food processing products. Indian businessmen found raising finances tough when they forayed into setting up industries and thus had to lean heavily upon the managing agency model.

Indian businesses also recognized the need for their collective voice to be heard on their concerns and demands and to engage with the colonial government for policy reforms. The Federation of Indian Chambers of Commerce and Industry (FICCI) was thus established on March 01, 1927, in the city of Mumbai (then Bombay) by prominent industrialists like GD Birla, Purshottamdas Thakurdas, and RP Goenka.

That most discourse around India's industrialization before, during and well after independence centred around the prominent political figure of Jawaharlal Nehru is not surprising. It was not just his stint as the prime minister for seventeen years since Indian independence (and a year before in interim capacity) or his position as the first chairman of the Planning Commission[98] but his ideologies and contribution as well, which shaped the course of Indian industry. It is well documented that Nehru advocated socialism of essential services and basic industries within the parliamentary framework of government as the best solution to eradicate poverty and ensure work for all. Simultaneously, he was attracted to the works of Marx and Lenin and the practical achievement of the Soviet Union. It is well known that the Five-Year Plans of India were modelled after the Soviet template.

Nehru's socialist leanings thus harboured a fundamental suspicion of capitalists much before independence. These were cemented with the findings of tax evasion and the personal aggrandizement of industrialists through the managing agents brought forth by the Income Tax Investigation Commission and the Commission of Inquiry.

---

98 The National Planning Commission of India, officially known as the Planning Commission, was established on March 15, 1950. It was created through a resolution of the Government of India and served as the apex body responsible for formulating and implementing the country's Five-Year Plans.

Independence of India in 1947 spurred the vision of nation building. The political mood was both hopeful and apprehensive as India debated on the best way to transform from an agrarian economy to an industrialized nation, creating employment opportunities and reducing poverty. The years between 1947 and 1966 (when the third Five-Year Plan concluded) were replete with discussions between businessmen and the dispensation on the path and construct of industrial development. On the one hand, roles of the public sector and the private sector were discussed, and on the other, the composition of ownership and control between Indian and foreign capital.

Even before, in January 1944, a fifteen-year economic plan for India was proposed by a group of eight industrialists and technocrats, under the moniker of "The Bombay Plan." It espoused import substitution and argued for a "mixed economy", where the state and private industrialists would be equal partners in progress. If it was curious why a group of industrialists would want the state to play a significant role, the answer lay in the government bailouts of crisis-ridden capitalist economy, notably the rebuilding required in the aftermath of the Great Depression of the 1930s in the industrialized Western world. Indian businessmen realised that to rapidly industrialize an underdeveloped country such as India, government support was necessary, as the private sector did not have the financial muscle to undertake long-gestation infrastructure projects. The Bombay Plan proposed that the government take control of "basic industries" such as rail and air transportation, shipping, chemicals, power generation, and engineering, and the private sector remain responsible for "consumer industries" such as textiles, glass, cotton, tobacco, and paper; essentially, where the business class had existing interests.

Signatories to the Bombay Plan included industry stalwarts such as JRD Tata, GD Birla, Purushottamdas Thakurdas, Lala Shri Ram, and noted economist John Mathai (who later served as finance minister in Nehru's cabinet). The Plan was hailed by Lord Wavell, the Viceroy of India, Jeremy Raisman, the finance member, and endorsed by the FICCI. It also dovetailed well with Nehru's socialist principles, and its strategy and methods foreshadowed the official Five-Year Plans some years later. However, it was never officially accepted by him or the Planning Commission. One of the reasons cited was that the Bombay Plan's targets were overwhelmingly more ambitious than anything the Planning Commission of the government of India ever attempted. The Plan's objectives included doubling the agricultural sector and a five-fold increase in industrial output. Furthermore, it envisaged the doubling of per capita income over the fifteen-year period.[99] Yet the real reason perhaps for the failure of the Bombay Plan was political. The Plan factored in social and human development; an area sorely neglected in the Five-Year Plans. This should have endeared the communist parties, the principal adversaries to the Congress at that point in time. They, however, remained steadfast in their opposition to the Plan, which they saw as a handiwork of the capitalist class. The Congress and Nehru were reluctant to declare that they were influenced by the business community since it would have given fodder to the communists to attack them.

There were other political developments too. Mahatma Gandhi's assassination in January 1948, the death of Vallabhbhai Patel (who arguably would have become India's first prime minister had it not been for Gandhi's support of Nehru) in December 1950, and the popular Rajendra Prasad's becoming the President of India, left

---

[99] The industrialists behind India's first national economic plan - Amal Sanyal, Quartz, November 15, 2018.

no centrist or right-leaning leader who had the ability to restrain Nehru. Not surprisingly then, independent India saw the growth of state-led socialism under Nehru's stewardship.

Nehru wanted to make the state a powerful engine of production and distribution so that equitable distribution of income and wealth would be assured. This philosophy finds place in the Industrial Policy Resolution (IPR) of 1948 as well. The IPR divided industry in the following categories: a) Strategic industry (public sector), b) Basic/Key industry (public-cum-privates sector), c) Important industries (controlled private sector), and d) Other industries (private and co-operative sector). The IPR was followed up by The Industries (Development and Regulation) Act 1951.

A significant feature of this Act required the private sectors to seek licences from the central government before setting up new industries and thus began the era of the infamous 'Licensing Raaj'. Trade restrictions were also part of the economic policy of the controlled industrialization of the Indian government. Imposition of tariffs and trade restrictions was thought to facilitate and accelerate industrialization in India to protect domestic industries from foreign competition.

The IPR of 1956 followed, which reaffirmed that India was set to follow the 'Public Private Partnership' i.e., PPP model for a longer period. All industries were divided into three schedules: a) Schedule A contained 17 industries: All new units in these industries would be set up only by the state, even if their establishment in the private sector had already been approved. b) Schedule B industries contained 12 industries: Though not barred to the private sector, these would see progressively greater government participation and state ownership, and c) Schedule C industries: All remaining industries fell in this category; the future development of these industries would be determined by the initiative and enterprise of the private sector. Clearly, IPR 1956 sought a greater and more dominant role for the public sector (state) rather than the partnership of equals envisaged by the Bombay Plan. The IPR 1956 was further strengthened by the second Five-Year Plan, which focussed on growth driven by significant public investment in large and heavy industrialization owned by the state. The other significant accent of the IPR 1956 was the importance accorded to the role of foreign capital in a country's development and as necessary to supplement domestic savings. The country therefore welcomed the inflow of foreign capital but subject to the conditionality that the major share in management, ownership, and control would be in Indian hands.

As discussed earlier, the private sector balked at the large investments required by large industries and infrastructure as other than short-term working capital finance, little long-term finance was available till 1948. They thus went along with their support that large industries remain under the ambit of the public sector. The banks providing working capital included the three Presidency banks – Bank of Bengal, Bank of Bombay, and Bank of Madras – which eventually got merged into the Imperial Bank, the precursor to the State Bank of India. Commercial banks neither had the capital nor the risk-taking appetite to offer loans over a tenor of seven to ten years to help large-scale industrialization, nor was there a great demand from the business for setting up and commissioning huge plants with a large component of machinery. Stock markets were still developing and the Indian investors of the 1950s and 1960s neither had the risk appetite nor the funds to underwrite large public offers of the size of Rs 5 crores plus, especially for projects of long gestation and uncertain returns. And long-term capital, whether debt or equity, became a crying need.

The solution to fortify Indian business groups with long-term debt at affordable interest rates became a reality with the birth of

India's three premier DFIs, discussed in Appendix 1. Funded by the government at low interest rates, these DFIs gave wings to the dreams of corporate houses to set up large ventures.

In addition to benign interest rates on loans, the DFIs were lenient in terms of their loan covenants.[100] The debt-to-equity ratio of major industrial projects was generally 2:1 or even 3:1, which meant that entrepreneurs could start a venture with a minimal amount of their own funds/raise other equity. Importantly, if the garnered equity was sufficiently fragmented and spread over many investors, the business group could retain a controlling shareholding over the venture. The Indian entrepreneur groups could thus control large companies despite having relatively little skin in the game.

Excluding a few corporate houses like the Birlas and the Bajaj group, which insisted upon majority ownership, most business groups began to control several large, listed companies under their wing with equity ownership of 15 per cent or less. Such groups included the Tata group companies, the Mafatlal group, the Mahindras, etc. Many of the Indian business groups thus were able to exercise disproportionate control over larger corporations while remaining exposed to the risks of small shareholding in terms of facing hostile takeovers.

And their sharp practices grew. A favourite methodology employed which started in the late 1960s was the "gold plating" of projects; whereby the overseas suppliers of machinery and capital goods would over-invoice (inflate) the cost of the imported machinery into India and the difference received by the overseas seller would be channelled to accounts of the Indian businessmen

---

[100] Terms and conditions of the borrowing which the borrow must adhere to. Failure to do so can lead to an event of default and prompt the lender to recall facility or resort to recovery procedures.

abroad. Given the accounting standards of that time, rarely was such diversion discovered.

Many were critical both of the 'License Raaj' as well as the Nehruvian socialist model of growth. BK Nehru, one of India's distinguished civil servants who served as India's ambassador in the US and high commission in the UK and was Jawaharlal Nehru's first cousin once removed, writes, "...the industrial policy resolution of 1956 which put Indian industry in a complete strait-jacket. Nobody could start or continue any kind of industrial enterprise without getting an industrial license and an industrial license was granted only for the manufacture of specific goods up to a certain capacity. It was an offence punishable under the law to manufacture in excess of that capacity making us the only country in the world where the production of goods badly needed by the people was punishable by law!

"...With the benefit of hindsight, it seems totally absurd there a country wanting to develop its industry should prescribe for its establishment conditions which were guaranteed to strangle it. But at the same time there was hardly any experience in the government apparatus whether at the political or the administrative level, of how industry was actually run. The Prime Minister's desire was that the "commanding heights of the economy" should be in the public sector. The commanding heights, i.e. the basic industries of oil, steel, and power had already been nationalized; so had one of the airlines and a number of lesser heights which were not so "commanding"' The insurance companies, both life and general, were nationalized under TTK's stewardship of the Finance Ministry. It seemed natural in the prevailing philosophy of the times that where the private sector was 'allowed' to operate, it should do so only within a framework prescribed by public authority... to ensure honesty and eliminate profiteering private business should operate under strict government control. The final result was of course that rapidly enough, private dishonesty was transferred to the public sector."[101]

Keen to address the upsurge of industrial and commercial activity on an unprecedented scale in India and large profits earned by Indian business during and immediately after WWII (1939-1945) as well as the other developments in the IPRs and the Five-Year plans, the government of India sought to revise company law which was the Companies Act 1913 and its subsequent amendments up to 1936. These were based upon English Companies Consolidation Act, 1908.

In 1950, the government of India appointed a committee of twelve members, representing various interests under the chairmanship of Shri HC Bhabha. The Bhaba Committee, in its report of March 1952, recommended far-reaching changes to the Companies Act 1913. After many deliberations by the FICCI, trade associations, professional bodies, leading industrialists, shareholders, and representatives of labour and both houses of the parliament, the Companies Act, 1956 came into force. Principal changes were made in the promotion and growth of companies, their capital structure, company meetings and procedures, company accounts and its presentation as well as the powers and duties of the auditors of the company, inspection, and investigations of the affairs of the company, the constitution of the board of directors and their powers and functions of director and the administration of the company law. Despite the sharp focus on corporate governance in this avatar of company law and the many amendments thereafter, legislation has seldom been able to reign in the ambitions of business capital.

---

[101] Nehru, BK, *Nice Guys Finish Second: Memoirs*. Gurugram, Haryana: Penguin Random House, 2012.

Thus, India travelled along a dual track of industrial growth, with major integrated steel mills and heavy engineering and electrical plants being set up as central government enterprises. Simultaneously, industries like jute, tea, coal, cotton textiles, cement, sugar, and lighting continued to grow as did medium engineering units under the ownership and control of private entrepreneurs.

APPENDIX 3: RECOMMENDATION OF THE COMMISSION OF INQUIRY

The Commission of Inquiry submitted its report on the investigations to the central government on June 18, 1962. Their observations covered irregularities, frauds, or breaches of trusts or action which disregarded honest commercial practices and contraventions of law. Any contraventions, in respect of which criminal proceedings were pending in a court of law, were excluded by the COI. They also detailed items, which needed to be actioned to prevent recurrence of such cases.

Some of their main observations and recommendations were as under:

1. Objects Clause of the Memorandum of Association:

   Observation: A company would choose to keep this scope as wide as possible to allow them to participate in activities far removed from either the main or the ancillary objectives (example: DJ Airways). Several committees had approached the above issue. The expert committee on company law, i.e., the Bhabha Committee (discussed earlier), had considered imposing restrictions was unable to evolve a practical method to distinguish between the 'real' and the 'apparent' types of businesses and recommend effective legal provisions.

   Recommendation: The COI underscored the importance of management responsibility along with periodic vigilance by the shareholders, at the time of company formation as well as when subsequent amendments were sought to the objects clause.

Observation: The prevalent system of inter corporate taxation of dividends at each stage, discouraged companies from setting up different subsidiaries under a main holding company. Companies thus preferred to amend their objects clause or empower their memorandum activities outside their principal engagement rather than set up separate companies.

Recommendation: Tax laws and Companies Act to be amended in line with global practices.

2. Underwriting Commission:

   Recommendation: Commission to be paid only for the *unsubscribed* portion of any share/debenture issue, and not on the portion already subscribed to at the time of filing the company's prospectus/statement in lieu. A copy of the contract for commission payment to be delivered to the register simultaneously with filing the prospectus/statement in lieu (Ref: Rs 8 lakhs gifted in DJ Airways where share application monies had already been received).

3. Issue and allotment of shares in the names of fictitious/non-existent persons:

   Recommendation: Share applications/transfers in fictitious names to be punishable with imprisonment up to five year (Ref: 114 non-existent shareholders application for the Rs 16 lakh public issue in DJ Airways).

4. Holding of shares on "Blank Transfers" and nominee holdings:

   Observation: The COI drew on the Thomas Report.[102] In the

---

[102] Report on the Regulation of the Stock Market in India - PJ Thomas,

blank transfer deed, only seller details are filled and not those of the buyer nor the date of sale. This allows multiple transfers without stamp duty payment until someone seeks to register ownership in the company's books. For this ultimate transfer and registration, the first seller will be treated as the transferor, even if it happens years after his death.

Stock Exchanges' recognition of 'blank transfer' as a valid delivery, helped in concealment of the identity of the real beneficial owners behind their nominees and the evasion of tax by suppression of 'secret' profits invested in holdings on blank transfers. This practice was also misused to window-dress balance sheets of companies by reshuffling of shares held on blank transfers between associated companies with the object of substituting intercompany loans and advances. Also fictitious or antedated transactions could be recorded in company accounts to create fictitious losses in investments for the purpose of reducing taxable profits.

Recommendation:

a. Companies Act 1956: Far-reaching changes recommended by the COI to:

   i. Mandate beneficial owners holding 5 per cent or more of the equity capital in a public company, having the right to vote at general meeting, notify the company the extent of their holdings and for any transactions by them or on their behalf in such shares within 15 days of their knowledge of such transactions. (Amend Section 307 and 308)

1948: Parekunnel Joseph Thomas was the first economic advisor of independent India. He was a Member of the Madras Legislative Council and later Member of the upper house (Rajya Sabha) of the Indian Parliament.

ii. Wilful failure to notify beneficial interest to be penalised by fine or imprisonment. (Amend Section 308(3)

iii. The company to record the identity and transaction details, in a new register, within 7 days of receiving the notification.

iv. Such register to be open for inspection and to be reported/filed with the registrar of companies along with its Annual Return under Section 159 of the Companies Act, 1956

v. Penalty for company's default in complying with any of the requirements above on the lines of Section 307(8).

vi. Extant provisions of Sections 247 and 248 of the Companies Act for investigating of real ownership of shares to be extended to empower the central government to appoint an inspector/conduct an investigation when warranted.

vii. Above requirements not applicable for private companies.

b. Section 137 of the Income-tax Act, 1961, be suitably amended in line with provision a(ii) above.

c. Blank transfer forms be permitted only for a limited period of 6 months. Applications for registration to be made to a company before six months in the case of listed securities and two months in the case of non-listed securities. Shares held in a fiduciary capacity or as a security by financial institution (provided the share was in the name of the borrower with a blank transfer executed in favour of the institution) to be excluded from this requirement.

d. Stamp duty charges on transfer of shares to improve compliance. Loss of governmental revenue would be compensated by increased transfers registered.

5. Dummy directors:

   Observation: First the rampant use of steno typist, personal secretaries etc., as dummies who would be subservient and merely carry out diktats of those in control who remained opaque, especially in instances of malpractices. Second, the Companies Act's definition of 'deemed directors' was limited and applicable only if the board of directors *collectively* acted in accordance with the directions of such persons. Thus, if a person acted through most nominee directors on the board but not all of them were his nominees, he could escape the definition and hence the responsibilities of a 'deemed' director. The Bhabha Committee of 1952 had suggested the use of the word 'directors' only rather than 'board of directors' if the enlargement of the penal provisions of the Act to the 'deemed' directors was to be effective.

   Recommendation: Expand the Bhabha Committee recommendations to expand the definition of "officer" contained in Section 2(30) of the Act by adding a sub-clause to include (as an officer) a person in accordance with those directions or instructions the *directors* of a company or any of them were accustomed to act.

6. Appointment and termination of sole selling agents:

   Observations: Provisions for the appointment of managing agents, managing directors etc., and remuneration/ compensation to them upon termination had been tightened up in the Companies Act, but similar safeguards were absent for selling agents. (Ref: Textile mills, SSB and MDM, paid large amounts of tax-free compensation to the agent/recipient company while denuding their reserves)

Recommendations: Companies Act to be amended to bring selling agents at par with managing agents, i.e. no compensation payable if their appointment was disapproved in the general body meeting of the company or where they resigned upon the reconstruction/amalgamation of the company with any other corporate, and were appointed as sole selling agent of that entity, or if found guilty of fraud/ breach of trust/gross negligence in duty or when the sole selling agent had, themselves initiated the termination of the sole selling agency.

Any compensation payable for loss of office to selling agent not to exceed the remuneration payable for the unexpired residue of the term or three years, whichever shorter.

7. Power and obligation to acquire shares of dissenting shareholders under a scheme or contract approved by the majority (a scheme or contract involving the transfer of shares or any class of shares in a company ["the transferor company"] to another company ["the transferee company"])

   Observation: Though Section 395 of the Companies' Act dealing with powers and obligations to acquire shares of dissenting minority shareholders had been tightened up to safeguard the position of minority shareholders, the COI had seen an instance wherein shares of a flourishing company worth lakhs were acquired by a newly floated private company with insufficient means (paid-up capital Rs 50,000 only). They had issued "deposit receipts", or its own shares as the consideration representing the price of the shares acquired. It was thus a case of a "takeover" bid by a bidder without having the necessary resources/cash.

For acquisition with cash, The Jenkins Committee[103] had suggested that a statement, binding on the transferee company (bidder), providing details of source/availability or such cash to be provided. The Committee also recommended that a part/whole of the consideration could be by exchange of shares rather than cash, subject to certain provisions.

Recommendation: In line with the Jenkins Committee report, the COI recommended that suitable provisions should be made, in the Companies' Act Section 395(3) and 395(4). The central government to have powers to frame rules for disclosure in every scheme by the transferee company, including statement for cash availability and source for cash acquisitions. The scheme to be registered by the registrar of companies before their circulation. The registrar to be empowered (subject to appeal to the court) to refuse to register any such scheme not having the requisite information or having misrepresentations. Current provisions allowed for transferor (target) company to receive funds from the transferee company for shares of dissenting shareholders to be sequestered in a separate bank account, to be held in trust. However, there was no requirement for the transferor company to either intimate the shareholders of the receipt of

---

[103] Committee, in the United Kingdom headed by Lord Jenkins, was appointed in December 1959, to review and report upon the provisions and working of the Companies Act, 1948, and the Prevention of Fraud (Investments) Act, 1958 (excluding matters relating to industrial and provident societies and building societies), and to consider what should be the duties of directors and the rights of shareholders. Their Report was published in June 1962.

such sums nor pay them unless a demand was made. The COI sought suitable amendments to the Companies Act to provide that the transferor company would, within a month from the date of registration of the transferee company as holder of the shares (of the dissenting shareholders), intimate to the dissenting shareholders of such registration, the receipt of the amount/other consideration payable to them by the transferee company and pay the money without delay.

8. Liquidation

   The COI stated that despite formalities and procedures being followed in the liquidations and in the schemes of arrangement proposed by the liquidated companies, courts were unaware of all the facts and circumstances, perhaps on account of collusion of those who appeared. Hence, their judgement/decisions were detrimental to the interests of the investors. Though the central government had adequate machinery through the department of Company Law Administration to handle representations to the court, such representations came only in cases of "oppression" or "mismanagement". The COI thus recommended an amendment to provide for issue of notice to, and consideration of any representations, submitted by the central government before the court passed its final verdict/orders.

9. Recovery of taxes on income from companies in Liquidation/Amalgamation

   Observation: Though income tax dues were given preference for debt settlement under Section 530 of the Companies' Act, there were considerable delays pending completion of assessment proceedings, raising, a notice of payment demand on the assessee and the expiry of such period. Thus, often, the tax on a company's income of one or two years preceding the commencement of liquidation couldn't rank as a preferential debt. The Direct Taxes Administration Inquiry Committee (DTIC) had sought to correct this lacuna by incorporating Section 178 in the Income Tax Act, 1961, the specific obligation on the liquidator to intimate his appointment to the income tax officer and to set apart assets of the value equal to the tax.

Recommendation: To strengthen the income tax provisions, the COI sought modification of Section 530 of the Companies' Act to allow preferential payment of one year's assessment relating to a period prior to the winding up, notwithstanding that the assessment was made after the winding up. The COI was however circumspect that such a speedy assessment could be achieved. To overcome the problem of income tax recoveries against the company in liquidation on account of its assets being transferred to another, the COI recommended that the IT Act should authorise the issuance of a fresh demand notice on a transferee company and include it in the circumstances in which an assessee is "deemed to be in default," as it had taken over the income-tax liabilities of the transferor company. Sections 391, 394 and 396 of the Companies Act to be suitably amended.

10. Destruction of Books of Account

Observation: Though Section 209 (4A) and Section 550 of the Companies Act provided for the preservation of a company's books of accounts for a minimum period of eight years, preceding the current year and for the preservation of books in a winding up, it was silent in instances where a company was amalgamated with another company *without* being liquidated.

Recommendation: The COI proposed that the provisions of

Section 550 be corrected as well to make it applicable to a transferee company where the transferor was not liquidated.

11. Administrative Machinery

    Recommendation: The COI proposed greater coordination in the workings of government departments dealing with the corporate sector such as The Department of Company Law Administration (DCLA) and other departments dealing with which dealt the control over the capital issues, stock exchange regulation, etc.

While making these recommendations, the COI observed that Companies Act of 1956, and the Amendment Act of 1960, had certainly brought about far-reaching changes to the provisions existing of the erstwhile Indian Companies' Act, 1913 as amended in 1936, under which many of the misdemeanours of the DJ group had been perpetrated. Various deficiencies and malpractices had been lessened and the loopholes largely plugged.

Finally, the COI stated, "We feel that no law can provide absolute remedies to stop malpractices, and a balance has to be achieved between attempting to stop malpractices and imposing fetters on honest businessmen, particularly when legislation can be defeated by human ingenuity, as unfortunately sometimes happens. In such circumstances, the wrong doer succeeds anyhow, and the honest businessman is saddled with a considerable amount of technical difficulties."

REFERENCES

BOOKS

1. Tyabji, Nasir. *Forging Capitalism in Nehru's India: Neocolonialism and the State, c.1940-1970*. New Delhi: Oxford University Press, 2015.
2. Dalmia Adhar, Neelima. *Father Dearest: the life, and times of R.K. Dalmia*. New Delhi: Westland Ltd, 2017.
3. Dalmia, Seth Ramkrishna. *Some Notes and Reminiscences (A Guide to Bliss)*. Delhi: National Printing Works (The Times of India Press), 1959.
4. Nehru, BK, *Nice Guys Finish Second: Memoirs*. Gurugram, Haryana: Penguin Random House, 2012.
5. Chagla, MC. *Roses In December: an autobiography*. Mumbai: Bharatiya Vidya Bhavan, 2019.
6. Patel, HM. *The First Flush of Freedom: Recollections and Reflections*. New Delhi: Rupa Publications India Pvt. Ltd, 2010.
7. Setalvad Motilal, C. *My Life: Law, and other things*. New Delhi: Law & Justice Publishing Co, 2022.
8. Falk, Bertil. *Feroze the forgotten Gandhi*. New Delhi: Roli Books, 2016.
9. Writings of Parekh, HT. *India In Transition Through the Eyes of a Visionary, 1940-1990s: Volumes I & II: A Tribute by HDFC and ICICI*. Mumbai: HDFC and ICICI, 1995.
10. Goswami, Omkar. *Goras and Desis: Managing Agencies, and the Making of Corporate India*. Gurugram, Haryana: Penguin Random House India,2016
11. Timberg, Thomas A. *The Marwaris: From Jagat Seth to the Birlas*. Gurugram, Haryana: Penguin Random House, 2015.

12. Dalal, Sucheta. *AD Shroff: Titan of Finance and Free Enterprise.* Gurugram, Haryana: Penguin Random House India, 2001.
13. Mukhopadhyay, Tarun Kumar. *Feroze Gandhi: A Crusader in Parliament.* Mumbai: Allied Publishers Ltd, 1992.
14. Sahai, Shashi B. *Politics Of Corruption: The Goddess That Failed.* New Delhi: Gyan Publishing House, 1995.
15. Reddi, Dr Agarala Eswara. *The Mundhra Scam and TT Krishnamachari.* Chennai: Sri Mundhra Bhaskar, Mundhra Prints, 2007.

JOURNALS, REPORTS, AND PAPERS

1. Report of The Commission of Inquiry (Inquiry on the administration of Dalmia Jain Companies) – Govt of India, Ministry of Commerce and Industry, Department of Company Law Administration.
2. Report to the Nations: 2020 Global Study on Occupational Fraud and Abuse - Association of Certified Fraud Examiners (ACFE).
3. PwC's Global Economic Crime and Fraud Survey 2022 - PricewaterhouseCoopers International Ltd.
4. An Overview of India Capital Markets - BK Muhammed Juman and MK Irshad, *Bonfring International Journal of Industrial Engineering and Management Science,* Vol 5, No 2, June 2015.
5. Transfer of Economic Power in Corporate Calcutta, 1950–1970 - Tirthankar Roy, *Business History Review 91* (Spring 2017): 3–29. doi:10.1017/S0007680517000393, Cambridge University Press.
6. G D Birla, A legend in his lifetime – *India Today* archives, June 30, 1983, updated April 09, 2023.
7. Of Traders, Usurers and British Capital: Managing Agencies and the Dalmia Jain Case - Nasir Tyabji, Industrial Development and Globalisation, *ResearchGate,* November 2008.
8. How the cow came to be debated in Constituent Assembly and why Article 48 was added to Constitution – Adrija Roychowdhury,

Indian Express Research, January 25, 2021.

9. Corporate Law in Colonial India: Rise and Demise of the Managing Agency System - Umakanth Varottil, National University of Singapore, Centre for Law and Business, December 2015.
10. The Rags-to-Riches Story of Ramkrishna Dalmia – *Marwar India*, April 21, 2016.
11. Ramkrishna Dalmia first spoke out against cow slaughter – *Business Standard*, August 25, 2015.
12. How politicians should deal with businessmen – *Rediff News*, December 03, 2010.
13. The Politics of Industry in Nehru's India – Nasir Tyabji, Nehru Memorial Museum and Library, *NMML Occasional Paper*, History and Society, 2015.
14. The Bank and the Mundhra Affair - Reserve Bank of India, 25 Jun 2022.
15. Private Industry and the Second Five-Year Plan: The Mundhra Episode as Exemplar of Capitalist Myopia – Nasir Tyabji, Institute for Studies in Industrial Development, Working Paper 2010/04, May 2010.
16. Govt to proceed against officers. – *Hindustan Times*, February 20, 1958.
17. Afterthoughts on the Mundhra Affair – Ashok H Desai, *The Economic Weekly*, July 1959.
18. LIC-Mundhra Scam: Independent India's First Mega Financial Scandal - Ashok K Singh, *Peepul Tree*, September 01, 2021.
19. British India Corporation and Mundhra Affair: After the Raj - *The Bizdom*, December 12, 2020.
20. Long View: India's Very First Corruption Scandal – *The New York Times*, May 09, 2012.
21. The industrialists behind India's first national economic plan - Amal Sanyal, *Quartz*, November 15, 2018.

22. Discussion on the Government Resolution on the Life Insurance Corporation Inquiry, Rajya Sabha Papers, September 11, 1959.
23. Indian Financial Sector: Structure, Trends and Turns - Rakesh Mohan and Partha Ray, IMF Working Paper, January, 2017.
24. Report on the Regulation of the Stock Market in India – P.J. Thomas, 1948.
25. 'Badla': The Mumbai Derivative - Vivek Kulkarni, *Economic and Political Weekly*, October 1997.
26. Jawahar Lal Nehru's concept of democratic socialism - Prof. K.V. Viswanathaiah, *The Indian Journal Of Political Science*, Vol 26, No. 4, conference number XXVII Indian political science conference: Mysore 28th -30th December 1965, pp 91-99.
27. Margin Trading and Securities Lending and Borrowing – SEBI, March 19, 2004.
28. Learning Resources, The Partition Museum, Amritsar & Delhi.

LEGAL CASES

(By judgement dates. Cases relevant to Dalmia and Mundhra have been clubbed together.)

DALMIA

1. 23 April 1957: Dalmia Jain and Co Ltd Vs The Commissioner Of Income Tax I, 1957 Equivalent citations: AIR 1957 Pat 424, 1958 33 ITR 294 Patna.
2. 29 April 1957: Ram Krishna Dalmia Vs. Justice S R Tendolkar, Equivalent citations: (1957) 59 BOMLR 769.
3. 29 March 1958: Shri Ram Krishna Dalmia Vs. Shri Justice S. R. Tendolkar and Others (and connected appeal), Equivalent citations: 1958 AIR 538, 1959 SCR 279, AIR 1958 Supreme Court 538, 1959 SCJ 147, 1961 BOM LR 192.

MUNDHRA

1. August 08, 1958: Richardson and Cruddas Ltd Life Insurance Corporation of India Vs. Haridas Mundhra and Others, Equivalent citations: AIR 1959 Cal 695, 63 CWN 439.
2. November 30, 1961: Tulsidas Mundhra … Accused-Petitioner; Vs. The State of West Bengal, Crl. Revision Case No. 1117 of 1961.
3. February 14, 1962: Life Insurance Corporation of India Vs. Hari Das Mundhra and Others, Special Appeal No. 299 of 1961 with Special Appeal No. 296 of 1961.
4. April 05, 1962: R K Dalmia Vs. Delhi Administration, Equivalent citations: 1962 AIR 1821 1963 SCR (1) 253.
5. May 16, 1962: G Subrahmanyam Vs. H D Mundhra and Others, Crl. Appeal No. 219 of 1960.
6. July 10, 1962: Haridas Mundhra Vs. Indian Cable Co Ltd, A.F.O.O. and D. No. 56 of 1964.
7. September 14, 1962: Bhagwati Prasad Vs. British India Corporation Ltd, Civil Misc. Appln. No. 232 of 1962, Special Appeal No. 299 of 1961.
8. May 05, 1964: Rameshwar Daga Vs. The State of West Bengal, Equivalent citations: AIR 1965 Cal 38, 1965 Cri LJ 26, 69 CWN 292.
9. May 05, 1965: Champarun Sugar Co Ltd & Another Vs. Haridas Mundhra and Others, A.F.O.O. No. 163 of 1964.
10. June 16, 1970: The State Vs. Haridas Mundhra and Another, Criminal Revn. No. 650 of 1967.
11. September 14, 1970: Hungerford Investment Trust Ltd Vs. Haridas Mundhra and Others, Appeal No. 148 of 1969 (Suit No. 600 of 1961).
12. March 09, 1972: Hungerford Investment Trust Ltd (In Voluntary Liquidation) Vs. Haridas Mundhra and Others, Civil Appeal No. 488(N) of 1971.
13. March 09, 1972: Turner Morrison and Co Ltd Vs. Hungerford Investment Trust Ltd, Civil Appeal No. 1223 of 1970.

14. March 30, 1972: Richardson & Cruddas Ltd Vs. Haridas Mundhra and Others, Suit No. 1540 of 1960.
15. September 06, 1974: Haridas Mundhra Vs. Mahabir Prasad Juthalal and Others, A.E.O.O. No. 76 of 1973 Decided on September 6, 1974.
16. June 20, 1975: F & C Osler (India) Ltd (In Liquidation) Vs. State of West Bengal, Matter 310 Of 1957 (C. A. No. 166 of 1964).
17. December 06, 1978: Turner Morrison and Co Ltd Vs. Shalimar Tar Products (1935) Ltd and Others, Company Petitions Nos. 204, 205 and 206 of 1973.
18. February 28, 2014: Angelo Brothers (in liquidation) Vs Nawdeep Singh, CA 401 of 2013.